Praise for the Triple Threat Novels

"Who killed one of the Triple Threat? Look into the Eyes of Justice. You'll be shocked by what you see."

—Bill O'Reilly, FOX TV
and radio anchor

"Book three in the wonderful Triple Threat Club series is a fast-paced thriller full of twists and turns that will keep you guessing until the end. What makes these books stand out for me is my ability to identify so easily with Allison, Nic, and Cassidy. I truly care about what happens to each of them, and the challenges they face this time are heart-wrenching and realistic. I highly recommend!"

—Deborah Sinclaire, editor-in-chief,
Book-of-the-Month Club and the Stephen
King Library regarding *Heart of Ice*

"Beautiful, successful, and charismatic on the outside but underneath a twisted killer. She's brilliant and crazy and comes racing at the reader with knives and a smile. The most chilling villain you'll meet . . . because she could live next door to you."

—Dr. Dale Archer, Clinical
Psychiatrist regarding *Heart of Ice*

"As a television crime writer and producer, I expect novels to deliver pulse-pounding tales with major twists. *Hand of Fate* delivers big-time."

—Pam Veasey, writer and
executive producer of *CSI: NY*

"With *Hand of Fate*, author Lis Wiehl has crafted a thriller that is unmistakably authentic and irresistibly compelling—both streetwise and sophisticated, and a flawless reflection of this former prosecutor's own expertise in law, life, and broadcasting."

—Earl Merkel, author of
Virgins and Martyrs and *Final Epidemic*;
cohost of talk radio's *Money & More*

"A talk show host with a long list of people who want him dead? Has Lis Wiehl been reading my e-mail? Talk radio fans and mystery lovers alike won't rest easy until they discover who had a hand in the fate of Fate."

—Alan Colmes, host of *The Alan Colmes Show*
on radio and FOX News contributor

EYES OF
JUSTICE

Other Books by Lis Wiehl with April Henry

The Triple Threat Novels
Face of Betrayal
Hand of Fate
Heart of Ice

Also by Lis Wiehl with Pete Nelson

The East Salem Trilogy
Waking Hours
Darkness Rising* Coming October 2012

EYES OF
JUSTICE

A Triple Threat Novel

LIS WIEHL
with APRIL HENRY

THOMAS NELSON
Since 1798

NASHVILLE   DALLAS   MEXICO CITY   RIO DE JANEIRO

Published in Nashville, Tennessee, by Thomas Nelson. Thomas Nelson is a registered trademark of Thomas Nelson, Inc.

Thomas Nelson, Inc., books may be purchased in bulk for educational, business, fund-raising, or sales promotional use. For information, please e-mail SpecialMarkets@ThomasNelson.com.

Scripture quotations are from the *The Holy Bible, New International Version*®, copyright © 1973, 1978, 1984, 2011 by Biblica, Inc.™ Used by permission. All rights reserved Worldwide.

Publisher's Note: This novel is a work of fiction. Names, characters, places, and incidents are either products of the author's imagination or used fictitiously. All characters are fictional, and any similarity to people living or dead is purely coincidental.

ISBN 978-1-40418-353-7 (IE)

Library of Congress Cataloging-in-Publication Data

Wiehl, Lis W.
Eyes of justice / Lis Wiehl ; with April Henry.
p. cm. -- (A triple threat novel ; 4)
ISBN 978-1-59554-708-8 (hardcover)
I. Henry, April. II. Title.
PS3623.I382E94 2012
813'.6--dc23

2011051155

Printed in the United States of America
12 13 14 15 16 QG 6 5 4 3 2 1

For Jacob and Dani. With all my love, from Mom. And for every Triple Threat reader. Your support and kindness is inspiring and humbling. Thank You.

Leave room for God's wrath, for it is written:
"It is mine to avenge; I will repay," says the Lord.
—Romans 12:19

CHAPTER 1

When the authorities questioned Channel Four's receptionist later about the phone call, Marcy King couldn't recall a single distinguishing characteristic about the voice of the person who had made it. Age, accent, attitude—all she could remember was that it belonged to a man. A man insisting that he had to speak to Cassidy Shaw, the TV station's crime reporter.

Cazdeshaw," Cassidy said into her headpiece, fast enough that her name ran into a single blurred word. Her hands never stilled on her keyboard. She was finishing a piece for the evening news, a terrible story about a man who had killed his two children rather than see his ex-wife get full custody.

"Is this Cassidy Shaw?" A man's voice, so soft it was nearly a whisper.

"Yes." She lifted her fingers, straining to hear. That sixth sense she had, the sixth sense that had never steered her wrong, told Cassidy it would be worth her while to listen.

"I've got a story for you." He hesitated and then said in a rush, "About a cover-up."

Her elation slipped away as fast as it had come. A cover-up? It sounded like some sort of boring malfeasance. "You know I handle the crime beat, right? I could transfer you to the business reporter." Her hand was already hovering over the button on the phone.

"No!" Panic edged his voice. "I only want to talk to you. It's about the Portland Police Bureau. And what's being covered up is . . . well, I don't want to get into it on the phone. Something bad."

The Portland Police Bureau? Cassidy's antennae were quivering again. "What's your name?"

"I can't give you my name over the phone. If they find out I talked, I'm in big trouble."

"Come down to the station then." She opened a new document, typed in the words *police cover-up*, and hit the save key. "I would love to talk to you."

His voice arced higher. "Are you crazy? If I'm seen walking into Channel Four, something will happen to me. I could end up being shot in the back and they'd rule it an accident."

What could be bad enough that this man feared being murdered? Whatever it was, it had to be juicy. Cassidy hoped he couldn't hear the soft tap-tapping of her fingers on the keys.

"Then we can meet someplace else—a Starbucks, a restaurant, a shopping mall," she said in a soothing tone. "You name it."

"You're not listening to me. It can't be anywhere out in the open. Not where people can see me. If anyone sees me talking to you, I'm as good as dead."

"I could wear a baseball cap," Cassidy said as she typed in the words *as good as dead*. "And dark glasses."

"That won't work. Everyone in Portland knows who you are!"

Cassidy smiled, but was careful not to let it color her voice. "So why'd you call me?"

"Because you're the only one who has the guts to break this story.

We all saw how you stood up to Rick. Everyone wanted that hushed up, but you wouldn't step off."

Rick McEwan was Cassidy's old boyfriend. And a cop. Over time he had changed from a generous and loving boyfriend to a man who kept her in line with well-timed outbursts of violence. Finally Cassidy had gathered her courage, pressed charges against him, and gone public with her story. She had laid her heart bare on live TV, spoken honestly about how even a smart woman could find herself cowering and afraid. The piece had won some local awards.

But what she really dreamed of was an Emmy.

"I watch you," the caller said now. "Even when you went after Rick, you were fair. You didn't throw mud at the whole bureau, just Rick, and everyone knows he's bad news. I figure you'll be fair here too."

From the way this guy talked, he had to be a cop.

"Okay, maybe we don't have to meet," she said, as she typed in *Rick McEwan* and a question mark. Was he hinting that Rick was involved? "You can just tell me what you know."

And then later she could talk him into being filmed in silhouette with his voice artificially deepened.

"But I have proof. Proof I need to show you."

"What kind of proof?"

"Proof that they planted that gun on that homeless guy. He was just a crazy transient, but they lost control and killed him."

This story was vaguely familiar. Cassidy hadn't covered it because it had been an open-and-shut case. In a new computer window she opened Channel Four's website and typed in the words *homeless*, *Portland*, *police*, and *shooting*. A few seconds later she found the story: *Homeless Man Shot Dead by Police*. Her eyes quickly scanned the three short paragraphs.

Two weeks earlier, just before midnight, an officer responding to a prowler call had been dispatched to northeast Martin Luther King, Jr. Boulevard. When the cop spotted the suspect, the guy ran. The officer gave chase and was joined by five other cops. According to Sgt. Joe Morton of the police bureau's media relations division, at some point during the foot chase the suspect produced a handgun. After pointing it at the responding officers, he was shot by one of them, Kevin Craine.

Cassidy leaned closer to the screen. Rick McEwan had been one of the other officers on the scene. At the sight of his name, the hair rose on her arms.

The story went on to say that the prowler, Vernell Williams, a black man who normally lived in a ravine underneath a freeway overpass, had been declared dead at the scene. Records revealed that he had spent time in prison, in mental health treatment, and in rehab.

Mentally ill, black, homeless, an alcoholic, an ex-con. Any of which could be problematic when it came to the local police. The Portland Police Bureau had an unfortunate history of occasionally treating crazies like criminals, seeing danger when there might not be any, and miscommunicating among themselves.

In the last year the city had made three expensive settlements: two for using excessive force and one for a wrongful death. And the chief of police had been working to change the perception that Portland cops would rather shoot first and ask questions later.

In the news brief, Williams's family said they couldn't believe he'd had a gun. But without evidence there was no way it could be proved that he hadn't. Now Cassidy was being offered that proof.

"How do you know what really happened?" she asked.

"Because I was there," he said, confirming Cassidy's suspicion. "We all promised to tell the same story. The chief has been wanting to make an example of someone to prove he's serious about shaking things up. If you shoot an unarmed civilian, at the very least you could lose your badge. Maybe even go to prison. So they planted a piece on this guy."

"A throw-down gun."

"Right."

"Who supplied it?" Cassidy wondered if she already knew the answer.

"I'm not saying that on the phone. But it was a spur-of-the-moment decision. And now we're all in too deep to go back. If the others knew I was talking, they might feel like they had no choice but to . . ." His voice trailed off. "But I keep thinking about the poor guy they shot. If someone like you starts asking questions, maybe the truth will come out."

This story was dynamite. They had to meet. Someplace private. Someplace safe. Someplace where people wouldn't notice them.

Her condo building.

Riverside Condominiums was a great place to go if you wanted to be unobserved. The builders had broken ground at the height of the real estate mania, when property was appreciating 15 percent every year. Everyone had wanted in. The management held lotteries to choose who was allowed to buy, and Cassidy had felt lucky when her number came up. Six months later the bottom fell out of the market. Roughly half the units in her building remained unoccupied. A lot of investors ended up walking away from the debt, giving their units back to the bank. As a result, the building was often eerily silent.

"Okay," Cassidy said. "How about this? There are a couple of meeting rooms in my condo building. No one ever uses them." It had been one of the perks of the building, but the parties and business meetings the owners had envisioned never materialized. She had signed her mortgage agreement in one of them, and that might have been the last time it had been occupied.

The caller finally agreed, reluctantly. Cassidy added up the time in her head. She agreed to meet him at six forty-five, after the last broadcast of the local news. She was supposed to be joining Allison and Nicole for dinner at seven thirty, but like her, they were professionals. They'd understand if a story caused a delay. She sent a quick text to each of them.

Might be a bit late—following a lead. Save some chips and salsa for me.

As she drove home, Cassidy's hands were slick on the wheel, and it wasn't just from the oppressive August heat. There was no doubt this story could be dangerous. Cops—even good cops—tended to band together when one of them was under attack. And Rick was far from a good cop. The story had so much potential. And she would be the one to break it.

What Cassidy didn't realize was that this story would really break her.

CHAPTER 2

I can see why Cassidy likes this place," Allison Pierce said as she lifted a tortilla chip laden with bean dip to her mouth. She bit down with a satisfying crunch.

Puerto Marquez was a wild riot of colors, from the purple carpet to the bright seascape murals decorating the walls. Each of the restaurant's chairs was a different color of the rainbow—green, purple, orange, yellow—and the backs were covered with paintings of flowers and birds.

The sounds were nearly as overwhelming as the colors: Mexican folk music drifting from the kitchen fought with Spanish-language infomercials playing on two of the dining room's big-screen televisions. The other two TVs were broadcasting Spanish telenovelas with the sound turned down. Overlaying the music and advertisements was the rattle of three aging air conditioners turned on full blast.

Nicole Hedges nodded, looking a little shell-shocked. Whenever it was Nicole's turn to choose a restaurant for the three of them, she tended to pick places where the loudest sound was the clink of ice cubes.

Puerto Marquez was located in a strip mall in a less-than-glamorous part of outer Southeast Portland. Without Cassidy's recommendation, Allison wouldn't have given the place a second look, but their friend had sworn that the restaurant had the best Mexican food in Portland. It didn't hurt that free chips, salsa, and refried beans had appeared on their table as soon as they sat down.

Allison thumbed through the huge menu, pages and pages encased in clear plastic. Despite the aggressive air-conditioning, her fingers slid on the pages. It was nearly eight o'clock, and she bet the temperature outside still hadn't dropped below eighty-five. Because of the heat, she had left most of what she thought of as her "court uniform" in the car—the suit jacket, white blouse, and pumps—and was now wearing just a white camisole, a dark blue skirt, and flip-flops. Her hair was still pinned up from this morning, but tendrils kept falling in front of her eyes or, more annoyingly, finding their way between her lips.

She hooked a strand out of the corner of her mouth and took another sip of her margarita, wondering just how late Cassidy would be. Maybe she'd sent a second text? But when Allison checked her phone again, there was nothing new.

Nicole put her hand on Allison's wrist. At the touch of her cool fingers, Allison set her phone back on the table.

"Stop checking," Nicole said. "You know that in ten or twenty minutes Cassidy will come running in, knocking some poor customer in the head with that big old black tote of hers. That girl is always late." As she spoke, Nic managed to dip a tortilla chip into the bean dip and the salsa without snapping it in half.

Nicole's description of Cassidy was on the money. Cassidy was always multitasking, always looking for a shortcut, always in a hurry, and always, as Nicole had said, late.

"Maybe I should start telling her we're meeting half an hour earlier than we really are," Allison suggested. "That way she might actually be on time for a change."

Nicole shook her head. "The leopard doesn't change its spots. Cassidy is Cassidy, and that means she's always late. It means a lot of other things too, but right now it means we shouldn't wait for her before we place our order."

The three of them had been friends for six years, though they had been acquainted with each other for much longer. Sixteen years earlier they had graduated from Catlin Gabel, one of Portland's elite private schools. In high school they had barely known each other. Cassidy had been a cheerleader. Nicole had stood out by virtue of being one of the fewer than a half-dozen African American students. And Allison had captained the debate team.

At their ten-year high school reunion, the three women realized they now had something more than an alma mater in common: crime. Cassidy covered it for Channel Four, Nicole investigated it for the FBI, and Allison prosecuted it for the federal government. At the time, Nicole had been working out of the Denver FBI field office, but a few months later she was transferred back to Portland and started working cases with Allison.

Soon after, the three women met for dinner, and a friendship began over a shared dessert called Triple Threat Chocolate Cake. In its honor, they had half jokingly christened themselves the Triple Threat Club. Now whenever they got together they always ordered the most decadent dessert on the menu—but just one serving, and three forks.

Allison wasn't sure, since most of Puerto Marquez's menu was in Spanish with no translation, but she thought the only dessert available here might be a flan.

Their waiter came up, and the two women ordered. After he left, Nicole said, "Some idiot almost ran me over today."

"What?" Allison straightened up.

"Yeah, I was out for a run at lunch, and some guy in an old beater came out of nowhere." Raising her hands, Nicole made a shoving motion. "I managed to push myself off his hood. Somehow I stayed on my feet and made it to the other side of the car. I'm lucky he didn't break my legs, or worse. As it is, I know I'm going to be really stiff tomorrow."

Despite the air-conditioning, Allison shivered. "Did you get his license plate number?"

Nicole grimaced. "The car was filthy. There was mud all over the plate."

Allison replayed her friend's words. "Wait—did you say you were running? It must have been ninety degrees by lunchtime."

The city was on the second day of over one-hundred-degree temperatures, and coping poorly. While most businesses had air-conditioning, a lot of older homes didn't. It was also an oddly muggy heat for Portland, which usually didn't have much humidity. The weathermen had promised a thunderstorm the night before, but it never came.

Nicole shrugged. "Lunch is the only free time I have. It's not that bad if you wear sunglasses and drink lots of water."

"I'll take your word for it. I can't stand this heat much longer." Allison made a face. "When I got in my car to come here it was like getting into a blazing oven. A blazing oven that was on fire. Inside a volcano."

Nicole smiled. "Don't you guys have air-conditioning at home?"

"Only in our bedroom. It's either turn the air-conditioning on and listen to it rattle, or turn it off and baste in your own sweat."

Nicole took another sip of her margarita. "Which one are you— the one who prefers silence or the one who would rather be cool?"

"We alternate." Allison pushed a piece of hair out of her eyes. She was starting to sweat again just thinking about it. "One hour I just want to cool off and who cares about the noise, only Marshall can't take it. The next hour I'm the one who can't stand listening to the fan bang around in that metal box, and Marshall's the one begging to turn it back on."

Nicole sighed. "I've been sleeping in the basement on a cot. I'm just thankful that Makayla's at that sleepaway camp. It's always cool at the coast."

"You must miss her a lot," Allison said. "Is it hard to have an empty house?"

"I do miss her." Nicole took another sip of ice water. "At the same time, it's a nice break not to be juggling child care or asking my parents to keep her for the night when something breaks. And if I come home too tired to do anything but eat a bowl of cereal, I don't feel guilty for not serving a meal made from however many food groups there are now."

Talking about food made Allison think about Cassidy. She checked her watch again. Cassidy was now forty-five minutes late—a record, even for her.

Their food came. Allison had ordered spicy shrimp with a side of rice and beans. The shrimp made her sweat too, but with the air-conditioning and the ice water and the margarita, she didn't mind. Every bite or two, she glanced at the front door.

"I'm going to call her again," she said when her plate was half empty, already pressing buttons on her phone. After four rings, Cassidy's voice mail kicked in. Disconnecting the call, Allison said slowly, "She doesn't have a new boyfriend, does she?" It was the only reason she could think of why their friend wouldn't even pick up.

"Not that I know of." Nicole shrugged. "But you know Cassidy— that can change in a minute."

"One thing that will never change is how much she likes her phone. You know she'll always answer. It doesn't matter whether she's sleeping or sick or super busy." They sometimes joked that Cassidy should just cut out the middleman and have her phone surgically implanted. "So why isn't she answering now? It's not like she's on the line and it's going straight to voice mail. It's like it's ringing and no one is answering." The shrimp Allison had eaten felt like they were alive and squirming in her gut. "Nic—I think something's wrong."

"Let's give it five more minutes," Nicole said. "If she doesn't show by then, we'll see if we can track her down."

CHAPTER 3

Without discussing it, they took Nic's Crown Victoria. As she slid behind the steering wheel, Nic's fingers hovered over the switches that activated the siren, the alternately flashing lights in the grill, the red-and-blue light bar in the rear window. Then she lifted her hand and put it back on the wheel. A friend not showing up for dinner didn't qualify as an emergency.

At a red light she cut a sideways glance at Allison. Her friend's eyes were closed, her lips moving silently. Nic knew what she was doing. Offering up a prayer for Cassidy's safety. The old Nic would have rolled her eyes at Allison's gullibility. But that was before breast cancer had shown her just how impossible it sometimes was to stand only on your own two feet.

Traffic was light. A second before the signal turned green, Nic was halfway across the intersection. She knew she was driving too fast. Tailgating. Switching lanes every few seconds. She cut off a young guy driving a white cube-shaped car, ignoring his rude gesture. Two blocks later they hit a speed bump so hard they were momentarily airborne, their teeth clacking together when they landed. Finally they were flying down the freeway toward downtown Portland. Five minutes later Nic took the off-ramp for Cassidy's neighborhood.

Located in the shadow of one of Portland's eleven bridges,

Riverside Condominiums had been envisioned as the first stage in the redevelopment of an old industrial area. When Cassidy bought her condo a few years back, artist renderings had pictured the area filled with shops, restaurants, and bars. Most of those businesses had never materialized. Instead the area was filled with boarded-up former warehouses and light manufacturing plants that had been bought and gutted but never rehabbed.

With few cars parked on it, the street that led to the condominiums seemed unnaturally wide. Adding to Nic's sense of unease, there wasn't a soul in sight. In the fading light, the whole area looked deserted. Of course there was no one around, she scolded herself. That's what this part of town always looked like.

When they reached Cassidy's condo building, Nic drove down the ramp into the underground parking garage. As soon as she got out of the car, the hot air immediately wrapped her in a smothering blanket.

"Look." Allison pointed. "There's her car."

"So she's here." Nic should have felt relief, but she didn't. She was aware of her Glock in its shoulder holster. She wore the gun everyplace except at home, and sometimes even there. She undid the button on her jacket.

They walked over to Cassidy's car, heels clacking on concrete already veined with cracks, and bent down to peer inside. It was the same mess it always was—brightly colored suits still wrapped in dry cleaner's plastic, red Netflix envelopes, a mascara tube or two or three, celebrity gossip magazines, and enough empty silver Diet Coke cans to fill a couple of cases.

"Maybe she forgot something and had to stop by her place to get it before dinner," Allison suggested. "Or she spilled something on her clothes and had to change."

Nic didn't answer. There was no point in speculating. They would find out soon enough. Something inside her was building a wall between her thoughts and her emotions.

While they waited for the elevator, Allison pressed the redial button on her phone. She held it to her ear for a long moment, then ended the call without speaking. Her lips thinned to a white line.

The doors opened on the fourth floor. The hall must have had some sort of air-conditioning, because it was slightly cooler than the elevator. A plant in a dark brown ceramic pot sat next to the silver doors. Even though it was fake, it looked like it was dying. Dust furred its sagging fabric leaves.

Nic knocked on Cassidy's door. She and Allison were both silent, listening for music, for footsteps, for their friend's voice.

Nothing.

Allison pressed the redial button again. Through the door they heard the faint first few notes of a song turned ringtone.

Cassidy never went anywhere without her phone.

"She has to be in there." Allison bit her lip.

"You don't have a key, do you?" Nic asked, but Allison shook her head.

With luck, the manager lived on-site. Nic would flash her badge. She would talk fast. She would say whatever she needed to say to get him to open this door. As she was thinking this, she put her hand to the doorknob. In her fingers, the handle turned.

Her mind split in two. One part was yammering that it was a bad sign, a bad sign indeed, that Cassidy's door was unlocked. The other, more rational part, the part that made her a good FBI agent, was thinking about fingerprints. If there were any, she had probably just obliterated them. Not that it was easy to lift prints from a doorknob. The twisting motion turned prints into long smears.

Allison's eyebrows rose. "It's unlocked?"

Nic nodded. Cassidy could be absentminded. It was possible she'd been in a hurry to get home for whatever reason and had forgotten to lock the door. She was probably sick, Nic told herself. They'd find her huddled miserably in the bathroom or curled up on the bed. It would explain everything. The unlocked door, the unanswered phone, the missed meal.

With her toe she nudged the door open. Her mouth was suddenly dry. She moistened her lips with a tongue that felt like leather.

"Cassidy?" She waited. "Cassidy?"

Nothing. Nothing but silence.

Nic elbowed the door wider and they both stepped inside. The room was shadowed, the light from the windows melting into dusk. Allison made a move toward the light switch, but Nic laid a hand on her arm.

"Fingerprints."

Allison's eyes went wide, as if reality was just sinking in. Nic took a pen from her purse and flicked up the switch.

"Cassidy?" Allison called out again. "Cassidy?"

No answer. The word fell flat, absorbed by the willow green walls, the flat cream-colored Berber carpeting.

It was staggeringly hot. So hot and stale and close. Why hadn't Cassidy turned on the air-conditioning? Why hadn't she at least opened a window?

Without moving from the entryway, Nic turned her head, taking it all in. Cassidy's mail had been tossed on the entryway table. Next to it were her keys and her black tote. A tall vase held a thick bouquet of tiny white flowers that smelled sickeningly sweet. A few of the blossoms had drifted down.

Nic thought of weddings, of flower girls in beribboned dresses, sprinkling pale petals before them. Of how Cassidy had had boy-friend after boyfriend but never married.

The white leather couch and matching armless chair in the liv-ing room were a sleek Danish design, with deep-seated cushions and steel legs. Nic couldn't imagine sitting on leather in this heat. Let alone owning white furniture. It was the kind of furniture that only a woman without kids would buy. Between the couch and chair lay a curved smoked-glass table shaped like half a heart. The pedestal was made of twisted wood that looked tortured.

Nic sniffed. Nothing. No smells, no sounds, nothing unusual to see.

Her nerves thrummed. Something working below the level of consciousness was screaming at her to run.

"It's a little messy." Allison swept out one arm to indicate the room, the pair of pumps kicked off in front of the couch, the book left facedown on the chair. Her voice shook a little bit. "But no mess-ier than any of the other times I've seen it."

"If anything, I'd say it's cleaner," Nic said. She'd been here plenty of times when discarded outfits had draped the furniture, when newspapers, magazines, and pizza boxes littered every flat service.

The kitchen-dining area was partly visible from where they stood. Nic walked into the kitchen. Empty. There were dirty dishes on the counter and in the sink. On the floor was a small garbage can full of coffee grounds, takeout boxes, and a blackened banana peel. When Nic accidentally nudged it with her toe, a swarm of fruit flies rose up.

She turned and walked down the short hall. In five steps she was at the end, Allison trailing silently behind her. No one was in the bedroom. Or the bathroom. The counter was covered with makeup, hair products, and jewelry. A scent lingered in the air, a light, grassy smell that Nic had always presumed was Cassidy's natural smell, but what must be, she now realized, perfume.

"She's not here," Allison said. "That's good, right? She's not here."

Nic tried to feel relief. There must be a reason Cassidy wasn't home, a reason her door was unlocked, a reason she hadn't answered her phone. Maybe she had gone down the hall to visit a neighbor. Although Cassidy always complained about how quiet the building was, how empty. How she could scream her head off and no one would hear.

A shiver danced across Nic's skin. She walked back into the living room, remembering the other times the three of them had been here. Laughing. Talking. Sharing gossip and information and treats. The time they had polished off three boxes of Girl Scout cookies and two bottles of wine.

There had been other times, too, like the time she and Allison had confronted Cassidy about Rick, about what he was doing to her.

"Nicole?" Allison's voice shook. "Nic?"

Nic followed Allison's pointing finger. Underneath the dining room table, half hidden in shadow, lay Cassidy's phone—the latest, sleekest, thinnest model, all matte black and shiny silver.

Nic crouched down to look closer, not touching it. It was face up. A spiderweb of cracks spread out from one bottom corner of the screen.

Behind her, Allison said, "Maybe that's why Cassidy's not here. She's probably at the phone store. That doesn't even look usable. She dropped it, it broke, and she couldn't call us."

Nic didn't even bother to answer her. They both knew that the keys, the purse, the unlocked door—all put the lie to Allison's last hope.

Just past the phone, something glinted in the fading light from the dining room window. Three drops, each of them shining, oily, and thick. Blood.

When Allison saw what Nic was looking at, she caught her breath in a gasp.

Nic bent closer. The drops were nearly round. Passive spatter, meaning the drops had been formed by the force of gravity acting alone. Not high-velocity blood spatter, like that from a gunshot. Not cast off from a bloody weapon being raised again and again, flinging drops with each strike. If Cassidy had cut herself on the broken phone, it was possible that the blood had slowly dripped from her fingers until she noticed it and staunched the bleeding.

It was possible, wasn't it?

Nic realized she was being as bad as Allison. Forcing the pieces together to make a picture of a sunny, happy scene.

She swallowed back a sudden nausea, the taste of chips and salsa burning and sour on the back of her tongue, and fought the unreasoning urge to run. How many crime scenes had she walked into? Hundreds? Her life had been in danger dozens of times. And she had never faltered. But now something told her that what had happened here was bad. Very bad indeed. And she most definitely didn't want to see it.

Straightening up, Nic took her gun from its holster. The weight of it settled her. Her eyes swept over the floor around the blood and the broken phone, but she saw nothing else out of place. She turned her head to scan the rest of the condo again. Everything was as neat as it got at Cassidy's. There was no trace of anyone else in any of the rooms.

But there was the broken phone.

Nic went back to the bathroom, Allison trailing. The blue shower curtain was pulled across the tub.

Was there a shadow behind it? Taking a deep breath, she pushed it back with the barrel of her Glock. The plastic curtain rings rattled.

Nothing. The white tub was empty except for a yellow rubber duck.

Nic's breath came out in a rush, and she realized she'd been holding it.

They went back to the bedroom. The sheets and lightweight duvet were only messy on one side, mute testimony to the fact that Cassidy had been sleeping alone. Allison dropped to her knees, reminding Nic of prayers. Of prayers it felt too late to say now. Allison looked under the bed.

"Nothing."

Nic reached for the closet door and then hesitated, thinking of the front door. Even though heavily handled objects didn't usually yield good prints, the only way not to corrupt a latent print was not to touch it. Taking a tissue from her purse, she was careful to twist just the connection between the knob and the door shield.

She pulled the door open, her gun at the ready. It was stuffed full of clothes. No beige or gray for Cassidy, and very little black. Just the bright colors she loved: turquoise and orange and bright blue. With her free hand, Nic pressed on the jackets and skirts, looked underneath the hanging hems. Discarded clothes lay on top of dozens of shoes. But there was nothing that shouldn't have been there.

She walked back into the center of the condo and stood tapping her toe, the sound *click*, *click*, *click*ing on the linoleum.

Finally she spotted it.

A tiny puddle of blood was pooled on the floor in front of the sink, hidden by the lip of the cabinets. It didn't even look dry. She took two slow steps toward it.

Allison stayed where she was, her eyes wide.

Taking a deep breath, Nic hooked her pen into the metal loop of the door and pulled.

Cassidy lay on her side, stuffed under the sink. Her body was curled around the silver U of the drain pipe. She barely fit, her knees against her chin. The front of her coral jacket was soaked in dark blood the color of the wine she liked to drink.

With unseeing blue eyes, Cassidy Shaw stared at her two friends.

CHAPTER 4

Allison tried to connect the empty blue eyes, the still form, to Cassidy. But Cassidy was never still.

"Maybe we should try CPR?" Her voice sounded as if it were coming from someone else. Someone far away. She had bent over when Nic opened the cabinet, and now it was as if she couldn't move, couldn't take her hands from her knees, couldn't lift her head from where she crouched with her face just three feet from Cassidy's.

A horrible gasping sound filled the air. It took Allison a second to realize that she herself was making it.

Cassidy couldn't be dead. She was a force of nature. There must be something that could be done, some procedure or drug that could bring her back from the brink. Maybe not to the point where she would immediately crawl out from underneath the sink, smiling at how it had all been a misunderstanding or a sick joke, shrugging back her bloody jacket to reveal unblemished skin. But still, there must be *something* they could do that would bring her to consciousness, leave her moaning and thrashing while one of them frantically dialed an ambulance and the other sought to comfort her.

Nicole gently pressed her fingers on the side of Cassidy's neck. Finally she looked up at Allison and shook her head.

Cassidy was dead, Allison tried to tell herself.

Dead.

The word was meaningless. But then she looked at Cassidy's face again, her dull eyes. Really looked. Whatever this lifeless waxy thing was, it wasn't Cassidy. Every bit of it was dead, every cell, every atom. It wasn't Cassidy at all.

Allison straightened up. A wave of dizziness washed over her. Despite the oppressive heat, her teeth were chattering.

"She's still warm." Nicole's face looked perfectly composed, but her breath was coming in short gasps, as if she had been running. "And there's no rigor. This didn't happen that long ago."

So they had been what—laughing? eating chips? drinking margaritas?—when someone punched a knife into Cassidy's belly?

Allison's legs were suddenly too weak to hold her. She groped blindly behind her for a place to sit down. Sit down before she fell down.

"Don't!" Nicole cried out. "Don't touch anything."

Allison pressed her hand to her chest and tried to concentrate on breathing. The air was too heavy. It resisted being sucked into her lungs.

Slipping her gun back into its holster, Nicole pulled her cell phone from her belt and punched in 9-1-1. Her face was a mask.

"This is FBI Special Agent Nicole Hedges. I need to report a homicide at the Riverside Condominiums. Unit 414. The victim's name is Cassidy Shaw."

As she half listened to Nicole's words, Allison stood frozen in the middle of the kitchen floor. Like an inflating balloon, her head felt like it was getting bigger and lighter and emptier. The dirty dishes on the counter seemed far away, tiny, fit only for dolls.

Don't look at Cassidy's face, Allison told herself, but against her will her gaze was drawn back to the open, staring eyes. Horror choked off the thick breath in her throat, tightened across her chest like a band.

Her fingers groped for and finally found the small silver cross her father had given her for her sixteenth birthday, three weeks before he died. The cross was the only anchor Allison could find in the world, a reminder that this world was not the only one.

What would happen to Cassidy's soul now? She had always been a seeker, flitting from belief to belief. *Lord,* she prayed, *please accept Cassidy's soul into Your keeping.* Allison's next breath was slightly easier, even though it still shook. *And help us find justice for her here on earth.*

Nicole was still talking with the 9-1-1 dispatcher. "You need to notify detectives that this is clearly a homicide." Impatience edged her voice. "I'm here with Allison Pierce. She's a federal prosecutor. We're both friends of Cassidy's. She was supposed to meet us for dinner but never showed up. We came here to check on her, and we found her body." She listened for a second and then said, "There's no one here but us. We came in through the underground parking garage and took the elevator to the fourth floor. We didn't pass anyone."

Allison tried to remember. Had she seen anyone on the street outside or through the glass doors of the lobby as they drove past them and down to the underground lot? Could there have been a shadowy figure watching from a dark corner of the garage? Had the murderer seen them? Could he still be in the building?

Nicole hung up and turned to Allison. "They're dispatching a patrol car here first. And then we'll have to wait for the uniform to get the homicide detectives out here. But this scene is fresh. The longer it takes, the less fresh it will be."

She crouched back down on her haunches, just inches from Cassidy's limp form, then looked up at Allison. "She was stabbed with something. Don't touch anything, but see if there's a knife missing from the block."

Thankful to turn away, Allison looked at the wooden knife block sitting on the counter next to the stove. "There're two empty slots."

Nicole stood up and scanned the dirty dishes. "There." She pointed and then pointed again. "One's in the sink and the other's on the counter."

Allison followed her finger, being careful not to let her gaze drop any farther. She couldn't bear to look at Cassidy again. One blade was smaller, a paring knife, the other a long serrated bread knife. Neither seemed like the kind you'd use to kill someone.

"There's really not that much blood," Nicole said, almost to herself.

"What do you mean?" Despite her best intentions, Allison looked down again. The front of Cassidy's jacket was red and sodden.

"There's blood, sure, but if she had died from being stabbed, I think we would have noticed a big pool first thing." Nicole pointed at the floor, at the small circle of blood that was not more than three inches across. "That's nothing. A couple of tablespoons."

Allison thought of another scenario. "Or maybe she was stabbed someplace else and moved here?"

"If they did that, there should be blood between here and wherever they killed her. And all we've got is a few drops." She bent down again to look at Cassidy. Her voice muffled, she said. "I don't see any stains or marks on her clothes. But her skirt's bunched up, like she's been moved."

Allison hoped Cassidy hadn't been raped. She tried to work it through. "Maybe they cleaned up."

"There should be evidence of that too. But I didn't see any wet or missing towels in the bathroom. And the tub and sink were dry." Nicole leaned down. "The kitchen sink's dry too."

While she heard Nic's words, Allison's brain kept toggling back and forth between the terrible now and the past that now could never be anything but past.

Cassidy's empty, staring eyes. The Mexican restaurant where she and Nicole had just eaten while complaining about Cassidy's lateness.

The blood that now soaked the front of her friend's coral-colored jacket. Cassidy's habit of twisting the back of her hair—a place the camera never saw—whenever she was lost in thought. How Allison and Nicole had chattered away while their friend must have been dying.

She had a thousand memories of Cassidy laughing, joking, eating, gesturing, and talking. Always talking, her words coming a mile a minute.

Then Allison's eyes would again find the real Cassidy, absolutely still and absolutely empty, looking like a clever doll fashioned from pale wax.

For the dozenth time, she tore her gaze away from those flat eyes. "I just don't understand how this happened. We know that Cassidy sometimes took risks. But to be killed here, in her own condo. It feels personal. I mean, I wouldn't have been surprised if she was in an accident driving too fast to a story or if some suspect she was interviewing turned on her. But to die here, in her own home . . ." She let her words trail off.

"I didn't see any signs of forced entry—no tool marks or anything on the doorframe," Nicole said. "And I don't think the lock was broken."

Allison walked back into the living room and looked at Cassidy's things. "Okay, she came in here, she put down her keys and her purse and her mail and then what—someone knocked on the door and she answered it?"

Nicole came out to join her. "Maybe. Or she could have come home and surprised a burglar."

Allison surveyed the room. "Only if that's what happened, where's the mess? Nobody's gone through things. There's no sign of a struggle."

"Maybe it was someone she knew, and when she let them in, they suddenly attacked her." Nicole's eyes were slitted like a cat's. "And if it was someone she knew, you know who I keep thinking of? Rick."

Allison blinked. She was still considering the idea when there were two sharp raps on the door.

"Open up," a woman's voice said. "Police."

Taking from her pocket the tissue she had used earlier, Nicole opened the door by turning the section between the knob and the door. The cop who stepped over the threshold was young with short dark hair. Half-moons of sweat darkened the underarms of her short-sleeved blue uniform shirt.

Twenty-five at the most, Allison thought.

"I'm Officer Santiago with the Portland Police Bureau. The 9-1-1 dispatcher reported you found a body?"

Nicole said, "I'm Nicole Hedges, FBI. And this is Allison Pierce. She's a federal prosecutor. We're the ones who found Cassidy Shaw. She's our friend. And she was definitely murdered."

Santiago swallowed and pulled back her shoulders. "Where's the victim?"

"In the kitchen," Nicole said.

The three of them walked back to stand at the entrance to the kitchen. When the cop saw Cassidy's body wedged under the sink, she let out a tiny gasp. Allison wondered if it was the first dead body she had ever seen.

"It looks like she was stabbed," Nicole said. "How long until your backup officer and the homicide detectives get here? We need to canvass the area immediately. The body is still warm."

"Are you sure she's dead?" Under brows plucked to a thin line, the cop's eyes were wide. She started forward.

Nicole put a hand on her arm. "Yes. I checked. You shouldn't go near her. We don't want to disturb any trace evidence. There are some drops of blood by her phone on the floor over there and more blood in front of the sink." She pointed.

Santiago nodded, but her eyes never left the body. Finally she said, "I need to notify dispatch." She reached toward the landline phone sitting in a cradle on a side table.

"What are you doing?" Nicole's voice rose as she grabbed her wrist. "You've got a radio and a phone on your belt, and you're going to use the victim's landline? Didn't they teach you about fingerprints at the academy?"

"Nic—" Allison said, but Nicole shook her head. Earlier she had been calm and methodical, but now she was so tense she was nearly vibrating. Nicole rarely got angry, but Allison realized her friend would rather surrender to anger than to sorrow.

Santiago pressed her lips together, then pulled her radio from her belt. "Dispatch, I'm on scene at Unit 414 of the Riverside Condominiums. We have one victim, deceased, apparent homicide, no fire or ambulance needed. No suspects on scene."

After putting away her radio, Santiago took a pen from her breast pocket and a notebook from the back pocket of her pants. "May I see some ID, please." Her voice was chilly. "I'll need your name, address, date of birth, and phone numbers."

"Why are you wasting time? Cassidy's body is still warm—whoever killed her could still be in the building or on the block! What you need to be doing is searching the area."

Office Santiago acted as if she hadn't heard. Moving with deliberate slowness, she flipped back a page and turned to Allison as if Nicole wasn't even there. "Name? And spell first and last."

"What?" Allison realized that Santiago must be so unnerved by the body that she was falling back on her training.

"We need to be able to get hold of you in the future. Witnesses have a habit of disappearing."

"Are you kidding me?" Nicole asked. Her voice rose. "We're not just some bystanders who happened to be walking by on the street. We're in law enforcement. And Cassidy Shaw is one of our best friends. You can bet that we will see this thing through to the end, until whoever did this to her is in prison. And you need to be helping us achieve that goal. You need to get the homicide detectives and some more officers out here as fast as possible. I will not have this investigation messed up by some girl who has no idea what she's doing."

Allison saw a muscle flicker in the cop's face and knew that Nicole had pushed her too far. "Look, you can't take what she's saying personally," she said hurriedly. "Cassidy's our friend. Nicole's very upset."

Ignoring Allison, Santiago set her jaw. Slowly she put away her notebook. Then she drew herself up to her full height, which was probably no more than five foot three.

"Nicole Hedges, I am placing you under arrest." The cuffs were already in her hand.

"What?" Allison couldn't believe this was happening. "Why?"

"For obstructing an investigation."

"But—"

"You watch it or you'll be next." Santiago's gaze swung back to Nicole. "Now turn around, Ms. Hedges, and put your hands together behind your back."

Nicole just observed her calmly, her tip-tilted eyes making her look like a cat, inscrutable and haughty. "You're joking, right? Let me advise you, Officer Santiago, that this is a very, very poor career move."

And then Nicole turned her back and presented her wrists.

CHAPTER 5

The metal cuffs slid around Nic's wrists and clicked into place. Anger burned in her like a cold fire.

Anger at Santiago, the rookie cop who was impeding the vital work of investigating Cassidy's death.

Anger at herself, for doing the same.

She had to shut up. She had to bite her tongue and not say a thing. She owed Cassidy justice, not a three-ring circus.

Nic was so busy lecturing herself that she didn't notice that a new person had entered the condo until she heard his gruff voice.

"What's going on here?"

She turned. The speaker was a Portland homicide detective she'd crossed paths with at some point in the past—Johnson, Johanssen, something like that. He was a tall man with sandy hair going silver and receding at the temples. His eyes turned down at the ends, and Nic remembered him as having a gentle expression.

Not now. Now his mouth twisted and he shook his head in exaggerated disbelief at the sight of Nic in cuffs.

Officer Santiago threw back her shoulders. "Sir, this woman is interfering in an investigation."

"This woman also happens to be an FBI agent." He sighed. "What exactly did she do?"

"She was yelling at me and trying to give me orders."

Allison started to interrupt, but Santiago raised her hand sharply and continued. "Once I arrived on scene, I was the officer in charge. In this situation, this woman is nothing but a civilian, and she was interfering."

The detective wore a crumpled white short-sleeved shirt and a shiny polyester tie that was already loose. Now he tugged at it as if it were strangling him. "She's also on the FBI's Evidence Recovery Team, if I remember correctly. So she could probably teach you a thing or two. Uncuff her."

The cuffs sprang open. Nic refrained from massaging her wrists, even though the cuffs had been too tight. No point in making things worse. Instead she held out her hand to the detective. "Thank you, Detective . . ." She hated to admit that she didn't remember his name.

"Jensen." His gaze moved past her to Allison. "And you're . . ."

"Allison Pierce. I'm a federal prosecutor."

Allison sounded better than she had earlier, but Nic could see the shadow in her dark eyes. She seemed to be relying on a certain level of formality to prop her up. Just as Nic was relying on a certain level of anger to keep her from falling to her knees.

Allison continued, "In some ways she's right, Detective Jensen. Nicole and I aren't here in a professional capacity. Cassidy is our friend. She was supposed to meet us for dinner, but she never came, and she didn't answer her phone. That's not like her, and we got worried about her. We came here, found the door unlocked, and then discovered her . . ."—she stumbled a bit and then recovered—"her body stuffed under the sink. Understandably, we're both upset. And understandably, we're anxious that steps be taken immediately to find whoever did this to her and bring him to justice."

"Understandably," Jensen echoed. He squinted at the officer's name badge. "Look, ah, Santiago, when you signed up to be an officer, it means you signed up to deal with other people's problems. And that means you need the patience of Job. Nobody thanks you. Everybody argues with you. You need to develop thicker skin."

"Yes, sir." Santiago hung her head.

Unexpectedly, Nic felt a flash of empathy. "I pushed her buttons pretty hard. But this murder didn't happen long ago, and we need to get moving."

Jensen raised his arm and wiped his forehead on the edge of his sleeve. "Who else lives here?"

Nic knew why he was asking. "You don't need a search warrant. This condominium is owned by the victim, she lives here alone, and she has never shared the space with anyone else at any time."

She wanted to scream at him to hurry. Jumping through hoops to procure a search warrant would mean someone had to get hold of a district attorney, who would then have to get hold of a judge, who would then sign the search warrant. Meanwhile, precious moments would be ticking away.

But screaming, as Nic had already experienced, would do no good at all. Instead she added in a mild tone, "Only about half the units here are occupied. You should ask the manager if there's an empty unit on this floor that you can set up as a command post."

"Thanks for the tip," Jensen said, not sounding particularly thankful. His eyes roamed past her. "Where is it?"

It took Nic a long second to realize that by *it* he meant Cassidy's body. Cassidy was just an *it* now. She met Allison's eyes and knew she was thinking the same thing.

"In the kitchen." The four of them walked to the edge of the carpet.

"Oh," Jensen said, and Nic heard the shock in his voice. *"That*

Cassidy. Cassidy Shaw from Channel Four. She's covered most of the cases I've investigated."

Nic realized that Cassidy might be personally acquainted with nearly everyone who would be assigned to solve the mystery of her death. She tried to view the kitchen as if it were just another crime scene. "The body's still warm."

"Yeah, and . . . ?" Jensen ran the back of his hand across his shiny forehead. "It's also about a hundred degrees in here. That doesn't mean it just happened." Still, he took out a notebook and jotted something down.

"We both got texts from her only a couple of hours ago," Nic said, although she knew it was possible that someone else had sent them. "I really don't think she's been dead long. That means whoever did this could still be in the vicinity."

"Don't worry, dispatch has scrambled a few dozen officers," Jensen said. "We'll have people doing canvasses of the building and the neighborhood in five minutes."

That many cars would be sure to draw a crowd, even in a neighborhood that only a few minutes ago had looked deserted.

"Don't forget to have someone take photos of any spectators," Nic said.

The shots might identify not only witnesses but even a potential suspect. After the body of his victim had been discovered, "Preppie Killer" Robert Chalmers had sat on a stone wall in Central Park and coolly watched as the detectives investigated.

Jensen let out a huff of exasperation. "I don't need to be reminded how to do my job. You can be sure we'll do what's necessary."

Nic took a deep breath and reminded herself to stop pushing. This guy was an old hand. He would want to clear this thing as badly as she did. And unlike Santiago, he would have a good idea of how to do it. She wished she could remember what case it was they had both worked on.

He turned his head to look up the hall that led to the bedroom and bathroom. "Besides the body, did you notice anything missing or out of place? Anything unusual?"

"Her phone's underneath the dining room table." Allison pointed. "The front's cracked."

"And there are three drops of blood near it. Passive spatter," Nic said. "That's why I was trying to keep Officer Santiago out of the area."

He nodded, and Nic was glad they were back on easier ground.

"I'll let the criminalist know. Since you've been here, what have you touched? We're going to need elimination prints. Oh, and I'll need photos of the bottoms of your shoes in case we turn up any shoe prints."

"It's possible we didn't touch anything at all except for when I initially knocked on the exterior door and then turned the knob." Nic went back through it in her mind. "We were pretty careful. I used a pen to turn on lights and open the cabinet under the sink, and when I opened other doors I used a tissue to twist the connection between the knob and the door shield."

Jensen's eyes narrowed. So much for easier ground.

"Just because your friend was late for dinner, that was reason enough for the two of you to walk in here already treating it like a crime scene? And if you were thinking that, why didn't you call 9-1-1 right away?" As if to punctuate his words, sirens began to sound in the distance.

"There weren't any signs of forced entry, but the front door wasn't locked," Nic explained. "Cassidy can be absentminded, but you put together an unlocked door with her not answering her phone, and we got hinky."

"Hinky?" he repeated dubiously. "So you just went inside instead of calling someone?"

Nic took a deep breath. "And are you telling me that if you thought your friend was in danger, you would have just hung out in the hall and called 9-1-1?"

His mouth crimped. "Leave me out of it, Special Agent Hedges. You should have called us first thing. As soon as you saw the door was unlocked. As soon as you found that broken phone. We had one chance to perform an untainted search. We didn't need you corrupting any evidence."

"You don't understand." Allison took a step toward Jensen. Her voice shook. "She's our friend. Our priority was helping her. We were hoping she was still alive."

"Look." Jensen spoke through gritted teeth. "I appreciate that the deceased was your friend. But it would have been better if the scene's integrity had been kept intact. Instead you both go in and play detective. And this is not the FBI's jurisdiction. This is a Portland Police Bureau matter."

Nic took a half step toward Jensen. "This isn't about which agency has jurisdiction. This is about bringing a murdered woman's killer to justice."

Behind them, the building's hall was suddenly full of voices and radio transmissions. The troops were here.

"Let me tell this to you straight, Special Agent Hedges." Jensen's skin was red and blotchy. "You both are going to go downtown for interviews and then you are going home. Right now, you're not law enforcement. You're not even witnesses. You're bystanders. Nothing more." He took a step forward until he was nose-to-nose with her. "I don't need your help."

"She's my friend, and I will see justice done." Nic bit off the words.

She was close enough that she could smell the pepperoni pizza Jensen had eaten for dinner.

"Trust us that it will be." His eyes were so narrow they had nearly disappeared.

Nic took a deep breath. "Come on, Allison."

Jensen shook his head. "No. I don't need you two comparing notes; I want you in separate cars. I want your memories fresh and untainted."

"We're professionals," Nic protested. She was so angry she could barely speak. How dare he think she would do anything to jeopardize this case.

He said nothing, just stared at her from under puffy lids. Nic knew she was one word away from feeling the cuffs back on her wrists. And that wouldn't do Cassidy any good.

Still, there were a million things she wanted to remind Jensen's team to do. She knew the criminalist would remember to bag Cassidy's hands in case there was skin under her nails, but what about getting a sample of the blood on the front of her jacket for DNA testing? The blood on the jacket and the floor might not necessarily even be hers, not if Cassidy had tried to fight someone off.

Nic wanted to impress upon Jensen the importance of every step. To make sure the responding officers asked Cassidy's neighbors if they had heard or seen anything unusual: a stranger's voice, an argument, a phone ringing, the sounds of a struggle. To hand out business cards in case memories surfaced. To search the halls, stairwells, and surrounding streets looking for anything that might have been discarded: the knife, bloody clothing, other weapons, other evidence. To record the license plate of every vehicle parked within a few blocks, in case the perpetrator had left his car behind.

Instead she turned and left without a word, swimming upstream against the suits and uniforms that now filled the hall. Behind her, she could hear Allison talking again to Jensen, but Nic couldn't stay in the same room with him any longer. He was just trying to do his job, part of her knew that, but he didn't understand that Cassidy was far more than a job.

In the elevator, Nic slipped her phone from her belt and pressed and held a single digit to speed dial. It was late, but she knew he wouldn't mind.

"Leif, it's me."

CHAPTER 6

Wait here," Detective Jensen told Allison as Nicole stalked out the door, and the hall outside the condo continued to fill with officers. "And do me a favor and don't touch anything."

Allison nodded, trying to remember if she had handled anything earlier. She didn't think so. But she had been here often enough that her fingerprints would probably still turn up.

Jensen quickly took charge of the responding officers. Some he dispatched to canvass the neighborhood, others to talk to condominium residents. As Nicole had suggested, he sent one to track down the manager to commandeer an empty unit. Officer Santiago's assignment was to stand just outside Cassidy's door and jot down the name and ID number of everyone who responded, noting if they entered the condo.

Half listening to the controlled chaos behind her, Allison stood rooted in the living room. The air was still and close and incredibly hot.

A dark-haired man dressed in black pants and a charcoal polo spoke briefly to Santiago and then entered the condo. Allison wondered how he could stand to wear long sleeves, but he looked cool and composed.

"I'm Kyle Binney, the criminalist." He shook her hand, then began to put on vinyl gloves.

"Allison Pierce. I'm a federal prosecutor."

His eyebrows pulled together. "Wait—this is a federal case?"

"No," she said quickly, hoping Jensen hadn't overheard. She didn't want him getting angry again. "Just a coincidence. I'm a friend of the victim's. We—another woman and I—found her about half an hour ago."

"Oh." He looked uncomfortable, and she guessed he seldom dealt with anyone but the official and the dead. "Sorry for your loss. So, um, where's the body?"

"In the kitchen." Would Cassidy's lifeless blue eyes haunt her dreams? "Under the sink. There's also a broken phone under the dining room table with some blood drops near it."

"Yeah, they briefed me on that." Binney started to open the case he carried over his shoulder. "Would you mind standing in the hall for a bit? I need to document the room."

Allison stepped outside. Santiago nodded at her, expressionless. Jensen was talking to two men dressed in street clothes, whom Allison assumed were also detectives. She turned back. Flinching at the flash, she watched as Binney took several photos from different angles. Finally he beckoned her back in. He moved to the edge of the room and looked into the kitchen.

"Oh," he said in surprise. "That's the lady from Channel Four, isn't it? Cassidy Something?"

"Shaw. Cassidy Shaw." Allison suppressed the crazy urge to smile. Cassidy always liked being recognized. But then again, she wouldn't want to be seen like this, undignified, her skirt rucked up, the front of her jacket sodden.

She wouldn't like being dead.

Allison started when Jensen touched her shoulder from behind. "Okay, I need you to go down to the station and answer some questions."

"I don't have a car. I came here with Nicole." She tried to pull herself together. "Look, I apologize for how she reacted. It was just such a terrible shock. I mean, we're only used to dealing with this kind of thing when it involves someone we don't know. Not when it's our best friend."

And Allison realized it wouldn't end here, with hers and Nicole's devastation. Cassidy's death would keep rippling out, like a heavy stone thrown into a pond. Her coworkers, her family, her other friends—all of them would be devastated by the news. In addition to the emotional loss, there was also the bruising impact her absence would have on the physical world. Her death was going to mean so much work, not just for the investigators, but also for the people she left behind. Just thinking of the clothes filling Cassidy's closet, the dishes in her sink, the jumble in her car—it all made Allison tired. Who would take care of all of it?

Cassidy's family would have to be told soon. Her parents lived in town, as did her brother.

"What about her folks?" she asked Jensen. "They still need to be notified, right?"

He looked at her for a moment before giving a short nod.

"Please let me go along. I promise I'll keep it professional. It will be better hearing it from me than from a stranger. I've known Cassidy since we were teenagers."

It was true, as far as it went. Allison was leaving out the fact that her friendship with Cassidy really only stretched back six years. But she knew Cassidy's parents well enough to know they would not take the news well. Allison mentally shook herself at the absurdity of the thought. Of course they wouldn't take it well. Who would?

Jensen let out a growl of exasperation. "When will you two stop trying to inject yourself into the process? This is a matter for the Portland Police Bureau, nobody else."

Allison laid a hand on his forearm, ignoring the sweat.

"I'm not asking you this as a federal prosecutor. I'm asking you as a person. This is the hardest news a parent could ever receive. Their child is dead. Please do them a kindness and let me make it easier for them."

Again Jensen's eyes narrowed to the point of almost disappearing. In the end he didn't say yes or no, just, "This is against my better judgment." He stuck his head out in the hall. "Halstead, can you take Ms. Pierce with you when you go to notify the Shaws? She's a friend of the family." He turned back to Allison. "And don't say one word that will screw up this case. Not one. Do you hear me?"

"I do." Allison looked him steadily in the eye. "And thank you."

In the elevator, the detective held out his hand to her. "I'm Sean Halstead." He had a thin face and large eyes that looked as though they had seen a lot. "Derrick Jensen's partner."

"Allison. Allison Pierce." After shaking his hand, she pushed a sweaty piece of hair off her forehead. "Thanks for letting me come along."

"Sure. I'm sorry for your loss. How close was your friend to her family?"

She chose her words carefully. "Their relationship could be a bit . . . fraught."

What would Cassidy's mother be like when she was really given something to fall apart over?

When the elevator doors opened into the lobby, two uniformed officers were already dusting the glass exterior doors for prints. Outside, the formerly empty street was now full with more than a dozen marked and unmarked vehicles. Halstead's car was a brown Crown Vic, sagging on its wheels, that could be cousin to Nic's own. To get to it, they had to walk through a small crowd that had already gathered.

As he started the car, Allison gave him the address.

"So how long have you known Cassidy Shaw?" he asked as he pulled away from the curb.

"We went to Catlin Gabel together, but we've only been close friends for about six years." She found it easier to be honest with him than with Jensen.

"That's still a long time. You must have some theories on the case."

The case. Well, Allison supposed that was what it was. A case.

"Covering the crime beat put Cassidy in touch with a lot of low-lifes," she said. "And she was in the public eye, so that can sometimes bring out the crazies."

"How about her love life?"

"As far as I know, the last person Cassidy dated seriously was Rick McEwan." She watched the side of Halstead's face carefully. "You probably know him."

He nodded noncommittally.

"Last year Cassidy spoke about their former relationship for a special on domestic violence. He was furious about it."

He looked over at her and then back at the street. "Has he threatened her?" His expression was unreadable.

"I don't know," Allison said. "I know she occasionally gets threats, but they're almost always anonymous. And she doesn't take them very seriously, any more than she takes the proposals of marriage from complete strangers. When you're on TV, it comes with the territory."

"What about her friends and family? Statistically, they're the most likely suspects."

"You're not saying you think—what—that her parents did it? Her brother?" Allison laughed and heard how it bordered on hysteria. "Nicole Hedges? Me?"

"I'm just saying we can't rule anything out."

He signaled for the Lake Oswego exit, the upscale suburb where the Shaws lived. Their house was dominated by a three-car garage. Allison could see lights in the living room. As they parked and went up the walk, she wished she were anywhere but here.

Halstead rang the bell. "Let me do the talking, at least at first."

"Of course." This was one bit of news Allison wished she could let someone else give.

David Shaw answered the door. He was a tall man in his early sixties, with aggressively erect posture and gray hair cut in a flat top. For all that he looked like a retired military man, he had actually made his money building up a small chain of grocery stores. Two years ago he had sold out to a much bigger chain. According to Cassidy, having free time and money had done little to improve his mood.

"Allison?" He looked from her to Halstead, trying and failing to make a connection between the two of them. "What are you doing here?"

"Mr. Shaw, I'm Sean Halstead, with the Portland Police Bureau. Is your wife home, sir?"

Something changed in Cassidy's father's face then, a faint flicker. "Why?"

From behind him came a woman's voice with a slight Southern accent. "Who is it, dear?"

A slender woman in a turquoise track suit appeared in the hall. She had Cassidy's blond hair, or at least the color was from the same bottle.

"I'm Sean Halstead with the Portland Police," he repeated. Allison noticed that he didn't say anything about being a homicide detective. "Could we please come in and sit down?"

"Why? What's wrong?" Mrs. Shaw clutched her husband's shoulder. Under her smooth forehead, the rest of her face suddenly sagged. "Why is he here? What's wrong, Allison?"

"If we could all just sit down . . ." Unbidden, Halstead stepped inside, and Cassidy's parents automatically shuffled back. Allison followed him in and closed the door. They were in a formal entryway, all dark polished wood.

"Has something happened to Cassidy?" Mr. Shaw asked. "Is she hurt?"

The detective spoke slowly, as if to let the words sink in. "Yes. I'm afraid so."

"How bad is it?" Mr. Shaw looked like a hawk, his eyes glittering.

Halstead didn't look away. "It's very bad, I'm afraid. Now if we could just sit down . . ."

"How bad?" Cassidy's father demanded again. "Just tell me. Tell me now."

Halstead managed to look as if he was there and not there. "I'm afraid Cassidy has been killed."

"No." Mrs. Shaw looked back and forth from the detective to Allison. "No, no, no." Her hands went over her ears as her voice got louder. "I just talked to her this morning!"

Suddenly she crumpled and fell against her husband's chest. He supported her as they went into the living room and sat down together on a green silk couch. Allison looked at Halstead to see whether they should sit too, but he remained standing.

"Was it a car accident?" Mr. Shaw asked. "I told her that car had terrible safety ratings."

"Actually, I'm sorry to have to tell you this, but your daughter was murdered."

"No!" Mrs. Shaw shook her head again.

"Murdered?" Mr. Shaw asked. His jaw was set, his eyes slitted.

Mrs. Shaw put a hand to her mouth, her blue eyes huge. "How do you know it's her? It could be just someone who looks like her."

Halstead glanced at Allison, and she realized it was her cue.

"Nicole and I were the ones who found her, Mrs. Shaw. I'm sorry, but it's definitely Cassidy." Maybe it would have been better after all, Allison thought bleakly, if they had heard the news from a stranger. She certainly wasn't doing anything to help them. "We found her in her condo."

"But . . . how . . . ?"

"It looks like she was stabbed."

Cassidy's mother got to her feet. "I need to go to her. She's always been afraid of the dark. I need to be with her so she's not all on her own."

Her husband grabbed her wrist. "You can't, Gretchen." His voice was harsh. Near, Allison thought, to breaking. "Don't you understand? She's dead. Our daughter is dead."

"That doesn't mean she won't know I'm there." Mrs. Shaw tried to tug free. "I just want to hold her hand, brush her hair."

"I'm afraid you can't, Mrs. Shaw," Halstead said gently. "We need to do an autopsy. Then we can release the body to you."

"What—you're going to cut her open?" Her eyes widened. "Saw the top of my baby's head off? No. You can't. I won't allow it. She's not police property. She's my child." She was shaking as if she would fly apart.

Allison stepped forward and touched Cassidy's mother's shoulder. "Do you believe in God, Mrs. Shaw?"

Halstead shot her a quick look, and she knew she was going wildly off-script. So be it. This would be on her head.

Mrs. Shaw's eyes slowly focused on Allison's face. There was a long pause, then she nodded.

"I know this is devastating news, Mrs. Shaw. God never promised that we won't experience loss or heartache, but He has promised peace and His presence in the midst of our pain. I'll be praying that you find that peace."

For a moment Allison thought Mrs. Shaw had heard her. Then the other woman's face changed, revealing all the years she had managed to keep at bay. "How would you understand? You've never lost a child!"

Allison bit her lip. She *had* lost a child. A year ago she had had a miscarriage, early enough in the pregnancy that most people hadn't known about it. But then again, Allison had only dreamed of holding her baby. Cassidy's mother had had her daughter for thirty-four years before she was cruelly ripped away.

"I promise you both that we will find justice for Cassidy," she said, ignoring the look Halstead gave her—the look that said there were no promises on heaven or earth that would bring peace to the Shaws.

CHAPTER 7

Nic had been in dozens of interview rooms—but never like this. Never as the interviewee.

The walls were blank. A long table had been shoved up against one corner of the room. Two chairs were the only other furniture. One had straight legs, the other wheels.

The whole setup of "the box" was deliberate. Bare walls meant that a bad guy had zero distractions, forcing him to focus on the person questioning him.

When it came to the chairs, the one on rollers would normally be occupied by the interrogator, who would then have the suspect brought in. The cop might start off four feet away from his quarry, but when it was time to coax a confession, he or she could roll forward to reduce the distance to inches.

As soon as she walked into the box, Nicole claimed the rolling chair.

And she dared anyone to try to take it from her.

She checked the time on her phone. Again. It had been over an hour since she had been put in this room. She rubbed her hands up and down her goose-pimpled arms. Her jacket was still in her car. The tank top that had been barely tolerable in the smothering heat offered little protection against aggressive air-conditioning.

Cassidy was dead. *Dead*.

Last year Nic had worried so much about dying. She had found a lump in her breast, undergone surgery and then radiation. She had been forced to come to terms with the idea that she could die. Even with the idea that she *would* die, someday.

But seeing Cassidy stuffed under her own sink, turned into an ugly sack of flesh—it was almost impossible to believe. Nic's mind kept replaying it. The blood on the floor. Opening the cupboard door. Finding her friend. Even seeing the horror on Allison's face had not made it any more real.

The friendship among the three of them—the Triple Threat—was like a fulcrum, with Allison in the middle and Nic and Cassidy occupying opposite ends. Allison was the glue that held them together.

Cassidy was so different from Nic. Talkative while Nic was quiet. Brash while Nic was reserved. Jumping in with both feet while Nic decided whether it was worthwhile to commit at all.

How many times had Cassidy caught Nic rolling her eyes, quirking her mouth? Her face went hot with shame. Couldn't she have been more patient? Couldn't she have realized that the very traits that annoyed her about Cassidy had been the same things she had liked in the first place? Nic should have cut her more slack.

And now, with Cassidy gone, would Allison grow tired of Nic's dark moods?

Allison was probably in another interview room somewhere nearby. Was she also waiting, or was she already being questioned?

Nic started when the door opened. It was Jensen. The smudges under his eyes made it look like he hadn't slept in a week. The knot of his shiny tie had been pushed back up. He had a notebook in his hand and a pen behind his ear. Without comment, he took the straight-legged chair. She wished she could remember where she knew him from.

"So you're the lead detective?" Nic asked. If only she had thought of that earlier in the evening. She had to keep a lid on her emotions.

"Yeah. Sean Halstead will be working the case with me."

The name didn't ring any bells. Homicide detectives often worked in pairs, although in most cases they split up the tasks, working together only when they needed backup or a second witness.

"Did you find any more evidence besides the blood drops?"

Jensen's eyes narrowed even further. "I'm pretty sure I shouldn't tell you even if I did." A space stretched out between them, threatened to snap. Finally he relented. "No. And the canvass hasn't picked up anything, at least not so far." He flipped to a blank page in his notebook. "So could you tell me a little bit more about what you did today, starting at six p.m.?"

It was the kind of question you asked a suspect. But in the interests of harmony, Nic decided to overlook how ridiculous it was. "I finished up at work and then I drove out to Puerto Marquez in Southeast Portland to meet Allison Pierce and Cassidy for dinner." She summarized how they had waited for Cassidy, their attempts to reach her, and the anxiety that had begun to grip them.

Jensen looked back over his notes. "But you just mentioned that Cassidy was known for being late. Why were you worried tonight?"

"First of all, she's never been that late before. But what really bothered us was that she didn't answer her phone. Cassidy always has her phone with her, and she always answers it. She even sleeps with it next to her. I'm not talking on the night table—I mean right next to her pillow."

"When was the last time you saw her?"

"About a week and a half ago the three of us got together for lunch." Nic tried to keep the memory at arm's length so it wouldn't swamp her. "I've talked with her on the phone a couple of times since then, and we've texted each other. But not about anything important."

"What about the text she sent you saying she was working on a story?" Jensen raised his eyes to hers. "Do you know what story that was?"

"No. It could have been anything."

Nic knew Jensen would be ordering a trap and trace on Cassidy's phone. The phone company would turn over a record of the numbers she had called and those that had called her, but of course they wouldn't have the actual contents of the calls. Jensen would also be getting any text messages that were still available. Depending on the phone company, texts were saved anywhere from forty-eight hours to a couple of weeks. But if Cassidy had kept her texts and they were recoverable from her broken phone, they could date back much earlier.

"As you drove up to her building, did you see anyone on the street or in a vehicle?"

"Not that I can remember."

"How about in the parking lot?"

"No." The skin on Nic's face felt tight. "You already asked me these questions."

Jensen continued as if she hadn't said anything. "How did you get inside? Did you have a key to Cassidy's apartment?"

"No. When we got there, we found the door unlocked."

"Ajar?"

"No. I put my hand on it and was surprised when it turned."

He made a note. "Now, what I could use your help on is understanding a little bit more about Cassidy and what might have happened to her. Does she keep any cash around?"

Did he really think this was some burglary gone bad?

"Cassidy? No." Cassidy was like the grasshopper in the fable. She lived for today and didn't worry about tomorrow. The condo had represented most of her retirement funds. It struck Nic, sickeningly, that Cassidy hadn't been wrong. Because for Cassidy there would be no tomorrows. At least not on this earth.

"Jewelry?"

"Strictly costume, as far as I know." Nic realized she was tapping her fingers on the table and made herself stop.

"Prescription drugs?"

"She used to take Somulex, but she quit. And nothing since then, at least that I'm aware of."

"Illegal drugs?"

"Cassidy? No. She liked her appletinis and lemon drops, that's all."

"Could you tell me more about what kind of person she was? What were her best and worst traits?"

Nic bit the inside of her mouth. Was this really a good use of Jensen's time? But arguing would probably get her nowhere and take up even more time.

"Cassidy has a lot of energy, a lot of imagination. And she'll never take no for an answer. But she's not a big detail person. Not the kind to read the fine print."

"So if she came home and someone was burglarizing her condo, she might not notice at first?"

"Please don't tell me you're looking at that angle."

He gave her a slit-eyed look.

"All right, it's possible, sure, that she might not notice right away. But Allison and I didn't see anything missing or out of place."

"Could you describe your relationship with Cassidy?"

"The three of us have been good friends for about six years. We're not only personal friends, but we also end up working a lot of the same cases. Cassidy covers them, and Allison and I work together to get convictions."

"Seems like it'd be pretty easy to cross some lines there." Jensen gave her a knowing look. "Give her information she shouldn't have."

Nic took a deep breath. Was he baiting her?

"Allison and I are more than aware of our relationship's challenges. We would never jeopardize an investigation. At the same time, Cassidy sometimes has sources we don't, or we can use her to leak a story and control how it's shaped."

Jensen stiffened. "So does that have anything to do with how she got the story about the jail smuggling ring?"

"What?" And then Nic remembered. Six months earlier Channel Four had broken the story of a Multnomah County inmate running an illegal business from his cell, funneling thousands of dollars of drugs and cigarettes into the jail. Of course, the inmate hadn't been able to do it on his own—three guards were also implicated.

The DA's office had already been investigating. Cassidy had been doing a routine check of public documents, trawling for story ideas, when she ran across the search warrant. A search warrant that should have been sealed, but had been filed in the wrong place.

How could Jensen think she or Allison had anything to do with that?

"No. Of course not. She did that on her own. We were upset with her too."

Nic's words didn't seem to register. Jensen spoke through gritted teeth. "She tipped off the bad guys and ruined our investigation. The confidential informant got scared. The DA had to pull the plug. The whole case, months of work"—he made a spiraling motion with his hand—"down the drain."

Nic remembered how the three of them had argued about it. After the fact. Cassidy hadn't dared tell them what she planned to do, knowing they would have tried mightily to talk her out of it.

As if anyone could talk Cassidy out of anything.

Her argument—and the one that Channel Four later made when it got push-back—was that it was important to run the story based on the jail's recent problematic history. Only a few weeks earlier the jail had been on lockdown after a gun had been discovered hidden in a hollowed-out space in a wall.

Nic crossed her arms. "You're not going to let that color your hunt for her killer, are you?"

He pressed his lips together. "I am a professional, as you are, Special Agent Hedges." He turned a page in his notebook. "Does Cassidy have a boyfriend?"

So he was finally getting to the heart of the matter, or at least circling around it.

"No." She amended it to, "I guess it's possible. Cassidy liked men, and men liked Cassidy. But as far as I know, she hasn't dated anyone new for months." Nic took a deep breath. "Look. You and I both know that you have to look at Rick McEwan. It doesn't matter that he's a cop. They dated, and it became an abusive relationship."

Jensen blew air out of pursed lips. "Whatever was between him and Cassidy is long over."

"So? She dragged his name through the mud. After that special on domestic violence aired, people figured out who he was. It was an open secret. And I heard that the chief ordered him into counseling. Knowing Rick, all of that must have been humiliating. And I still remember the way he treated her. We were over there once and found all her bras and panties in the garbage. Rick had made her cut them up in front of him, because he thought they were too sexy. And whenever they were out with other people, he would accuse her of flirting with other men. He pushed her around. I saw the bruises he left. Are you telling me that someone like Rick just forgave and forgot and moved on? I don't think so. That's not the Rick McEwan I remember."

"If you're saying whoever did this had a long memory, what about any of the people she covered? It seems like they were all rapists and murderers and molesters." Jensen pointed his pen at her. "Maybe one of them wanted to get back at her. It wouldn't be hard to figure out where she lived. And then all he would need to do is pretend to have a delivery that needed a signature. Show up in any kind of uniform, and people will let you in."

It was true that Cassidy had never kept her guard up as much as she should have. Nic tried to picture it. Cassidy stopping by her condo on her way over to the restaurant, a knock at the door, and then—

"But whoever did it hid her body. Like he was ashamed. I don't think whoever killed her was a stranger. You need to at least take a look at Rick."

His face reddened. "Look, I want to remind you again that when it comes to this case, you are a civilian. We already have investigators. We don't need you muddying the waters. We don't need you running your mouth about Rick."

Nic's spine stiffened. "You're supposed to be listening to my answers, not challenging them. If you have personal feelings about this, maybe you shouldn't be the one asking the questions."

Jensen shook his head. "You're a piece of work, do you know that? You don't remember the other time we worked together, do you?"

Nic was so tired. Suddenly it was as if she could lay her head right down on the pale laminate of the table and fall asleep. "To be honest, no. No, I don't. But don't let whatever happened in the past between us affect what you do here."

He slapped his hands on his knees. Hard. "Look. You are going to have to trust me, Agent Hedges. Trust me that I will get this right.

Because it's not about you. It's not even about Cassidy Shaw. It's about justice."

They both jumped when the door opened. Leif Larson walked in. He was well over six feet, with the muscled body of a warrior. The interview room suddenly seemed very small.

"I think we're done for tonight," Leif said. "Okay, Detective Jensen? If you need to talk to Agent Hedges again, you can do it in the morning. After everyone's gotten some sleep."

Nic stood up on legs that were suddenly almost too weak to hold her. Head high, she followed Leif onto the elevator.

It was only when they were safely in a shadowy corner of the parking lot that she let herself crumble.

Leif caught her in his arms.

Victoria Avenue Library

4848 Victoria Avenue
Niagara Falls, ON L2E 4C5
905-356-8080

PUBLIC LIBRARY

my.nflibrary.ca

Welcome to the Victoria Avenue Library!

Card # 28080001800200

You checked out the following:

1. Eyes of justice : a triple
   threat novel
   Barcode: 38080101558516
   Due: March 2, 2020

================================

Overdue Fines per item:

Books => Child ~ 10¢/day

Books => Adult ~ 25¢/day

DVDs/Video Games ~ $1/day

Lucky Day Books ~ $1/day

Boardgames ~ $2/day

Launchpads ~ $2/day

================================

Feb 10, 2020 3:38 PM @ VIC

CHAPTER 8

It was after midnight when Allison finally tried to put her key in the lock of her front door. Tried and failed.

Two hours earlier, after she and Halstead had left Cassidy's parents' house, she had called Marshall from the Shaws' driveway to let him know what was happening. She'd thought nothing could be worse than breaking the news to Cassidy's parents, but telling her husband had nearly breached her defenses.

She had wanted to go home immediately, but first Halstead took her to the police station to formally interview her. Afterward she looked around the station for Nicole, but all she found was Detective Jensen, who said Nic had already left. Judging by the way he said it, things hadn't gone well.

Allison hitched a ride with a patrol officer to retrieve her car from Puerto Marquez's otherwise empty parking lot. The meal she and Nicole had eaten there seemed like it had taken place in another year. Another century. She drove home in a blur, too beaten down to offer more than an inarticulate prayer.

Help us. Help them get through this, help them find who did it, help Cassidy get the justice she deserves.

Now Allison's hand shook so badly that the key danced over the lock, making a scratching sound. Suddenly the door swung open, and she started back, her hand over her mouth.

"It's just me, Allison." Marshall's blue eyes were full of sadness.

She opened her mouth, but no words came out.

Cassidy was dead. Cassidy was dead, and the world didn't make any sense.

Marshall held out his arms. Allison stepped forward, and he wrapped them around her. She tucked her head under his chin. With a jangle the keys fell from her hand and landed on the mat. The veneer of professionalism that had been the only thing holding her together for the past few hours crumbled. Tears choked her throat, clouded her eyes. Marshall tightened his grip until he bore most of her weight, and she pressed against him, skin on skin, heartbeat to heartbeat.

"Oh, Marshall, it was so awful," she muttered, her mouth against his damp, salty shoulder.

Even close to midnight, it was still too hot to touch, but she needed it too much to care. Marshall was wearing shorts and a tank top. If Lindsay, Allison's sister, hadn't been living with them, it probably would have been only shorts. For the past year Allison and Marshall had been living a slightly artificial version of their life, one that was braced for a third party at any time.

"I just can't believe it, Marshall," she finally said. "Who would do that to Cassidy?"

It was the same question she had explored with Halstead, both in the car and in the interview room. Cassidy had such a strong personality that it was pretty much guaranteed no one could ever feel neutral about her. But who in the world could possibly hate her enough to drive a knife into her body?

Marshall sighed and shook his head. "I don't know, babe. I don't know. It just doesn't make sense."

Finally Allison unpeeled herself from him, stepped back, and

wiped her eyes on her forearm. Her head ached. The door to the living room was still open, and she stepped inside after picking up her
keys. Lindsay had been stretched out on the couch. Now she sat up.
The TV was turned to the news with the sound on low. On the screen
were pictures of some war on the other side of the world—civilian
men being rounded up at gunpoint, the bodies of men and women
and even children sprawled in a dusty street. Allison grabbed the
clicker from the arm of the couch and turned it off.

Lindsay got up and ran her hands through her pink-streaked
hair, her expression tentative. "Ally, I'm so sorry about Cassidy. What
a terrible thing."

"Yeah. Thanks." Allison had no idea what to say back. The future
was sure to be filled with many such conversations. *Thanks* wasn't
right, but what was?

Looking at her sister, dressed in orange-and-white shortie pajamas that had once been Allison's, just made her even more tired. It
was selfish, she knew, but for a minute she wished she and Marshall
were alone in the house. She didn't have the energy for a third person,
not tonight. Sometimes Lindsay felt more like an observer than a sister, an anthropologist sent to study the upper middle class.

"Why are you still up?" Allison asked.

Lindsay gestured toward an open notebook on the couch. "I was
working on plans for my cart."

Lindsay's dream was to open a coffee and cookie cart in one of
Portland's food pods. The pods were former parking lots now filled
with food carts. They attracted everyone from businessmen to hard-
partying hipsters to foodies looking for something a little different
and eminently affordable.

Allison nodded numbly, incapable of small talk or of any talk
at all. "I'm going to take a shower." Moving like a robot, she went

upstairs. With each step, the heat seemed to rise a degree. Upstairs, all the windows were wide open, but there wasn't even the hint of a breeze, and the air was close and still. In the shower she let the cool water wash away the grime, sweat, and tears of the day. And then she wept, thinking of how she would never see Cassidy again, never hear her voice or her laugh.

Afterward, Allison toweled herself off. She left her hair wet in the hopes it would keep her cool. When she opened the door, she saw that Marshall was already in bed, a long dark shadow on top of the sheets. She tiptoed across the room and lay down beside him. She had imagined sliding between crisp and cool sheets, but instead the very mattress seemed to radiate warmth.

"It must have been terrible for you," Marshall said in the darkness, "finding her like that."

"Nicole knew right away that something was wrong, but I was in denial. Before she saw the blood on the floor, I was trying to tell myself that everything was okay. And even after we saw the blood, I kept trying to think of reasons that would explain it all away."

"It's pretty unbelievable. Cassidy was one of the most alive people I knew," Marshall said. "Do you think it had something to do with a story she's covering?"

"It could be. She texted us that she was going to be late because she was following a lead. But we don't know what that story was. Or maybe it had nothing to do with Channel Four. The cops were wondering if she could have surprised a burglar." Allison sighed, thinking of Halstead's questions. "But things at her condo were actually neater than they usually are. Nothing was really out of place."

She scooted closer to the edge of the bed, then rolled on her back and spread out her arms and legs so that nothing touched anything else. "One of the homicide detectives told me they found a knife under her body. If we're very lucky, maybe there are prints. If not, it's going to take a lot of work to figure it out. It could be Cassidy's personal life, her professional life, or just something random."

She felt Marshall turn on his side to face her.

"But it's not your job to figure it out, is it?"

"No." Hearing him echo Jensen's argument, she made a sound that wasn't quite a laugh. "That was already explained to us by the lead homicide detective. This is a case for the Portland police."

"He's right. Let them work the case, see what they come up with. They're responsible, Allison. Not you. Don't take this on too."

In the dark, her eyes opened. "What do you mean, *too*?"

"You can't fix everything, Allison. Or everyone."

She knew he meant her sister. "But I owe it to Cassidy, Marshall." She thought of the promise Nicole had made to Jensen, and that she herself had made to Cassidy's parents.

"You may owe it to her to *see* that justice is done, Allison, but you don't have to be the one to bring it about. Try to let go and put this in God's hands."

She closed her eyes again and tried to center herself. Marshall was right.

"What do you want?" Marshall asked, and for a second the question seemed global. What did Allison want? Justice? Revenge? To simply forget? But then he added, "Air-conditioning on or off?"

Maybe the rattling would drown out her thoughts, cover her memories. "On."

But it didn't work. Every time she was about to drift off, she would suddenly picture Cassidy's slack face and staring eyes.

Allison tried counting backward from three hundred but made it all the way down to one without relaxing a single muscle. She focused on her breathing, the air flowing into her mouth, filling her lungs and then being pushed back out, but all that did was remind her that Cassidy would never draw another breath. An hour passed, two, and Allison was no closer to sleep. Finally she slipped out of bed and padded downstairs into the living room.

She sat on the couch and picked up her phone.

At 3:13 a.m. Nicole had sent her a text. *Rick was best man at Jensen's wedding. How hard is Jensen really going to look at him?*

CHAPTER 9

Hey, Nicole—what are you doing here?"

Tony Sardella, Multnomah County's medical examiner, looked up at the viewing gallery in surprise. Dressed in blue surgical scrubs, his mask dangling around his neck, Tony had just walked into the autopsy suite carrying a stack of files.

Nic was standing in the special observation room that let law enforcement view an autopsy through a long window set in one wall. A color monitor also offered a bird's-eye view from a camera positioned over the autopsy table. The distance, the window, and even the monitor helped you pretend that what was happening was a movie. Something you could tell yourself wasn't real if it got too difficult to watch.

It was a little past eight in the morning, and Nic and Tony were completely alone. The waist-high, stainless steel autopsy table was still empty.

"I want to observe Cassidy Shaw's autopsy." Nic had put that on the sign-in form and had been lucky that no one questioned it.

Tony looked through the files in his hands, pulled one out, and opened it. Then he looked back up at Nic, his high forehead creased in confusion. "But that's a PPB case, right?"

Nic chose her words carefully. "It does belong to the police, but I have a special interest."

She didn't say more. Let him think it was a professional interest. She was pretty sure that Tony had no idea that she and Cassidy
were friends. Had been friends. She kept forgetting to use the correct
tense.

She didn't know if she could carry this off, but she wanted to try.
She wanted to know how Cassidy had been killed, because the how
might tell her the why. And with luck, Jensen would be relying on
Tony's report, not watching the autopsy himself.

"Shaw's not our first case. She's second."

"Oops." Nic shrugged. "I'll just wait. I have some paperwork I
can do." She had a notepad and pen, but it wasn't for anything to do
with the FBI.

Before driving here, she had argued with Allison on the phone.
Rick could have done it, Allison had reminded her, but he was just
one possibility. Nic decided to heed her words, or at least that one
sentence, while ignoring her next one, which was a reminder that this
wasn't their case at all.

She started a list:

Rape
Burglary
Serial killer
Rick
Another old boyfriend
New boyfriend??
Someone mad about a story
The story that made her late to dinner

When the assistant wheeled in the first body, Nic was still the
only person in the observation suite. It was a woman in her late

sixties, with lank graying hair and a swollen face. For the microphone overhead capturing everything for the official record, Tony
noted aloud that she had been found in the Willamette River and
reeled off some particulars about her eye and hair color. Then he and
the pathology assistant began to remove the woman's clothes. They
tugged off her T-shirt, rolling her from side to side. Next the assistant
lifted up the woman's legs while Tony pulled off her pants. After they
finished wrestling off her clothes, Nic looked away from the poor
woman's pale, bloated body. She closed her eyes when Tony made the
Y-incision in her chest and bit her lip when she heard the sound of
the circular saw.

Nic heard rather than saw Tony noting no signs of violence, just
heart disease. The older woman had died by drowning, but a death
investigator would have to look at the circumstances of her life to
decide if it was a suicide or an accident. Possibly it would never be clear.

They were still sewing the older woman back up when Nic's luck
ran out. Jensen walked into the viewing room. He didn't look much
different from twelve hours before—rumpled short-sleeved shirt,
loosened tie, eye sockets smudged with fatigue.

But his face was red with anger. "I couldn't believe it when I saw
your name on the sign-in list. You have got to be kidding me, showing up like this."

Nic reminded herself of what she had found last night when she
couldn't sleep. Rick McEwan wasn't on Facebook, but his sister was.
And her photos included some of a wedding three years earlier, a wedding in which her brother had acted as the best man. The wedding of
Derrick Jensen. The man who had warned her against running her
mouth about Rick.

In the autopsy room below them, a Portland police criminalist
Nic knew by face but not name had walked in. Alerted by the sound

of Jensen's raised voice, he and Tony were looking up at the viewing room curiously.

"Hello, Detective Jensen," Nic said, playing it cool. She looked past him to the two other men who were entering the viewing room. "Sol." She nodded at Sol Greenburg, the deputy district attorney, then held out her hand for the third man, whose large, light brown eyes were made more prominent by his thin face. "Nicole Hedges, FBI."

"Sean Halstead," he said. "Homicide."

Jensen took a step toward her. "Who told you when this autopsy was scheduled?"

"Is there a problem?" Tony asked from below.

Out of the corner of her eye, Nic could see Cassidy's body being wheeled in. She was still dressed in the coral-colored suit they had found her in the night before. The blood on the front of the jacket was dried to rust. Her hands and feet were covered with paper bags and her eyes were half open. Only a few hours ago she had been moving, eating, laughing, talking, typing. Probably all at once.

Jensen walked to the window of the observation room. "This isn't Hedges's case, Tony. The decedent is a personal friend of hers."

Tony's gaze swung to her. "Is that true, Nicole?"

"Well, yes, but, Tony, I need to know what happened to her. I won't bug anyone. I'll just sit here in the corner. You won't even know I'm here."

Jensen snorted. "I'll know you're here." He turned to Tony. "She and another woman reported finding the body, and she had to be handcuffed by the first responding officer last night because she flat-out refused to cooperate."

"How long had that girl been on the job?" The words burst from Nic's lips before she could call them back. "A day? I was just trying to make sure she didn't screw anything up."

"You can't run a parallel investigation, Agent Hedges." Jensen looked at her with narrowed eyes. "There is only one investigation. The official one. The one being conducted by Portland Police."

Tony's head swiveled back and forth as they argued.

"How do I know you're going to consider all the options? Including the idea that Cassidy might have been killed by her abusive former boyfriend, who also happens to be a Portland cop?"

Tony's eyebrows went up. Still, his voice rose over both of theirs. "Look, I don't really know what's going on. But it's my call as to who observes, Nicole. And I'm sorry, but if this isn't your case, it's not appropriate that you're here."

She could argue, but what would it get her? If worst came to worst, Jensen or even Tony would get on the phone with Lincoln Bond, the new special agent in charge of the Portland field office, and have Bond order her out. That wouldn't exactly start things off on the right foot with her new boss.

She was fighting a losing battle.

Nic held her hands up in surrender. "All right, I'm going, I'm going."

As she braved the already blazing sun to walk back to her car, she finally remembered where she and Jensen had crossed paths before. Eighteen months earlier a joint task force had been looking at the illegal drug trade in Portland. Nicole and Jensen had sat around the same table two or three times.

Then Jensen started investigating the death of a Mexican American found shot to death in downtown Portland. Roberto Delgado had taken one in the head and one in the heart, both at such close range they left powder burns.

It wasn't a murder. It was an execution.

But it turned out that Delgado had been a federal informant, killed before he could testify in a drug smuggling case. The FBI took over the case from Portland Homicide, but they had different priorities. Rather than focusing on solving a single murder, the FBI wanted to connect the dots and clean up a drug-trafficking web that stretched from Portland to Central America.

They were going after the big fish. If the little minnow who actually pulled the trigger on Roberto Delgado was caught along the way, fine—but only after he led them further up the food chain. What was catching one bad guy, when there were so many out there? And the victim had not been a shining beacon of innocence, as Nic had pointed out. Jensen had protested, but had been told he was serving a larger justice.

And soon after that, he asked that someone else from PPB be appointed to the task force.

When Nic's cell phone rang around one o'clock that afternoon, the display showed a number she didn't recognize. When she said hello, she wasn't completely surprised to hear Tony's voice.

"Do you know who this is?"

"Yes." There was no privacy in her cubicle. Nic walked down the hall and out into the stairwell. She leaned against the wall.

"This is all strictly off the record—do you understand me?"

Autopsy results were not a matter of public record in Oregon, so Tony was really going out on a limb calling her. But they had worked closely on a number of cases and had come to respect each other. Nic wondered where he was calling from. She bet it was a pay phone nowhere near his home or office. It was what she would do in his place.

"Okay, we weren't able to establish an exact time of death. We know she was probably alive when you got a text from her. Of course, it's possible someone could have used her phone. But assuming it was her, there are still too many variables to pin it down. Just her being under the sink with the door closed could have changed things, because the air wouldn't have been circulating around the body. She could have died any time between when she was seen leaving the television station at six twenty and when you found her body shortly before nine."

"All right." This was no surprise. "And?"

"There were fingertip-shaped contusions under her chin, and her airway had been compromised. There were no defensive wounds or marks, and nothing under her nails."

"So she was strangled from behind." Nic wondered why she hadn't fought. That didn't sound like Cassidy. "What about the blood?"

"That was from a sizable penetrating wound in her chest. The blade was about three-quarters of an inch wide, not quite an eighth of an inch thick, and, based on penetration depth, at least four inches long. It was a single-edged blade, not serrated. All of that's consistent with the knife found at the scene."

Allison had told Nic about the knife.

"So which was the cause of death?" Nic asked. "The strangulation or the stabbing?"

"Well, even considering the bloodletting on the clothes and the blood on the floor—that could have been from the way she was crammed in that cabinet, with her head and chest slightly elevated from supine . . ." Tony's voice trailed off. "It was hard to tell, but there might have been some reactive hemorrhage around the wound. But I'm thinking it was a perimortem strangulation and a postmortem stabbing."

Nic put it into English. "So you think she was strangled and then stabbed after she was dead?"

"It's just a guess. I'm listing both as causes of death. The stab wound would have been enough on its own to be fatal. It nicked her aorta. There's no evidence she was moving when she was stabbed, though, so she was quite possibly already unconscious or deceased. Maybe the killer just wanted to make sure she was dead."

Nic took a shaky breath. It was bad enough to think of Cassidy being strangled—but to suffer both . . . "I hope you're right that she wasn't awake to feel it. For her sake." Nicole's own heart was beating so loudly she could hear it in her ears. "How long would it have taken for her to die?"

"Not long. A few minutes. Once you deprive the brain of oxygen, everything starts to fail. She would have passed out before she died."

A few minutes probably had seemed like an eternity. Nic just hoped Cassidy had lost consciousness quickly.

She leaned her forehead against the cool concrete wall. "Was she sexually assaulted?"

"The rape kit was negative." Tony took a deep breath. "There was one other noteworthy thing about the body."

"What?" Nic suddenly knew this was why he had called her.

"We found a circular abraded and contused pattern on her wrists. It suggests she was restrained. My best guess is with metal handcuffs."

Metal handcuffs.

Just like the ones Portland police used.

CHAPTER 10

Cassidy's turquoise blue eyes looked directly into the camera. "While I was dating my ex-boyfriend, I felt so isolated. I was in the public eye, but it felt like I was cut off from everyone. Over time, my self-esteem was completely destroyed."

Her gaze was unwavering as she lifted her chin. "My ex-boyfriend manipulated me and got under my skin. He took every grain of confidence I had. He called me names. He belittled me. And eventually he began to hit me. He also isolated me from my family and friends. And it was the emotional manipulation that took longer to get over than the bruises."

Cassidy took a deep breath. "I am speaking out about my experiences to help any of our viewers who are being hurt and who hear this broadcast. You need to know that you don't have to live in pain and isolation. You are not alone. I have stood in your shoes, I have walked the paths you are walking, and I managed to come out on the other side. I've reclaimed my life, and you can too." She nodded once, her expression serene, not quite a smile.

And with that, the clip of Cassidy Shaw on YouTube came to an end.

Allison reached her fingertips toward her computer screen, stopping just short of touching the hard plastic. "Oh, Cassidy," she murmured. Hot tears filled her eyes, and she was crying again. Crying so hard she worried someone might hear her through her closed office door. She pulled another tissue from the box.

That morning she had finally fallen asleep just as the sun was rising. When she woke around nine, the oppressive heat flattening her to the mattress, at first all she knew was that something bad had happened. For a second, Allison had the luxury of not remembering exactly what it was.

And then it came crashing down on her. Cassidy was dead.

Unable to eat breakfast, she had managed a few sips of coffee, thankful that Lindsay was still sleeping and Marshall was already at work. He'd left a note saying how much he loved her and suggesting she take it easy. She'd paged blindly through the paper without focusing on the headlines. The story about Cassidy's murder was brief, headlined *Woman's Body Found, Foul Play Suspected*. It didn't mention her name.

Later in the morning, her head throbbing, swollen eyes hidden behind dark glasses, Allison had gone to work, thankful she wasn't scheduled to be in court. She spent most of the morning sequestered in her office, fending off a blur of people saying they were sorry. Even with little in the paper, details about Cassidy's murder seemed to have spread like wildfire throughout Portland. In a city where most killings were the result of domestic violence or gang members targeting other gang members, in a city filled with thousands of young women trying to make it on their own, the inexplicable murder of a well-known reporter was a shock.

Allison's coworkers were solicitous—and curious. There were only so many ways to respond to their questions and awkward condolences. She wanted to hold Cassidy close in her thoughts—the real Cassidy, warts and all—but the more Allison talked about her, the more she became a simpler and slightly smaller version of herself, more fit for public consumption.

Through a blur of tears, Allison stared at Cassidy's image, frozen on the screen. Could Rick McEwan really have murdered her for dragging his abuse out into the open? In the middle of the night, seeing that text from Nicole, Allison had been half convinced it was possible. Now, in the bright light of day, the idea seemed a stretch.

She got up and paced the office, thinking it through one more time. Everyone in Portland had known that Rick was dating Cassidy. He had liked to show her off. So when she came out with her accusations, his ego must have been bruised. Maybe more than bruised. But was Rick the kind of man to bide his time for a year?

This high above the city, the freeway sounded like a distant river. Allison was cocooned away in her office, cut off from the heat and sweat of the day. The pale blue walls behind her never witnessed raised voices. By the time the crimes she prosecuted reached her, they had been leached of emotion. Even the color photos of the horrific aftermaths were all neatly closed up in binders.

Pausing in front of the floor-to-ceiling window, Allison squinted in the bright sunlight. The steel-gray Willamette River was directly underneath her, cutting through the heart of the city. On the other side of the river, the city stretched for miles in an orderly grid. Mount Hood, pictured on a thousand postcards, loomed in the background, snowcapped even at this time of year. She had spent enough years with the spectacular view that now she seldom focused on it.

But Cassidy would never see it again. Allison remembered how her friend's eyes, dull and fixed, had stared out from under the kitchen sink. Stared at nothing. Cassidy would never see anything again, beautiful or ugly.

On Allison's desk, her cell phone buzzed. She walked over, ready to dismiss the call, but saw that it was Nicole and snatched it up instead.

"Where are you?" Nicole said without preamble. "We need to talk."

"At work, but I'm pretty useless. Why? Is there something new about Cassidy?"

"I'll tell you when I see you."

Fifteen minutes later there was a knock on the door. After Allison called out that it was open, Nicole nudged the door open with her hip. In one hand she held a white paper Starbucks cup that looked a foot tall, and in the other a second cup that was only slightly smaller.

Dan Wilcox, Allison's boss, was walking past, and he glanced over at them curiously. That morning he had expressed his sympathies and told Allison to "take as much time" as she needed. But he had been fiddling with a pen when he said it, and he hadn't met her eyes.

Nicole closed the door and handed Allison the second cup. "Here. You probably need this. I'm guessing you got just about as much sleep as I did." Only in an air-conditioned office did hot coffee on such a hot day make sense, but Allison took it gratefully. Nicole continued, "I was at the autopsy today."

"You watched? How could you stand to?" The few times Allison had witnessed autopsies she had gotten through them by pretending she was watching a particularly grisly movie—detailed but ultimately fake. And those times the bodies had all belonged to strangers.

"Actually, I didn't." Nic sat down. "Jensen turned up and wouldn't let me stay. He even threatened to go to Bond about it. Since I haven't even had my one-on-one with him yet, I didn't protest. I have a feeling that wouldn't get things off on the right foot."

"I hate to say it, Nicole, but if Jensen showed up on a case of ours and started acting like he didn't trust us to get it right, we'd kick him out too. This is a job for PPB. Not us."

"Do you really think that?" Nicole snorted. "Tony called me just a little bit ago. Off the record."

Allison blinked in surprise. "Why?"

"He said they found bruises around Cassidy's wrists. The skin was practically rubbed off in places." Nicole circled one wrist with her finger and thumb, then turned it back and forth before grasping the other wrist and repeating the motion.

Allison's scalp prickled. "Handcuffs?"

"Exactly. Now, who do you know who carries a pair of handcuffs on his belt every day?"

Allison ignored the question. "What was the cause of death?"

"She was strangled first and then stabbed. It's possible she was still alive when she was stabbed."

Cassidy, struggling to breathe. No way to defend herself. Her hands locked uselessly behind her back, wrists bruising as she writhed in desperation.

"Handcuffs aren't the only things Rick has on his belt," Allison pointed out. "If it was him, then why didn't he shoot her?"

"And have the ballistics match? Rick's too smart to do something that dumb. Besides, this feels personal. Killers who strangle their victims *feel* them die."

Nausea bubbled up in Allison, and she swallowed it back down. How could anyone stand to do that? "I don't know, Nicole. Why would Rick kill Cassidy now? Things have been over between them for more than a year."

"Maybe he waited until he figured no one would connect him to it. He's not the kind to forgive and forget. You remember how he treated her. And what kind of incentive do the cops have for looking at Rick too closely? If they have a murderer on the force, they'll never live it down. They were already mad at Cassidy for shaming Rick in public and then leaking that story about the smuggling at the jail. Do you think Jensen really wants to take a close look at his best man?"

Allison remembered the set of the detective's jaw. "Jensen seems like a professional. I think he'll be turning over rocks, even if one of them ends up having Rick under it. You really think he would let a killer go free to teach a dead woman a lesson?"

Nicole crossed her arms. "Cops tend to stick together."

"So do FBI agents," Allison pointed out. "So does pretty much any group. That's what makes them effective, because they know they've got each other's backs. But this is going to be a high-profile case, and they know people will be watching." Exhaustion crested over her like a wave. She raised the cup to her lips. "PPB knows they have to connect the dots and follow where they lead."

Coffee normally smelled enticing, but today it just smelled burnt. Nausea thickened her throat. Allison hadn't eaten since last night, and now the thought of those spicy shrimp made her hold herself very still for a few seconds, trying to decide if she was going to retch. Finally the urge receded. Swallowing hard, she set the coffee down and looked up to find Nicole watching her.

"Sorry. Just a little sick to my stomach. I've already drunk so much coffee I probably shouldn't have any more." She moved the cup to the far edge of her desk.

"Nauseated?" Nicole tilted her head.

"I'm not pregnant, if that's what you're thinking."

Allison and Marshall hadn't talked about trying again for months. The idea of actually having a baby seemed more remote with each passing day. She wasn't even disappointed anymore when her period showed up every fourth Friday, just like clockwork. She sighed. "Look, I get that you think it's probably Rick. But we have to look at the other possibilities."

"Oh, so it's *we* now." Nicole looked at her with hooded eyes.

"Come on, Nicole. No one is going to listen to us if we just have a gut feeling. We have to look at this logically. And looking at it logically, there are three choices. The first one is that Cassidy was just in the wrong place at the wrong time, and it's her bad luck that she's the one who ended up dead. That covers a botched burglary. Or even a serial killer who likes blondes."

Nicole wasn't buying it. "I pulled up the crime reports this morning. There haven't been any recent burglaries or break-ins in the area. And there's been no unsolved murder with a similar MO anyplace in the Pacific Northwest."

"Okay, then there's the second choice," Allison said. "It could have had something to do with who she is. Something personal. That means not only Rick, but any other past or current boyfriend." She thought of something. "Was she sexually assaulted?"

Nicole shook her head, and Allison felt the faintest relief.

"So it's possible it was even a woman, maybe someone who got mad thinking that Cassidy poached her man. Maybe that explains the handcuffs—someone who needed her incapacitated to make sure they were strong enough to kill her." Allison took a deep breath that shook at the end. "And the third choice is that this has something to do with her work. We need to figure out what stories she's covered that might have left someone mad at her."

"That shouldn't be too hard." Nicole raised one eyebrow. "Heck, you and I worked a lot of the same cases Cassidy did."

"I think our first priority is figuring out what lead she was working on when she texted us. I'm going to call Brad and see if he knows what it was about."

She picked up the phone, but she must not have been the only one calling Channel Four. The only way Allison succeeded in getting through to Brad Buffet was by using her title.

"Have you made an arrest?" he asked as soon as he came on the line. He must think she was officially on the case.

"Not yet," she said noncommittally. It wasn't really a lie. "Brad, Cassidy texted me and Nicole Hedges right before she died. She told us she would be late to meet us for dinner because she was following up on a lead. Do you know what story she was working on?"

"The cops already took away her computer and most of the contents of her cubicle."

"Oh." Allison should have expected as much.

"But I backed up her most recent files before they did."

"You did?"

"Hey," Brad said, sounding defensive, "I need to know what it is we're dealing with here. What if it's someone targeting the reporters at Channel Four? There are a lot of crazies out there. We never really take that kind of thing seriously, but maybe Cassidy should have. I mean, look how things turned out."

"What do you mean, Brad?" Allison asked as Nicole looked at her curiously.

"Don't you know?"

"No. What are you talking about?"

"Cassidy had a stalker."

CHAPTER 11

Nic had been so focused on Rick McEwan. Maybe, she realized now, too focused. Was it possible that the person who had killed Cassidy hadn't really known her at all, except in his twisted imagination?

"Someone like Cassidy was probably stalker bait," she told Allison as they drove to Channel Four. At the Denver field office, Nic had worked a couple of stalker cases. Both were women in the public eye, like Cassidy. "I should have talked to her more about whether she was having any problems. You know, Cassidy loves—loved—her fans, but sometimes they can cross the line into crazy, and you have to be careful."

Allison leaned closer to the air-conditioning vent. Her face was shiny with sweat. "What kind of crazy? Some kind of personality disorder?"

"Definitely not in touch with reality. These guys can't have normal personal relationships, so instead they retreat to fantasy ones."

A delivery truck had narrowed the road to a single lane, and they were forced to idle in place. Nic imagined she could feel the heat rising off the soft black asphalt. The people shambling by looked like zombies, with slack faces and half-open mouths.

"So you take a guy who's unbalanced and lonely. He turns on his TV, suddenly he's looking at a beautiful young woman. She's warm, she's talking to him and looking him right in the eye. Maybe he's the kind of guy who goes through his whole day—his whole week—and no one looks at him. But this girl on TV, she comes on every day at the same time and says hello and good-bye to him. That kind of thing is tailor-made for someone with a delusional disorder."

Nic managed to nose the Crown Vic into the other lane. The driver she cut off started to make a gesture, then abruptly stopped himself, probably noting the signs that the car belonged to law enforcement.

"These guys think they really have a relationship with their victims," she continued. "The problem comes when they try to act out their imaginary plots in the real world. Say this guy went to Cassidy's condo last night and tried to talk to her, maybe even kiss her. A guy like this is convinced that his victim loves him back. That she sends him signals by the words she chooses or how she wears her hair. He believes that the victim is his perfect match and they're destined to be together forever. It's not even really sexual. It's romantic. Idealized."

"That could explain why Cassidy wasn't raped," Allison said. "But if he romanticized her, why would he kill her?"

"Someone like this can go from a love obsession to a hate obsession in the blink of an eye. The love obsession validated his life, and when it's threatened, his very being is threatened. He panics. He might think, *If I can't have her, then no one can.*"

"So if this guy showed up at her condo, acting like they really were a couple," Allison said slowly, "and Cassidy managed to convince him that her feelings didn't match his . . ."

"If he realized he could never be part of Cassidy's life," Nic said grimly, "then maybe he decided to kill her."

Aside from Marcy, the station's receptionist, Channel Four's huge lobby was unoccupied. Empty overstuffed chairs and couches were grouped around a low table topped with a fan of the latest magazines. No one was watching the flat-screen TV—showing Channel Four, of course—that murmured in one corner.

Heels echoing on the wooden floor, they walked the fifty feet toward the reception desk. Even from a distance it was clear that Marcy's eyes were red, her nose swollen. She pushed back her chair and gave them each a hug. Nic submitted to it though her history with Marcy did not go much beyond hello and good-bye.

"I can't believe Cassidy's gone." Marcy sniffed. "I didn't even say good-bye to her last night."

"So she was still at work when you left?" Nic asked.

"I saw her walking out as I was pulling out of the parking lot." Marcy's gaze was unfocused. "That was about six fifteen. I waved, but I don't think she saw me. That's what I told the detective who was here earlier." Marcy seemed to think the two of them were there in their official capacity.

"A lot of leads are being followed," Allison said, neatly sidestepping just who was following those leads.

"Where can we find Brad?" Nic asked.

"He's in the makeup room getting ready for the five o'clock." Marcy plucked a tissue from a box and blew her nose with a loud honk.

Nic and Allison walked down a short hallway that doglegged to the right and then opened up into the newsroom. This room definitely wasn't meant for public consumption. A single large open space, the newsroom was crowded with cheap metal desks split up by a few waist-high partitions. It smelled faintly of sweat and stale food. The desks were cluttered with coffee cups, half-eaten bags of chips, family photos, and advertiser or station giveaways: logo-laden mugs, sports bottles, pens, lunch bags, and even bobblehead dolls.

Nic had always liked seeing behind the facade. She liked knowing that when Cassidy appeared on the news in the studio next door, the skyline behind her was a huge photograph framed by a fake window. A photograph that on closer inspection showed a few dings.

Normally the newsroom would be filled with the buzz of talk and the *click-clack* of computer keys. Now people stood in knots on the stained carpet, speaking in low voices while the air-conditioning labored mightily to bring the temperature below eighty degrees.

Heads turned and conversation stilled as Nic and Allison walked back toward the makeup room. Most of the women and quite a few of the men looked like they'd been crying. Nic nodded and made eye contact, but kept her expression unreadable. Her blouse stuck to the small of her back, and she reached back to pluck it free, wondering why she had even bothered to iron it.

Brad wasn't alone in the makeup room. Sitting next to him was Phoebe Sennett, his latest co-anchor. Both were using what looked liked turbo-powered silver pens to carefully apply spray-on foundation. Unforgiving HD cameras required perfect skin—or at least skin that appeared perfect.

When he caught sight of them in the mirror, Brad tugged a small white towel out of his shirt collar and set it and the airbrush on the long, cluttered counter. He got to his feet and gave them each an awkward embrace—the hug equivalent of an air kiss. Phoebe settled for nods.

Three months earlier Phoebe had joined Channel Four when the station once again passed over Cassidy for the co-anchor spot. The previous co-anchor, Alissa Fontaine, had only lasted nine months. While on vacation in Florida and under the influence of too much rum, she had entered a wet T-shirt contest that had degenerated into an impromptu striptease. Which, of course, ended up all over the Web. Rather than being hounded out in shame, Alissa had quit the station to star on a reality show.

After the station hired Phoebe, Cassidy had consoled herself with the idea that the other woman at least had a degree in broadcasting. Before the stripping incident, Alissa's sole claim to fame had been being a former Miss Connecticut.

Nic saw Brad press something into Allison's hand. A thumb drive, which she guessed held the stories Brad had surreptitiously copied from Cassidy's computer. He gave them both a nod and then shot a meaningful glance in Phoebe's direction. Nic took the hint and didn't say anything.

"How are you guys holding up?" Brad asked.

"We're in shock," Allison said. "Like everyone else."

"And yet the show must go on." Brad settled back down into his chair and regarded his jawline critically. "We're leading off the newscast with a special tribute to Cassidy."

Nic looked at her watch. It was 4:45. They'd have to talk fast. "I was surprised when you said Cassidy had a stalker. She never mentioned it to us."

"You guys really need to coordinate," Brad said. "This is like the third time I've said this stuff today."

Nic exchanged a glance with Allison. Allison, who never lied. Ever. But now she let Brad's supposition stand, the way she had Marcy's. They both did.

"Everyone has a crazy guy," Phoebe said. Her words were slightly distorted as she applied a layer of berry-colored lipstick. "They're just fans. Really, really eccentric fans. It was the same in Seattle. It can be a little disconcerting, but it's just one of the hazards of being in the public eye."

"It's more than that, Phoebe." Brad half turned toward her. "I've been in this business longer than you, and things are changing. Now people want to get up close and personal with the talent. It's not like the old days, when there was a little bit of privacy. Now if you refuse to sign an autograph or leave the house dressed in sweats, someone will film you with their phone and before you know it, you're viral on YouTube. Meanwhile, you're supposed to be using social media to promote the station. *Social media.*" He snorted. "You have no idea how much I hate that term. Jerry thinks they can turn around the decline in viewership by having us blog and Tweet and Facebook. Only I don't know how that leads to more *television* viewers."

Phoebe shrugged as she capped her lipstick. "TV stations aren't in the business of selling the news. Not anymore. Everyone else has the same news, and you can get it a lot sooner by going to the Internet rather than waiting for us to come on at five. So what they've got left is our personalities. They're basically selling us. And it's ten times worse for women. At least men don't get those head-to-toe body shots or have to worry about keeping their knees together when they're sitting. I mean, look at the things they say about Cassidy online."

"What do you mean?" Nic asked.

Phoebe picked up her smart phone. "Watch what happens when I type Cassidy's name into the Google search box." Her thumbs moved rapidly over the screen, typing in *cassidy shaw* and then she handed it to Nic. Allison leaned over her shoulder to look at how Google autocompleted the phrase with the most popular search terms.

cassidy shaw sexy
cassidy shaw dating
cassidy shaw nose job
cassidy shaw breasts
cassidy shaw married
cassidy shaw hot
cassidy shaw upskirt shots

"Ugh," Allison said. "It makes me feel creepy just looking at it."

Nic nodded, wondering whether Cassidy had known, and how much she minded being discussed as if she were a piece of meat.

Phoebe gave them a sad smile. "Mine are even worse. You don't get things like *Phoebe Sennett breaks story.* Or *Phoebe Sennett great reporter.* Instead, it's all about my body and whether I might be pregnant or if I'm dating anyone. It's all superficial and stupid." Her upper lip curled. "And the creeps who post sick stuff about us don't even necessarily live here."

"What do you mean?" Allison asked.

Phoebe took back her phone, typed something, and handed it back to Nic. It showed a website called hotnewsbabes.com.

Nic scrolled down through tiny photos of TV screens showing one female reporter after another. Each series of photos had a headline like *Randi Corlett shows great cleavage in tiny black dress*, or *Libby Worall looking sexy.* And under each photo was a line reading *Rate her* with check boxes for *Ugh, OK, Hot,* and *Smoking!*

"See the links at the bottom of the photos?" Phoebe asked. "If you click on them, they take you back to the reporter's bio at whatever station she works at. So in two or three clicks, you could be sending some pretty girl in another state an e-mail—and half the time, the station where she works will have a policy that she has to send a cheerful e-mail back, because they don't want to make the 'fans' angry. Fans? These guys have probably never seen the shows that these photos are taken from."

"That's why I say we've got targets on our backs," Brad said as he knotted his tie. "And the station is painting them there."

"These guys are annoying but harmless," Phoebe said. "They're just pitiful losers who can't get real dates. Half of them probably don't ever get off their couches."

"Oh really?" Brad straightened the knot. "Then what about that Texas TV anchor who was shot to death when some guy broke into her apartment? What about the Iowa reporter who called her producer to say that she was leaving for work and then never showed? All they found were her shoes, earrings, and blow dryer on the ground next to her car. And there was that sports reporter in Montana. Somebody ambushed him when he walked out to his car. They never caught the one who did that either."

"But bad things happen to people in all kinds of professions," Phoebe said. "And that guy who liked Cassidy was harmless. I saw the stuff he sent her. Cards and flowers and really bad poems that rhymed *love* with *move*. I don't think some guy who sent her a card with a white kitten on the front is going to be the one who stabbed her to death."

It was clearly the same argument Brad and Phoebe had been having all day.

"What was his name?" Nicole asked. "The guy who sent Cassidy all this stuff?"

"Roland." Phoebe raised an eyebrow. "Does that sound like the name of a guy who is ever going to have a real girlfriend? Roland Baxter. He called her and sent her weird letters and left messages on her Facebook page. Cassidy said he was harmless. Besides, there wasn't really anything she could do about it unless he threatened her. And he didn't. Not really. He mostly just said he loved her. Once he left a letter on her windshield calling her 'my fair lady.'"

Brad said darkly, "Don't you remember the rest of that one? He also said that if she ever noticed an unfamiliar car with tinted windows pulling in behind her, she had better hope it was him."

"But even that wasn't really a threat," Phoebe said.

"Yeah." Brad made a raspberry sound. "More like a promise. And now look what happened."

Nic shivered a little, thinking Brad had it right. It did sound like a promise. "You said he left the card on her windshield. Was that at the station or someplace else?" If it had been in the condo's parking garage, then that meant he knew where Cassidy lived.

"Here," Brad said. "In our parking lot. We don't have a fenced lot for employees, so anyone can get at your car."

"Do you know if he knew where she lived?" Allison asked.

Brad shrugged, but Phoebe said, "Last month Cassidy told me that when she opened her door one morning to get the newspaper, the hallway was littered with rose petals. But no note, no message. She didn't know who had done it. I think she thought it was halfway romantic."

"Can we see the card?" Allison asked. "Or anything else he sent her?"

"Like I keep telling you people, Cassidy didn't hang on to any of that stuff," Brad said. "She just looked and threw it away. Sometimes she showed things around and sometimes she didn't. But this one guy, this Roland, he was in love with her. Or something like love."

A woman Allison recognized as the producer for the five o'clock news stuck her head in the room. "We need you guys out on the set," she said.

"Why don't you stay and watch the show in the studio?" Brad offered.

"We're going to have to slip out at some point," Nic said. "We don't want to cause any distraction."

"We'll catch it in the lobby," Allison said. She was already halfway out the door.

CHAPTER 12

Back in Channel Four's lobby with Nicole, Allison felt too keyed up to sit down. She paced back and forth in front of the TV set, which was showing two women earnestly discussing bladder control drugs.

"Can't you stand still for one second?" Nicole snapped.

"Sorry." She stopped in her tracks.

"No, wait. I'm sorry, Allison." Her friend heaved a sigh. "It's all just too much, you know?"

Allison did know. Nervous energy still thrummed in her, but she willed herself to stay still. She lifted one hand and lightly rested her fingers on her cross.

God was in this situation as surely as He was in any other. Wasn't He? It was so much easier to rely on God when it felt like things could still be changed. Cassidy was gone, and nothing could bring her back.

Allison's days were normally filled with prayers, large and small, but Cassidy's death had rocked her. Her guts felt like they had been pulled out and replaced with twisting snakes.

On the screen, the theme song for Channel Four's nightly newscast sounded. File footage swooped dizzyingly around the city skyline before the camera cut to Brad Buffet, looking solemn.

"Tonight we're going to depart from our usual format to open with a tribute to Channel Four's own Cassidy Shaw, our crime reporter, who, in a terrible twist of irony, has become a crime victim herself. As you may have heard, last night Cassidy was found murdered in her Portland condominium. Police are investigating. All we know is that the death occurred sometime after she broadcast her last story. We'll be sure to bring you the latest information as it develops."

At Brad's words, Allison found her mind flashing back to that terrible moment when Nicole had opened the cabinet under the sink. She again saw Cassidy's flat blue eyes, staring at nothing. Someone had done that to her friend, discarded her like a piece of trash.

Brad continued, "Like our viewers and all of us at Channel Four, I am in shock and in mourning over this tragedy. I had the pleasure and the privilege of working with Cassidy for the last eight years."

As he spoke, a montage of photos appeared behind him. Cassidy laughing. Cassidy holding a mike. Cassidy at the front of a pack of press. Cassidy with both hands raised as she talked to a cop. Arguing, if Allison had to guess.

It was the photo of the impassive cop and the always-anything-but-impassive Cassidy that nearly brought Allison to her knees. Or maybe it was the finality of the unchanging words underneath the flurry of photos: Cassidy's name and the dates of her birth and death.

A choking sob forced its way out of Allison's mouth. She put the flat of her hand between her teeth and bit down. Hard. The external pain was a welcome distraction from what was inside her.

Nicole leaned in close. "That's right," she whispered. "Crying's not going to do us any good. We can't cry for her. We have to get whoever did this."

Allison freed her hand and took a shaky breath.

Meanwhile Brad was saying, "Cassidy had the biggest smile and the loudest laugh of anyone I've ever met. I can't imagine our newsroom, or my life, without her. She was the heartbeat of the station, and in many ways the heartbeat of our community." He paused to clear his throat, his eyes shining with unshed tears. "Cassidy was never afraid to ask the hard questions or tackle the tough issues. She exuded energy in everything she did. She walked fast, she talked fast, and"—he managed a shaky smile—"boy, did she love to eat."

Allison tried to hold on to that familiar image of Cassidy relishing a bite of food. Often it was a bite of someone else's food. Cassidy was never shy about sharing—or waiting for an invitation.

"I'd like to read you some tributes from viewers." Brad picked up the top piece of paper from a two-inch-thick pile. "This one comes to us from Diane Short of Portland. She writes: 'My husband and I felt like we knew Cassidy because we have watched Channel Four for so many years. When our son died from a drug overdose and we felt no one was paying attention to the terrible drug problem out there, to how these pushers are making thousands of dollars and their customers are dying, I contacted the only media person I "knew."'" Brad's inflection indicated the quotes. "'That was Cassidy. She took the time to e-mail me back with some good advice, and she helped us get in touch with a group working to toughen the sentencing laws. She touched our lives for a brief moment in time. But at a time when we needed someone, she was there for us. Thank you, Cassidy.'"

Brad looked into the camera and nodded, then set the paper aside and picked up the next. "Suzanne Sheffield writes, 'I am certain that God had a reason for your life and a reason for your death. Your life had a purpose and your work was part of His plan.'"

Allison felt a pang of something like jealousy. She didn't feel certain of anything. Instead she felt lost and alone. The only thing keeping her going was anger. Anger at the man who had done this to her friend. But was it also anger at God for allowing it to happen?

Even when she had lost her baby, Allison had been able to tell herself that there must have been a reason. Maybe something had been wrong with the baby. Perhaps God had spared them when He decided to take the child before it had even been born. But what purpose did Cassidy's death serve?

Last night Allison had cried and prayed in the darkest hours of the night. She had knelt on the oak floor of the living room, her elbows resting on the well-worn brown leather of the couch, stifling her sobs so they wouldn't wake Marshall or Lindsay. She had asked God why He had taken her friend.

And she had gotten no answers.

God's ways were not man's ways, she knew that. Could she be at peace without understanding why?

Maybe Nicole was right. Maybe peace would not come from the why, but the who. All they could do for Cassidy now was to find the man who had done this to her and bring him to justice.

Brad was still reading viewers' notes. "'You may be gone here on earth, Cassidy, but we know you are in heaven. You were loved and respected by many. Thanks for being part of our lives, and may your name live on.'" He glanced back up at the camera. "You'll find these comments and many more on our website, where you are welcome to leave your own.

"As for me . . ." Brad's voice hitched. "I'll always remember the time I asked Cassidy what her favorite was of all the stories she had covered. And she told me, 'The next one.' That is so like Cassidy. Always surprising. Always looking forward. And that is how I will always remember her."

Allison heard a muffled gasp. When she glanced over at Nicole, she was shocked. Nic's face was wet with tears. Nicole, who never cried. Nicole, who had perfected the art of wearing no expression at all. Nicole, who, even when Allison knew she must be angry or sad or worried, just retreated behind a stony facade until her eyes were looking out from little caves.

Allison put her arm around her friend's shoulder, at first tentatively, then more tightly when she felt how Nicole trembled. They leaned into each other.

"Well, isn't this a touching sight?"

They turned to see Detective Jensen.

"I can't believe my eyes. Didn't we just talk about jurisdiction last night?"

Nicole straightened up and wiped her hand over her face. Her expression was so cold that Allison shivered just looking at it.

"It's after five," Allison pointed out. "We're off the clock." It was true, as far as it went.

"Public servants are never off the clock," he growled. He had foregone the tie today, as well as the jacket. His badge was clipped to his belt.

"And you seem to keep forgetting that Cassidy was our friend," Allison said, "not just a case. Brad told us about Roland Baxter. Are you looking at him?" She wanted to put the focus back on finding Cassidy's killer.

Jensen bounced on his toes like a boxer in the ring. "Brad can't have told you everything."

"Like what?" Allison narrowed her eyes.

"Like how this Roland left Cassidy a voice mail saying how much he loved her, no matter what. But that she needed to be true to him."

Nicole's head snapped up. Allison waited for Jensen to say that he had arrested Baxter. Instead he just shook his head and said, "He left that message around eight o'clock this morning. Before news broke that Cassidy was dead. But way after she was."

"It could be a ruse," Allison said. "He could have left that message knowing it would throw everyone off the scent."

"It's possible," Jensen said in a tone that made it clear he didn't believe it was. "But while that guy's thinking is definitely twisted, I'm pretty sure it's not twisted like that. It's not twisted in a way that would lead him to commit murder. He was falling down and crying and begging us to tell him it wasn't true, that she wasn't really dead. Personally, I don't think he's that good of an actor."

Nicole started to say something, but the phone on Jensen's belt buzzed. He flipped it open and walked away from them. "Jensen," he said. And then after a long pause, "No." He repeated it. And swore. And listened some more. And when he turned back toward them, a muscle was twitching under his right eye.

"They made a match to the prints on the knife they found under Cassidy's body," he said. "They're only partials, but they matched them. They were already in the database."

"And?" Nicole prompted.

"They say they're Rick's." Jensen suddenly looked empty, as if he might dwindle and collapse like a leaking balloon. "They just arrested him for her murder." He scrubbed his face with his hands. "Rick and me came up together fourteen years ago. We were in the same class. That's not the Rick I know. Sure, he's got a temper. Who doesn't? But to do that? It just doesn't make sense."

"It most definitely does make sense," Nicole said. "It's like I tried to tell you last night. Cassidy exposed Rick McEwan to the world, and he found a way to get back at her."

"But he'd have to be crazy to do it the way he did. Stab her and leave the knife right next to her body?"

"Maybe even as he did it, he knew he was wrong," Allison ventured. "Maybe he wanted to get caught."

No one answered her. Both Jensen and Nicole were quiet, caught in their own thoughts.

So that's that, Allison thought. The hunt was over before it had even begun. Rick had killed Cassidy. He had bided his time and then he had killed her. Stuffed her under the sink like garbage.

Part of Allison had known the first day Cassidy had told her about how Rick threatened her in private and kissed her in public that something was very wrong. How he showered her with presents and apologies. If only Allison had spoken up about him earlier, maybe Cassidy would have left before things got bad.

Maybe then Rick McEwan wouldn't have handcuffed her, strangled her, stabbed her, and shoved her body under her own kitchen sink.

CHAPTER 13

When she and Allison walked out of Channel Four, the heat took Nic's breath away. The sun was so dazzling it hurt to even glance at the sky. The air above the sidewalk shimmered.

"So that's it," Nic said. "It's over." She felt emptied out, a hollow woman walking around on two matchstick legs.

"Want to go someplace quiet and have a drink?" Allison asked.

Nic turned in surprise. "Don't you want to go home?"

Allison sighed. "I just need a little time to catch my breath. Things are moving too fast."

Nic nodded. Twenty-four hours earlier Cassidy had still been alive. It seemed like another lifetime ago that they had waited for her at the restaurant. Waited while Rick stole the air from her lungs and the blood from her heart.

"How about the VQ?" Allison suggested. The Veritable Quandary, a downtown restaurant and bar, was a Portland institution.

"It's too hot to sit outside." Any other summer day the VQ's patio, which was surrounded by flowers and had a view of the Willamette River, would have offered an oasis. Now all Nic wanted to do was hide from the sun.

"I was thinking we could sit inside at the bar."

Nic imagined sitting in semidarkness, a cold drink sweating in her hand. "Let's go."

The interior of her car was even hotter than it was outside. It was like sitting on a griddle that had been cleverly fashioned to look like seats. Allison sat hunched forward so that as little of her body as possible made contact with the vinyl. After starting the car, Nic turned the air-conditioning on full blast. She maneuvered her way out of the parking lot, gingerly handling the steering wheel with just her fingertips. What she really needed were oven mitts.

Inside, the VQ was blessedly cool, with air-conditioning and fans overhead. They took a seat at the far end of the bar with its ranks of hundreds of bottles.

The bartender had a shaved head and one gold earring. Nic vaguely recognized him, but after he brought their drinks and snacks, he asked, "Where's your friend? That blond spitfire you two always come in with?"

Nic froze, and Allison's eyes widened. In choosing a familiar location, they hadn't realized it would result in its own special brand of pain.

Nic was too tired to soften it. "She was murdered last night."

The bartender took a step back and swore under his breath. "Really?"

"They just arrested her old boyfriend." Nic took a sip of her drink, sour and sweet. It was one of the VQ's specialties, a martini made with limoncello and lavender-infused vodka. It had been one of Cassidy's favorites.

He blew air out of pursed lips. "That is really hard to believe. She was just so, so—alive, you know?"

"We know." Nic suddenly wanted to put her head down on the cool, dark wood of the bar, close her eyes, and wish it all away. The bartender squeezed her right hand and Allison's left, then gave them a nod before going over to another customer.

Nic tried to put into words what was inside her. "I thought I would feel better when they arrested someone. Instead, I just feel kind of lost. Cassidy's gone. And now I can't even obsess over who killed her."

"You were right, though. You thought it was Rick." Allison picked up her magenta-colored VQ-8, the house Bloody Mary made with beet-infused vodka.

"Somehow that's not much of a consolation." Nic's sigh was so deep it shook. She took another sip to steady herself. "I didn't want to get in her business, but I should have. The first time I met Rick I knew things weren't going to go well. I should have said, 'Cassidy, you know he's bad news, girl. You need to stay away from him.'"

"And would she have listened?" Allison made a sound that was something like a laugh. "Do any of us listen when people give us advice?"

"I still should have tried to say something. But I figured she was a big girl. Only she wasn't, was she? I mean, in some ways Cassidy was like a little kid." Nic thought of their friend's enthusiasm, her petulance, her excitement.

"Yeah." Allison managed a half smile. "That was her good point—and her bad point. I guess that's the same for any of us. The trait that you love most about someone also becomes the trait you wish you could change."

What was *Nic's* bad trait, then? She was afraid to ask. Instead she picked up one of the stuffed dates they had ordered, along with a bowl of sweet and spicy cashews. "Cassidy really loved these," she said, before popping it into her mouth. The dates were stuffed with goat cheese and Marcona almonds, then wrapped in pancetta. They were a lovely mix of sticky, sweet, salty, crispy, and squishy. Perfect for nibbling alongside a drink.

"Was there a food Cassidy didn't love?" Allison smiled. "How many times did she eat more of our entrees than we did? Plus hers."

"Yeah." Nic felt her eyes get wet. "Nothing was safe from her. You didn't want to get between that girl and something she wanted to eat."

"And she loved it when someone recognized her." Allison glanced at the bartender who was now serving three Japanese businessmen.

"Yeah," Nic agreed, "but she wouldn't have liked that he didn't know her name."

"He probably works when she's on air." Allison paused. "Was on air. It's so hard to think she'll never be on again."

"You know what I'm going to miss?" Nic asked rhetorically. "Cassidy's purse. Her big black tote. That thing was as big as my garage. It was like a magician's hat—anything could come out of it, up to and including a rabbit." Now there would be no more magic purse. "I used to make so much fun of that purse," she choked out. "That and everything else about her. I rolled my eyes behind her back, and she caught me. More than once. And when I wasn't giving her a look, I lectured her. But I never told her that I loved her. I figured she knew, you know?"

Allison patted the back of her hand. "Oh, Nicole, I'm sure she knew."

"If I could go back, I'd be more patient. I'd be nicer. I'd tell her how much she means to me." Nic picked up her napkin and wiped her eyes, not caring if she smeared her mascara.

Allison gave her hand a squeeze and then released it. "All you can change is today. Today is tomorrow's yesterday."

It took Nic a second to figure it out. "That's good. Did you just think that up on the spur of the moment?"

"I'm pretty sure it's already a saying."

The bartender set down another drink. Nic was surprised to find that her first glass was empty.

"Oh, I didn't order another one."

"That's okay. It's on the house."

She thought about protesting, but instead she just thanked him and took a big sip.

"I hardly have any photos of Cassidy. That's one thing I'm going to start doing more," she told Allison. "Taking more photos." Someday Nic would lose her parents, maybe her older brothers. Nothing was permanent. Someday Makayla would lose her. Nic couldn't bear to contemplate that even ten-year-old Makayla wouldn't live forever.

"There're plenty of photos of Cassidy on the Web," Allison said. "And I was watching her on YouTube before you came by."

"But it's us I want to remember," Nic said. "The Triple Threat." She slipped her phone off her belt and pressed a few buttons to put it into camera mode, then she beckoned to the bartender. "Could you do me a favor? Could you take a picture of my friend and me?"

"Sure." He took a step back while Nic slung her arm around Allison's shoulders. Then the flash went off, and he handed back the phone while an older couple glanced over at them curiously.

Allison leaned in close, and the two of them regarded the photo. The sadness was still in their eyes, but their smiles were broad.

"That's perfect," Nic said. "Thanks."

As she put the phone back on her belt, she saw the bartender's eyes take in the holster and then skitter away. A minute later he brought her another drink. She thought about waving it away, but instead she drained the last inch of her old drink and picked up the new one.

"It's weird that we can watch videos of Cassidy anytime we want," Nic said to Allison. "In the old days, when you were gone, you were gone. Maybe someone cut off a lock of your hair and framed it. But that was it."

Allison popped a cashew into her mouth. "Have you ever seen

those scary old daguerreotypes they used to take of people lying dead in their coffins? Most of the time that would be the only photo of the person ever. Now even after you're dead you can live on forever on the Internet."

"Not to mention the billboards," Nic said. "I wonder how long until they take those down?" She had passed one this morning on her way to work. *Your Friends at Channel Four*, with pictures of Cassidy as well as Brad, Phoebe, and the sports guy whose name Nic could never remember.

"And I think they're on at least one of the MAX trains."

"Everything's going to change," Nic said, feeling the weight of the truth. "Not just the billboards, not just at Channel Four. The three of us—you and me and Cassidy—it just worked. She was lighthearted and fun, and I'm way too serious. And you're right in the middle. It's not going to be balanced anymore."

"That doesn't matter," Allison said. "You and I still need each other. Maybe even more than we did before."

Allison was probably just saying what Nic wanted—needed—to hear.

"Everything *is* changing. Makayla won't hold my hand anymore. She gets mad if I come into her room and she's not completely dressed. She wasn't even scared to go to sleepaway camp for two weeks by herself. According to her, ten years old is practically grown up."

A flicker crossed Allison's face, and Nic remembered the baby her friend had lost. Did it hurt her every time Nic mentioned her daughter? Had that flicker always been there, but she just hadn't been tuned in enough to see it?

"What about you and Leif?" Allison asked. "Is that changing?"

"He definitely wants things to change. He wants to get married. But you know me. I'm too independent and too old to change. Not that he's not great. He actually pulled me out of the interview room last night and told Jensen we were done. Then he followed me home to make sure I was okay."

Leif had stayed and held her for a couple of hours, listened to her cry, not interrupting as she tried to make sense of Cassidy's death. And when she was all talked out and all cried out, he had told her funny stories about a private investigator he was working with who was really more like a computer.

"This was your friend's favorite, right?" The bartender's voice interrupted Nicole's memories. He set down three forks and a chocolate soufflé that had grown over the top of the white ramekin. It was dimpled with melting chunks of chocolate and dusted with powdered sugar. Next to it was a small white pitcher of chocolate sauce. But it was the three forks that Nic couldn't look away from. Three forks, as if there was still a Cassidy to share it with them.

Nic nodded at the bartender, unable to speak. Instead she forked up a bite and lifted it into the air. "To Cassidy," she said.

"To Cassidy," Allison answered, lifting her own bite in a toast. The bartender nodded and then turned away.

They busied themselves, taking bites in turn. With no Cassidy to fend off, it felt strange. As Nic waited for the last of the sauce to drip out of the pitcher, she had a flashback so clear it made her gasp. The last time they had been here, they had eaten the ramekin empty. Then Cassidy had run her index finger inside the pitcher and licked it clean, declaring, "I'm not letting a single drop go to waste."

Cassidy hadn't let anything go to waste. She had thrown herself into every activity, from eating to covering a crime story, with unbridled enthusiasm.

And now she was dead. And only one person knew why.

"You know what I keep wondering?" Nic said. It wasn't really a question. "What were her last few minutes like? Did she suffer?"

"I hope it was fast," Allison said. Her eyes looked haunted.

"The only person who knows is Rick." Nic stood up, and for a moment it felt like her head kept moving even after she was on her feet. She put her hand on the bar to steady herself. "And I'm going to go talk to him. With or without you."

Before Nic could stop her, Allison snagged the keys from her hand. "It's definitely *with* me. And I'm driving."

"I'm not drunk," Nic said, but she knew it was a lie.

CHAPTER 14

Official visiting hours for the Multnomah County jail were only on weekends. But certain types of people, like clergy and bail bondsmen, could visit at any time. As could law enforcement personnel and attorneys. It wasn't unheard of for an officer to want to talk to a prisoner being held on an unrelated case. Bad guys were bad guys, after all, and tended to be involved in or have knowledge of more than one bad thing.

When Allison walked through the jail's double doors with Nicole, she was immediately assailed by the mingled stench of greasy food, sweat, and sewage. Her gorge rose and she swallowed hard, forcing down the suddenly nauseating mixture of cashews, stuffed dates, and alcohol. Even though the jail felt cool, almost clammy, the heat outside must somehow be intensifying the smells. She concentrated on breathing shallowly through her mouth.

Nicole managed to appear not only completely sober, but she had also tapped into her patented don't-you-dare-mess-with-me vibe. The corrections officer didn't ask them what their business was with Rick, and they didn't volunteer. While they were presenting their IDs—Nicole had left her Glock in the gun safe in her car—Allison asked, "So does McEwan have a lawyer yet?"

The corrections officer shrugged. "Word is he'll have Michael

Stone representing tomorrow at the arraignment. I guess Stone's out of town until then."

Allison and Nicole exchanged a glance. Michael Stone and Rick McEwan were meant for each other. No crime was too heinous to be defended by Stone. Past clients included a surgeon accused of operating while drunk, an actor charged with sexually abusing a middle-school student, and a Portland Trail Blazer who had shot his wife and then tried to make it look like a robbery.

And now a cop who had killed his ex-girlfriend.

They were ushered back to the empty visiting area, a cheerless row of windows separated by chest-high cinder block partitions. On either side of each section was a single battered chair. Allison dragged a second chair over to the first window and then sat down to wait for Rick. Under her fingertips, the scratched and scarred counter felt like some kind of reverse Braille. How many people had sat here? Their desperation, depression, and disappointment still hung in the stale air.

Accompanied by a guard, Rick appeared on the other side of the glass. He wore an orange jumpsuit over a white T-shirt. Allison stiffened. This was the man who had brutally killed her friend. Her hands curled into fists, her fingernails cutting into her palms. For a second time, her stomach rose and pressed against the bottom of her throat.

Rick normally strutted, but now he shuffled. When he turned to face them, Allison gasped. His left eye was purple and swollen shut, and the whole side of his face was bruised. When they came to arrest him, he must not have gone along quietly.

Staring at them through the Plexiglas, Rick slowly lowered himself into a chair. With his face so distorted, it was hard to tell what expression he wore. Allison's rage changed into something duller and heavier. It was all so stupid. Rick had taken Cassidy's life and ruined his own, and for what? For what?

She picked up the black corded phone from the wall, trying not to think about how many hands had handled it, how many lips had rested against the mouthpiece.

For a long moment, Rick did nothing, just stared at them with his one good eye. The guard stood off to one side, his hands clasped in front of him. Finally, Rick picked up his own phone. Allison tilted the receiver so Nicole could hear.

"Here to gloat?" He lifted his chin.

Allison didn't answer him immediately. Finally she took a deep breath. "What happened to your eye?"

Nicole pulled back and looked at her, but Allison kept her gaze on the man on the other side of the glass.

He gingerly touched his lower eyelid. "A little souvenir from an old friend."

She was shocked. "They put you in with everyone else?" Cops were normally segregated from other prisoners for their own safety.

"Oh, I've got my own cell. But the guy in charge of the uniforms recognized me." The undamaged side of Rick's mouth twitched upward. "I guess it wasn't a good memory."

Nicole grabbed the phone from Allison's hand. "You've made a lot of those, haven't you, Rick? Especially for Cassidy. Tell us what happened last night. Did she suffer? Did it take her long to die?"

His mouth twisted, and his good eye blinked rapidly. "I loved that girl once, you know?"

"Oh, please." Nicole made a sound as if she were spitting something foul from her mouth. "Love? What kind of love is that? The kind where you strangle someone and then when that's not good enough, you stab her? What kind of love is that, Rick?"

He straightened up, and there was a flash of the old Rick, always aggrieved. "You two never liked me. Not for one minute. You cheered when Cassidy dragged me through the mud."

The anger was back, stiffening Allison's spine, pushing back the sadness and the nausea. She took the phone from Nicole. "That's because we saw what you did to her. Like making her cut up her underwear because you thought it was too sexy."

"People were always looking online for shots of her with her bra showing or her skirt riding up when she sat down. I was just trying to keep her from embarrassing herself."

Allison thought of what Phoebe had shown them. Was there a kind of truth to what he was saying? But a guy like Rick would always have an excuse for everything. "Then what's your explanation for how you left those bruises on her when you were dating? Or how you broke into her condo and pulled a gun on her?"

He said nothing. Allison watched his body as well as his face, alert for the slightest change in expression. Even the best liars couldn't control everything.

Nicole took the phone. "So why didn't you shoot her last night, Rick? Was it just not hands-on enough for you? Did that make you feel like some big man, choking the life out of her? You must have seventy pounds on her."

Eyeing how tight the orange jumpsuit was over Rick's biceps, Allison wondered if he was taking steroids. Rage and 'roids went hand in hand. It was probably too late to do a urine test. Steroids cleared in a day or two.

Nicole continued her accusations. "So what—you came over, you two argued, and then things just went too far? Is that why you strangled her from behind, Rick? So you wouldn't have to look her in the eyes?"

"I don't remember." His gaze dropped to his hands.

"What do you mean, you don't remember?" Nicole's tone was sarcastic.

"I don't remember being there. I don't even remember talking to her last night, let alone killing her."

"What do you remember, then?" She issued the words like a challenge.

"Here's what I remember about yesterday."

Allison read Rick's lips as much as she heard his words through the receiver Nicole held between them.

"Yesterday I was called out to a house to do a welfare check. When I got out of my car, I could hear the flies before I even got up on the porch. The windows were black with them."

Allison's imagination obligingly supplied the details. She wished she hadn't eaten anything at VQ.

"I didn't want to go in there. I knew what I was going to find. But I'm the police. I don't get to say no. I'm the one who gets to find some old guy who died two weeks ago. So it was a very bad day. And then later I went to Diamonds."

Diamonds was a strip club.

"All I wanted to do was try to relax and take my mind off things. And then I must have gone home. That's all that I remember."

"What are you saying?" Nicole asked.

He brought his face within an inch of the glass. "As far as I'm concerned, I haven't even talked to Cassidy for months. I know what they say I did, but I have no memory of it."

Suddenly Allison saw the way it would go. Rick would claim post-traumatic stress. Or some kind of flashback. Or temporary insanity. Michael Stone would construct an elaborate theory to explain how Rick briefly went crazy, lost it so bad that once he regained his sanity, he didn't even remember the terrible thing he had done. Could you really be guilty if you didn't even remember the crime?

Meanwhile Stone would trot out stories of Rick's heroic actions as a cop, and a few more of the terrible things he had faced in the line of duty, things that would make a bloated dead guy in a fly-filled house look like a cakewalk. Whatever happened, Stone would say, was a terrible anomaly.

And a jury might even buy it.

"If I was thinking clearly, would I have left my fingerprints on that knife?" Rick demanded.

Nicole sighed theatrically. Her sigh said it all. That she wouldn't take any more lies from Rick. That she was bored by his lies.

Allison took the phone from her. "People do a lot of stupid things in the heat of the moment. You can't say that because you left your fingerprints on the murder weapon, *ipso facto*, you weren't in your right mind."

"I must have blacked out," Rick said. "It's happened to me before."

"What do you mean?"

Here came the lies. Allison waited for his hands to busy themselves. Liars unconsciously created jobs for their hands, like grooming or lint picking. Anything to fill the pause while they figured out what response was in their best interest.

Rick kept his free hand flat on the counter. "Last week I was out at Diamonds. The next thing I knew it was morning and I was in bed feeling like I had to hold my head together with both hands." He looked from Allison to Nicole. "I woke up with no idea what had happened the night before, who I was with, what I did. Luckily I still had all my money, but when I went outside, my car was parked in someone else's space at my complex. It was just a complete blackout. Last night wasn't quite as bad, but I still don't remember getting home."

"How much did you have to drink?" Allison asked.

"Three or four drinks. That's all. I'm not an alcoholic. But I've been on high blood pressure medication for six or seven years. It could have been a spike in my blood pressure."

So if the explanations about temporary insanity or post-traumatic stress or on-the-job horrors didn't work out, there was always his blood pressure. Allison had never heard of high blood pressure causing blackouts, but Michael Stone could probably find a physician for hire who would testify that it was possible.

But the strange thing was that Rick didn't *act* like a liar. His body hadn't contradicted his words once. But he had also been a cop for fourteen years. He knew the tells as well as Allison and Nicole did. He was probably practicing for the jury.

"Cassidy talked about you two, you know," he offered. "She said you were always interfering in her life."

Inwardly Allison flinched, but she tried not to let it show on her face. Had Cassidy really said that? Or was Rick just lobbing shots in the dark? There was no way to know.

Through clenched teeth, Nicole said, "If we had done a better job of interfering in her life, you would never have been part of it." She didn't have the phone, but Allison could tell Rick still understood what she had said. Nicole got to her feet, the chair scraping back on the floor. "I think we're done here."

Allison's next words surprised even herself. "I'll pray for you, Rick."

He snorted. "Thanks, but no thanks. I don't need your crocodile tears. I don't need you pretending that you care about my soul."

She was opening her mouth to reply when a voice spoke from behind them.

"What are you two doing here? Why are you talking to my client?"

Allison jerked around. It was Michael Stone, dressed in a charcoal-gray suit and looking as natty as if it wasn't several hours past quitting time. Rumor had it that he slept just four hours a day—and found ways to bill for all twenty-four.

He stepped uncomfortably close to Allison, close enough that she could smell his cologne, something with the mingled scents of musk and money. Bitter bile flooded her mouth.

"What are you doing here?" he repeated.

"We're here as citizens," Allison said flatly.

"Citizens who used their officially issued IDs to get in after hours?" Stone let out a two-note laugh. "I can't wait to find out how much weight that will carry with Dan. He won't like this much, will he, Allison? Especially if I leak it to the *Oregonian*. 'Federal prosecutor abuses powers to harass prisoner.'"

"We weren't threatening him." The calm in Nicole's voice was belied by the tiniest twitch under her left eye. "We just had a few questions."

"Just wait until I talk to your new SAC about it. One of his agents abusing her credentials, threatening and taunting a suspect. Do you know how many lines you both crossed just being here?"

"We were just leaving," Nicole said, and swept out past him.

Allison followed. She made it to the parking lot before she threw up.

CHAPTER 15

Allison was useless the next day. No matter how much she tried to focus on the case she was building—a Ponzi scheme that had masqueraded as a real estate investment—her mind kept jumping from thought to thought.

She had braced herself in the morning for a talking-to from Dan, but all he had done was pat her on the shoulder and ask her how she was holding up. Stone must have been bluffing, then. That was Michael Stone, all bluff and bluster.

Once inside her office, Allison had closed her door so no one would witness just how scattered she was. She would think she was working, only to come to with a jerk and realize she had been doing nothing but staring into space. She leafed through pages of bank transactions without seeing them, then found herself checking her computer for old e-mails from Cassidy. There were fewer than she had thought. Why hadn't she saved more? E-mail storage was practically free these days.

Cassidy had signed every e-mail with a series of Xs and Os. Looking at all those crosses and circles, kisses and hugs that would never be put into practice, Allison's eyes burned with tears. She forced herself to turn away from the computer and back to the reams of documents. "Focus, Allison. You need to focus!" she lectured herself.

Out loud. Her brain couldn't hold a thought. Or it could, but only the unceasing drumbeat that Cassidy was dead.

Dead. Dead. Dead.

Her stomach was still touchy. Food poisoning? The flu? It was probably exhaustion, her nerves shot from the stress and the heat. It had been another stifling night. Relief had flooded her when the rising sun finally lit up the blinds, because it meant she no longer had to wrestle with sleep.

Maybe what she needed to do was eat. She hadn't had any breakfast this morning or any dinner last night. The last thing she had eaten had been those spicy cashews and stuffed dates, and most of that had come right back up in the parking lot after the stress of confronting Rick and Stone.

Allison took out her purse. She was rooting for coins for the vending machine when her fingers closed on the thumb drive Brad had given her. Moot now. Cassidy's death hadn't been connected to her work.

But looking at the notes for her stories would be another way to remember her. Maybe an even more intimate way. The notes would show Cassidy's thoughts. Allison plugged in the thumb drive and clicked.

It held five Word documents that Cassidy had worked on the day she had been murdered. The first one Allison opened was the story of a man who had killed his two children rather than see his ex-wife get custody. It read like a finished story, and she guessed it had already aired on Channel Four, since she had heard about the killings on the radio while driving to Puerto Marquez. The world was a twisted place, one where children were smothered and a woman was left stuffed under the sink.

The next two files also seemed to be complete stories. One was about a sixteen-year-old boy shot by another teen, one whose getaway vehicle was a bicycle. The other was about a burglary suspect who had left his license at the crime scene. Allison thought those two also sounded familiar. But both were stupid people tricks, the kind she ran across again and again.

The fourth story, about a Portland music teacher charged with sexual abuse of a minor, was incomplete. Cassidy had written a list of questions to ask the teacher, but it didn't look like she had gotten any answers.

Then Allison clicked on the final story. And a piece of the puzzle fell into place.

Now she knew why Rick had been at Cassidy's condo—and even why he had killed her.

The day that Cassidy died, an informant had called her, saying there had been a police cover-up after the shooting of a homeless man named Vernell Williams. The tipster said he had proof that the cops had planted a throw-down gun on Williams after he was shot by one of the officers chasing him, a cop named Kevin Craine. The caller also said that his life could be in danger. In her notes, Cassidy had guessed that the informant *was* a cop. But it was the last sentence she had typed—maybe the last sentence Cassidy had ever typed— that stopped Allison: *Was Rick involved?*

She realized she had forgotten to breathe. She sucked in a gulp of air, all the while thinking, *Now it all makes sense.*

Cassidy had carried so much anger toward Rick. But even after she had gone public with her accusations, nothing much had happened to him. Sure, the chief of police had ordered an investigation. And Internal Affairs had conducted interviews and analyzed the facts.

Only it turned out that the facts were scant—Cassidy's word against a decorated veteran of the police force, with no photos or other physical evidence to back up her words—and there wasn't the necessary preponderance of evidence. It was a he said–she said affair. One of them had a badge and the other a microphone.

The chief had ordered Rick into counseling. And that was it.

After she got the tip about the throw-down gun, Cassidy must have contacted Rick. Frightened that the truth would come out, he had killed her.

Allison grabbed her phone and called Nicole.

"What's up, Allison?"

"I know why he killed her. It wasn't because he was holding on to a grudge. Or at least that wasn't the only reason. The day she died, somebody tipped Cassidy off that Rick was dirty. It looks like he planted a gun on an unarmed guy who was shot by the cops last week."

"Cassidy would be all over that. E-mail me the story, and I'll see what I can find out. But that has to be it." Nic sighed. "Are you going to the arraignment today?"

"I thought about it, but no," Allison said. "You know how it will be. Three minutes to exchange paperwork and statements. It would take me longer to find a parking place than to sit through it."

"Channel Four's going to cover it on the noon news," Nicole said. "How about if I grab some sandwiches and we watch it together in your office?"

Allison had thought about watching, but she didn't want to be alone. "That sounds good."

A few minutes before noon, Nicole showed up with deli sandwiches and small bags of chips. At the sight of the food, Allison's stomach rumbled. Hunger or a warning? She wasn't sure.

She clicked on the live stream for Channel Four. Phoebe was anchoring, and the story she led off with was the heat, with a warning that there was no end in sight. The city was setting up cooling centers for people who couldn't afford air conditioners, but already three elderly people had died and several more had been hospitalized. Workers who labored outside were being treated for heat stroke, and motels with air conditioners and pools had no vacancies.

Then the image over Phoebe's right shoulder changed from a cartoon sun wearing sunglasses to a photo of Cassidy. Allison stopped breathing. Nicole's sandwich froze halfway to her mouth.

"Police officer Rick McEwan was arraigned earlier today on charges that he murdered Channel Four's crime reporter, Cassidy Shaw."

Then Phoebe's image was replaced by a video showing Rick being brought out from the prisoner holding area to stand in front of Judge Zelda Fanconi, along with Michael Stone and the prosecutor, Tommy McNaught. The swelling had gone down on Rick's face, but the bruise had spread in lurid colors.

Phoebe spoke over the images. "The prosecutor said that investigators were very concerned that McEwan would flee if he was released, and that as a police officer he had a better understanding of how to do that successfully. Then defense attorney Michael Stone asked that McEwan's bail be set low."

On the video, Michael Stone said, "Your Honor, my client is very distraught by his ex-girlfriend's death. He has cooperated with the investigation by giving a voluntary statement and a DNA sample. Mr. McEwan has a fourteen-year career as a police officer. He has deep roots in the community. I ask that you would grant him reasonable bail to give him a chance to secure his release and seek medical and psychological treatment."

Judge Fanconi, who had a reputation for cutting to the chase, said, "Mr. McEwan is facing very serious charges. Those who are entrusted to protect and serve the people of Portland cannot expect to be treated with lenience simply because of their status. I consider

Mr. McEwan a flight risk and a possible danger to the community."
And then she set his bail at five million dollars.

Allison almost smiled. Five million dollars meant that Rick
would have to raise five hundred thousand to pay a bail bondsman.
Chances were better than good that he was going to stay in jail.

The next shot in the broadcast showed Stone standing outside
the courthouse facing a dozen microphones. Allison automatically
looked for Cassidy at the front of the crowd, then winced when she
realized what she was doing.

Stone said, "Rick McEwan is a good man and a good law
enforcement officer. It is a disappointment that he is being dragged
through this. But we are certain that the truth will prevail. The
whole truth."

Nicole snorted.

And then it was back to Phoebe and the story of a small plane that
had crashed near Cannon Beach.

Allison closed the browser window. "A disappointment? Stone
acts like Rick was arrested for jaywalking." She finally took a bite of
her sandwich. As the taste of roast turkey spread over her tongue, her
mouth filled with water. Hunger, then, not a warning. She chewed
and swallowed and hoped it would stay put.

"Yeah. He and Rick are a pair." Nicole tossed the half-eaten
remains of her lunch into the trash. "Rick will always have a million
excuses. High blood pressure, post-traumatic stress, temporary insanity, being kidnapped by Martians . . . He'll never admit the truth."

Allison finally put into words what had been bothering her since
their visit to the jail. "The weird thing was, it didn't seem like Rick
was lying. He wasn't all 'honestly' or 'truthfully'—you know those *ly*
words liars always use. It felt—" She hesitated, knowing Nicole would
not agree. "It felt almost like he was telling the truth."

Nicole shrugged. "Rick knows the same things we do. He knows the signs and the tells. He just edited himself. I'm sure all he's done since he was arrested is sit in his cell and figure out how to sell his bull."

"You're probably right." It was the same thing Allison had told herself. "But if Rick knows anything, it would be not to leave fingerprints. So why would he be stupid enough to stab Cassidy and then just toss the knife under the sink?"

"Who knows? This is the same person who thought he could plant a throw-down piece and nobody would notice. And somebody who's angry enough to murder is probably not thinking straight. And then by the time he was, it was too late." Nicole looked at her watch. "I'd better get back to the office."

Allison walked her to the elevator. As she was turning to go back down the hall, she heard Dan's voice.

"Allison, may I see you in my office?"

She was suddenly sorry she had eaten half her sandwich. At a nod from Dan, she closed the door and sat down across from him.

Dan's lean, boyish face was expressionless. Dapper Dan—as he was known only out of his hearing, since he hated the nickname—could easily have passed for a decade younger than his fifty-two years. For a long moment he said nothing, just steepled his fingers and skewered her with his gaze. Today, his pale blue eyes had all the warmth of marbles.

He tapped his index fingers together. "Allison, you are one of the best prosecutors I have working for me."

She said nothing. She knew there was a *but* coming.

Dan didn't disappoint.

"But I will not stand for insubordination. Last night you used your official credentials to get in to see Rick McEwan."

Allison didn't say anything. There was no excuse she could make that Dan wouldn't punch through like tissue paper.

"Do you see how this looks?" His chin jutted forward. "Do you know how poorly this reflects on me? I haven't made this public yet, but I'm planning on running for DA next year. You see my problem here, don't you, Allison?"

Allison did indeed. And it had nothing to do with Cassidy and everything to do with perception. Yes, she had been in the wrong last night, but she had been seeking answers, not acclaim. She nodded.

"I will not have your behavior be a millstone around my neck. What if the media gets hold of it? You are lucky that you are not losing your job. Michael Stone would have been happy to have your head on a spike. I had to call in a lot of favors to save your behind."

Allison swallowed. "I appreciate that."

"No, you don't." The bridge of Dan's nose was white. "You don't know what those favors cost me. They're gone now. And I wasted them because you couldn't let something go. Cassidy Shaw is dead, and yes, that is a terrible tragedy, but her murder is not a federal crime. This case belongs to the Portland Police Bureau. And PPB has already done their job and caught the guy who did it, even though he's one of their own. And now he'll go to trial and then to prison." He leaned forward. "Let me make this perfectly clear." His finger stabbed the air. "You are not any part of that process. Yes, you may be called to testify about finding the body. But I don't want to hear another word about you muddying the waters. Do you understand me?"

"Of course, Dan, but—"

He cut her off with a slashing gesture. "There are no *buts*. You are a professional, and I expect you to act like one."

Feeling like a sullen teenager, Allison muttered, "Yes, Dan." Not meeting his eyes.

CHAPTER 16

The heat was like a weight on Nic's chest, making it hard to draw a breath. The car's air conditioner was set on high, but the air coming from the vents seemed hotter than the air outside. Hoping to catch a breeze, Nic rolled down the windows and left the air conditioner setting where it was. It was too hot to care how much gas she might be wasting. Even if it was the government's dime.

The punishing heat couldn't distract her from wondering if Allison's hunch was right. Was it possible Rick had been telling the truth?

It was true that she hadn't seen him make any of the subtle body movements that usually accompanied lies. He hadn't touched his hair or wiped his index finger across his face. He hadn't looked up and to his left, the way most right-handed people did when they were lying. He hadn't even leaned back in an unconscious effort to put more distance between them.

How much energy and agility would it take to fake it? Was Rick capable of it? Was Rick capable of it even after the stress of having been arrested and attacked?

Besides, it was possible that he wasn't faking it—*and* that he wasn't truly innocent either. He claimed that he didn't remember that evening. Maybe that part was true. Maybe something inside Rick had snapped, had made him step across the line. After all, they knew he had crossed that line before, when he pulled a gun on Cassidy. And again when he planted the throw-down piece, as she had been about to reveal. Only this time, had Rick left his conscious thoughts behind?

When Nic came back into the office, Dixie, the FBI's long-term receptionist, stopped her before she went back to her cubicle. "Mr. Bond would like to see you in his office."

Nic's skin tightened. "Did he say what it was about?"

"No." Dixie pursed her lips and looked away. Nic could tell she didn't think it was anything good.

A few months earlier John Drood had finally retired as SAC—special agent in charge—of the Portland field office. His replacement, Lincoln Bond, had only been in the office for a week. Other than to shake his hand hello, Nic hadn't spoken to him.

"Lucky you, Nicole," Heath, another agent, had said to her after their first general meeting with Bond.

"What do you mean?" Nic gave him the evil eye, but Heath, as usual, was immune to it.

"Bond's black. Excuse me, African American." *Like you*, he didn't say, but he didn't have to.

"Do you think I'm going to flash him some secret signal?" Nic had said and then shut her mouth and hadn't said anything more. Heath lived to get a reaction.

Like all of them, though, Nic had been looking for clues as to what their new boss would be like. The press release announcing his hire had said that Bond had a bachelor of science degree in biblical/pastoral studies, which was an unusual background for an agent. Then he had become a cop and started studying criminal justice at night. Eventually he had become a special agent.

The way to get ahead in the FBI was to transfer from field office to field office, with a promotion each time, and that's what Bond had done. He had worked violent crimes in Detroit, Mexican drug trafficking at Quantico, organized crime in Cincinnati, and, most recently, held the position of assistant SAC in Tampa. Now he was in Portland, although chances were good he might not stay that long.

When Nic knocked on Bond's half-open door, he told her to come in and close the door.

It was the first time she had been in the office since Drood left. There was a new addition to the décor: over Bond's left shoulder hung a framed photo of J. Edgar Hoover. Nic blinked. Was it some sort of joke? Hoover had considered Martin Luther King, Jr., a Communist. And when Hoover died in 1972, less than 1 percent of agents were black—and there were zero female agents.

"It's Nicole Hedges, right?" Bond's expression conveyed that even this was suspect information.

"Yes, sir." She sat in the visitor's chair, but held herself erect. This was no social call.

"How long have you been with the Bureau?"

It felt like a trick question. A file with her name on it sat in the middle of his otherwise empty desk.

"Nine years."

"Nine years." Bond's voice somehow managed to convey disappointment. "I have just had a very disturbing phone call from a defense attorney named Michael Stone."

Nic kept her expression neutral. On her hip, her phone started to buzz. She silenced it without breaking eye contact with Bond. She didn't need to glance at the display to know it was Allison. Too late. But even if Allison had given Nic a heads-up, what could she have done?

"Mr. Stone accused you of interfering in a case that does not fall under the FBI's jurisdiction. Is his accusation true?"

One look at Bond's face, as cold as if it had been carved from ebony, and she knew there was no point in appealing to his emotions. To explain that Cassidy had been her friend.

"I know both Stone's client, Rick McEwan, and the woman McEwan is accused of murdering. I was trying to make sense of what really happened that night."

"So you decided to waltz down to the jail and harass him?"

"I just asked a few questions, sir."

He sat back in his chair and folded his arms. "If you think that because you're a sister that you're getting a pass, you're wrong."

"I don't think any such thing, sir." The only thing Nic thought was that Bond would never be accused of playing favorites.

"And just so I have all the facts correct, this case has nothing to do with you on a professional level. Is that right?"

Nic matched Bond, unflinching stare for unflinching stare. "While that's true, sir, I was only trying to ensure that justice is being done."

Was that what she had been doing? It had all made sense last night, the kind of sense things made when your friend had been murdered and you were operating on no sleep and three drinks.

"But I made an error in judgment in how I went about it."

"The Portland police are our partners. Honoring that partnership is one of my top priorities. If we don't work together, we could tear this city apart. I don't need one of my agents turning them into enemies."

"No, sir."

Rather than appearing mollified, Bond was looking angrier. "Too bad you didn't visit this McEwan while you were on duty. Then I could have had your badge. As it is, you can expect a letter of censure in your file."

Nic flinched. While a letter of censure was the lowest form of discipline, she had never been censured before. Never. Whatever the FBI required her to do, she did, and she usually landed in the top 5 percent. The letter would be placed in her files at both headquarters and Portland and could negatively impact any promotions for the next year.

Bond was looking at her as if he expected an answer.

"Yes, sir. And I apologize for my behavior."

"I'm going to be keeping my eye on you. If I hear of anything else untoward, you could be looking at a disciplinary transfer to Butte, Montana, where you can freeze your posterior off while pondering the beauty of the world's largest open-pit copper mine. So don't be a distraction, Hedges. Don't be a liability. Do I make myself clear?" Bond pointed his pen, something gold and expensive looking, directly at her heart.

"Yes, sir." She met his eyes, her face neutral.

"You've made an impression, Hedges. And it's not a good one. I don't want to hear one more word about you crossing boundaries." When she nodded, he said brusquely, "You can go now."

It was only after Nic got to her feet that she realized that her legs were shaking.

Yes, she had erred in going to see Rick. But something about Cassidy's death nagged at her. Nic had joined the Bureau to make sure that the bad guys got caught and got what they deserved. Wasn't that more important than the tiny print of rules and regulations, more important than dividing crimes up into city, state, and federal?

She had been in her cubicle for only a few moments when Leif Larson stepped in. Leif was six two, with red-gold hair and square shoulders. He looked like a Viking warrior. While the FBI had no rules about agents dating other agents, he and Nic normally kept their in-office exchanges polite and professional.

Until now.

She stood up and put her mouth close to his ear. In a low voice she said, "Allison and I went to see Rick last night."

Looking startled, Leif pulled back. "Why?"

It was the question Nic could no longer answer, even for herself. "I just wanted to understand why it happened. Then this morning Allison figured out Cassidy had been covering a story about a throw-down piece Rick might have used to cover up the killing of an unarmed, mentally ill guy."

"That would certainly give him a reason to go after her. And you're the one who thought it might be him in the first place. Everything fits."

"But it's like it's almost too perfect. Why would he leave his prints on the knife—and then leave the knife there?"

"People do stupid things all the time. You know that, Nic. Especially if they're drunk."

Leif was referring to Rick, but his words made her inwardly flinch.

"Well, Michael Stone showed up at the jail last night too, and I guess he complained about us this morning. Bond just gave me a talking-to. And a letter of censure."

"Nic, listen to me." Leif's voice was low and urgent. "You've got to stop trying to figure out this on your own. The Bureau will not back you up on this. And Bond could be looking to send a message to the higher-ups that he is willing to make the hard choices. You could be looking at a disciplinary transfer or even outright termination."

Nic didn't tell him about Bond's Montana threat. "I just want to know the truth."

"The truth might be that some part of Rick wanted to be caught."

"So why is he saying he doesn't remember anything now? If he wanted to be caught, why didn't he just call the police himself? Why did he stuff Cassidy under the sink like a piece of garbage and then leave?"

As Nic spoke, Heath sauntered past her cubicle. Was he trying to eavesdrop? Did everyone already know about the censure? She made her voice even softer.

"Even Allison believes Rick really doesn't remember what happened."

"Just because he doesn't remember," Leif said patiently, "doesn't mean he didn't do it."

"But what if he didn't? Or what if he didn't act alone?" Keeping her voice low, Nic quickly summarized for Leif the story Cassidy had been working on. "How many cops were on the scene when Vernell Williams was shot? If they knew about the cover-up and didn't say anything, their careers would be on the line. And then Cassidy started asking questions."

"Nic, listen to yourself. You know that murders don't have to make sense. Especially not if the killer is under the influence, which Rick probably was if he was at a strip club beforehand. But if you keep insisting that the pieces don't fit, then Bond won't look the other way. You have to let this go before he lets you go. Let PPB figure this out. No matter what happens, Cassidy won't be any less dead. And your career could be on the line."

Anger stiffened Nic's spine. She stepped back. "What about the truth? And justice? Aren't they more important than my career?"

As the afternoon wore on, Nic tried to work, but she kept having brief flashes of Wednesday night. The broken phone. The small dark pool of blood under the cupboards. The cool slack skin of Cassidy's neck.

A half hour later she slapped her hand on her desk when she suddenly realized what had been bothering her about that night.

But was it a clue or just a coincidence?

Her cubicle was too open. She thought of Heath. It was too hard to have a hushed conversation on a cell phone. Anyone walking by could hear her, even if she kept her voice low. Nic took her phone and went out into the stairwell.

When Allison answered the phone, Nic said, "Can you talk?"

"Yeah."

"I got the same talking-to you did, but that's not what's important."

"It's not?" Allison sounded surprised.

"No," Nic said. "What's important is I just realized what was bugging me about the murder scene."

"What?"

"That knife block of Cassidy's had just two empty slots, right? And remember how you pointed out that there were a paring knife and a bread knife on the counter?"

Allison caught on. "So where did the knife come from that was next to her body?"

Nic gave voice to the argument she knew she would hear if she shared this observation with anyone else. "Cassidy could have extra knives that didn't fit in the block."

She didn't believe it, though, not for a second. Cassidy was no cook. She might slice a baguette or a brick of Tillamook cheese, but that was as far as it went. Cassidy was the kind of woman who hid old newspapers in her oven when company came over.

Allison said, "Rick must have brought the knife with him. But if he did, that means it's premeditated."

"We need to find out if the knife matched the knives he had at home. And if it does, the question is: if he was thinking clearly enough to bring the knife there to kill her, why didn't he think to take it away? Or at least wear gloves. It just doesn't make sense."

"Yeah, but what murder ever does? And remember, Nicole— we've both been told to stop asking questions."

"Don't we owe it to Cassidy to find out the truth?" Nic asked.

Allison's reply was a long time in coming. "Of course we do. We've just got to think of some way that doesn't end up with both of us fired."

CHAPTER 17

As she walked into the funeral home's already crowded chapel, clutching a program with Cassidy's picture on it, Allison suddenly stopped short. Marshall bumped into her. Behind her, she could hear Nicole's gasp as they all saw what had made Allison halt in her tracks.

A mahogany casket, trimmed in gold, stood at the front of the chapel. Silhouetted by the open top of the lid, Cassidy lay on a white satin pillow. More white pleated satin edged the casket and lined the lid.

A wave of dizziness passed over Allison. She steadied herself on Marshall.

"I haven't been to an open casket funeral since I was a kid," he whispered.

Allison forced her legs to start moving again. "I think they do them more in the South. And her mother's from . . ." Her voice trailed off when she couldn't remember. Mississippi? Georgia?

Lindsay's mouth was still open in shock. "Why did they do that?" Her voice was loud enough that a few heads turned.

Letting go of Marshall's arm, Allison turned back and drew Lindsay to her. "I think some people believe it helps bring closure. It lets them say their good-byes."

Her sister's nose wrinkled as she peeped again at Cassidy and then pointedly turned her head away. "Do you think she would like to be lying on display?"

"Well, maybe," Nic said from behind them. "She looks good."

Leif nodded agreement.

"But she doesn't look like herself." Lindsay shivered. "I'd rather be cremated than end up looking like some kind of life-sized doll. It's creepy."

Halfway down the aisle, the five of them—Lindsay, Marshall, Allison, Leif, and Nicole—found a pew that had room for all of them. As they settled into their places, Allison found it impossible to take her eyes off Cassidy. The expanse of unsullied white framing her denied the grim reality of her death and its aftermath. Cassidy was even dressed in white, wearing a dress cut high enough to cover the Y-shaped incision from the autopsy. Her hands were folded demurely on her chest.

Cassidy was a bride and a beauty queen, all rolled into one. Or Sleeping Beauty. Her hair was like spun gold. It had been teased and fluffed to twice its normal volume, presumably to hide the black stitches where Tony had cut open her scalp.

Allison half turned to watch new mourners file in. At the sight of the open casket, nearly every face registered a degree of shock. Now that no one died at home, people were so insulated from death. No one washed the bodies of the dead, straightened their limbs, closed their eyes. Even the realities of dying—the pain and stink and mess of it all—often took place behind closed hospital doors under the impersonal gaze of paid caregivers. Cassidy's corpse, with its pink lips and carefully arranged hair, represented another way to deal with death, another way to make it palatable. But for Allison, the pretty shell could not erase the memory of what she had seen crammed under the sink.

The chapel was nearly full. It was a long, windowless, wooden box lit by a row of sconces along the side walls. Even the ceiling was made of dark polished wood. The lack of windows made Allison claustrophobic, as did the people crowding into the pews. The air tasted as if it had already cycled through a dozen people's lungs. Within a few minutes the remaining spaces had filled and ushers were directing people to an annex where clattering folding chairs were being set up.

"Standing room only," Nicole said. "She would have liked that."

Allison thought of Tom Sawyer eavesdropping on his own funeral. Too bad that Cassidy's body could no longer hear or see. And her spirit—did it care about the size of the crowd, the prestige of the mourners, the way people caught their breath when they first saw her laid out in her coffin? Did it care about the TV camera set up in the back corner?

Among the mourners were many people Allison recognized, at least by sight. There were prosecutors, defense attorneys, cops, PR flacks, minor political figures, crime victims, staff from Channel Four, and other media folks from radio, newspapers, and even rival TV stations. Derrick Jensen and Sean Halstead were seated near the back. On the other side of the chapel was a guy Cassidy had dated five or six years ago. He spotted Allison and waved. She lifted her hand. She couldn't remember if he was the surfer or the vegetarian or the dentist.

But as many people as Allison recognized, even more faces were unfamiliar. Were these the people who handed Cassidy her lattes and dry cleaning? Or strangers who had only seen her image on a TV screen?

The crush of people meant that the time listed for the service came and went. Nic leaned over to Allison. "Just like Cassidy to be late," she said, a smile tugging at the corners of her lips.

Finally the pastor, a man with a silver tonsure and plain dark suit, came in through a side door. He started by leading them in the Lord's Prayer, with the audience's usual hesitation and stumbling over "trespasses" or "debts."

Allison's debts to Cassidy weighed on her. She could have been a better friend. She could have warned Cassidy about Rick. Chided Cassidy more about the chances she took. She also could have said yes more when Cassidy suggested they get together. How many times had she begged off, citing a pressing case? Those cases had come and gone, and no matter what, she would have gotten all the work done somehow. But the time with her friend? That she could never recapture.

"The death of Cassidy Shaw reminds us that all of us will die," the pastor said. "This is a thought we usually try to keep far away. Someday each of us will step from this life into another, a life without end, and leave our earthly body behind. It is not that we *are* a body and *have* a soul. It's that we *are* a soul and *have* a body. Cassidy has left the temporal body you see here, but her soul still lives."

He opened up a Bible and began to read:

> *"There is a time for everything,*
> *and a season for every activity under the heavens:*
> *a time to be born and a time to die,*
> *a time to plant and a time to uproot,*
> *a time to kill and a time to heal,*
> *a time to tear down and a time to build,*
> *a time to weep and a time to laugh,*
> *a time to mourn and a time to dance,*
> *a time to scatter stones and a time to gather them,*
> *a time to embrace and a time to refrain from embracing,*

a time to search and a time to give up,
a time to keep and a time to throw away,
a time to tear and a time to mend,
a time to be silent and a time to speak,
a time to love and a time to hate,
a time for war and a time for peace."

When he was finished, he cleared his throat. "Despite his honest acknowledgment of the pain and tragedies and challenges of life, the writer of Ecclesiastes also wrote about the good things: healing, rebuilding, laughing, dancing, embracing, love, and peace. All those things are still possible in the world and in our lives.

"We give heartfelt thanks to God for His gift of Cassidy. We remember with joy and delight that there was also a time for Cassidy to be born. The evil we now suffer does not cancel out the joyful memories. Instead, it makes them sweeter. Thank God for the gift of Cassidy."

His gaze swept out over the crowd. "We do not know what the future holds. But what we can do is make sure the people we love know it. Show and tell them today. Tomorrow may be too late."

Marshall squeezed Allison's hand. Nicole smiled at her. She was surrounded by people she loved. Cassidy was dead, and nothing could change that. But if her death inspired more love, more joy, more laughter, more people who took the time to see what was really important, then a blessing could come even from evil.

"Now Cassidy's family would like to share a few words about their precious daughter."

Gretchen Shaw's face was drawn, as if she hadn't eaten since Allison brought her the bad news.

"Ever since she was born," Mrs. Shaw began, "Cassidy was just the sunniest little thing. Her smile could light up a room. When we gave parties, she would sneak out of bed, and I'd catch her in the kitchen entertaining a group of grown-ups." With every word her Southern accent grew more pronounced. "Cassidy was my baby. A mother is not supposed to outlive her child."

Before David Shaw spoke, he took a long look at Cassidy in her coffin. "As you can see, my daughter was beautiful. She was a light in this world. And now that light has been put out. Put out by some scumbag who wasn't worth her little finger." He addressed the still figure of his daughter. "But don't worry, honey, we'll make sure he gets what's coming to him. He'll never hurt another woman again. In your name, we'll make sure justice will be done. And we'll never, ever forget you."

Duncan Shaw was the last of Cassidy's family to speak. Her older brother had something of Cassidy in the shape of his nose and chin, although he had brown hair instead of blond and he was at least six inches taller. An engineer, Duncan did something in the aerospace industry that Allison had never quite understood. His words were so low that the audience stilled, straining to hear him.

"How could he hurt you like that, Cassie? How could he? He took you from me and for what? For what?" He stopped, his head hanging low, his breath rattling with the beginning of a sob. He scuffed his palms over his eyes and left the microphone without saying another word.

Allison was reminded by his words what the end must have been like for Cassidy, her lungs screaming for oxygen, her hands unable to do anything but twist helplessly in the handcuffs. Others must have been thinking similarly dark thoughts. Sniffles and even sobs broke out. The stale air was still and hot, smelling of dust and mothballs and sweat. People were fanning themselves with their programs, dozens of photos of Cassidy's face moving back and forth, back and forth. Allison tried to breathe more deeply. Her chest rose, but it was as if no air went in or out.

After hearing from the Shaws, it was a relief to listen to Cassidy's coworkers, who were more accustomed to putting a spin on things, to neatening up the rough edges of real life so they could turn them into stories.

First up was Phoebe, the new co-anchor. "I only worked with Cassidy for a few months, but I saw firsthand how fierce she was when it came to pursuing a story. She wasn't above using her charm or her high heels or both." Laughter rippled through the chapel. "And when Cassidy walked into a room, heads turned. She owned every room she was in. Not because she demanded our attention, but because we chose to give it to her. She was so alive—and just watching her made you feel more alive too."

Brad brought his own star power to the microphone. The room fell silent as he waited a beat before speaking. Even the fluttering programs stilled.

"Cassidy was tough and fair, yet always kind," he said solemnly. "For those who were victimized by crime and injustice, she was sensitive and caring. So many people whose stories Cassidy covered have told me that she called them after their pieces ran. Not just to follow up, but to sincerely check on their condition. We have lost a friend who touched every one of us. Cassidy loved Portland—and as the outpouring we see here reminds us, Portland loved her back."

The pastor took Brad's place. "Now if you would like to share a memory of Cassidy, we have a microphone set up at the front."

A steady parade of people came to the microphone, including a young woman with dramatic black bangs who declared, "I grew up watching her."

Allison and Nicole exchanged a wordless glance. Cassidy would have hated to hear another adult say that. She always complained that older women mysteriously disappeared from TV, and that lines only added character to a face if you were a man.

After a couple of dozen more people spoke, someone began making his way from the back. Walking up to the microphone, he looked like a boy, but when he turned to face them, his face was that of a man in his thirties. He was about five foot five, with cropped curly brown hair. His shadowed eyes reminded Allison of a puppy that had been kicked too many times to count.

"Cassidy was an angel here on earth," he said. "We did not appreciate her. We did not see her for what she was." After each pronouncement, he took a laboring breath. "We all know that's true. She was a perfect woman."

People were beginning to shift and murmur. Allison raised her eyebrows at Nicole, wordlessly asking if she recognized him, but Nic just shook her head.

Suddenly, he pulled the microphone from the stand and then took two steps back until he was standing next to the head of the coffin. There was a collective gasp as he reached down and stroked Cassidy's cheek. "My darling," he murmured, "you are so beautiful. I should have saved you. Can you ever forgive me?"

Then his free hand slipped inside his jacket.

"Look out!" a woman screamed. "He's got a knife!"

It appeared in his hand like a magic trick, glinting in the light. He held it, pointing up, about six inches in front of his face.

Leif, who was sitting on the aisle, got to his feet, saying, "It's okay, buddy. It's okay. What's your name?"

The man didn't answer. Instead he put the blade to his throat. The point dimpled his skin.

Allison began to pray. Asking God for protection. For all of them.

Now Nicole was on her feet as well, her hand resting on the butt of her gun. But there was no point in shooting someone who was determined to hurt himself.

A tiny red drop appeared at the tip of the knife. It trickled down his pale neck.

"We'll be together in death, as we should have been in life," he said, leaning down to address himself to Cassidy. "We'll be together for all of eternity."

A woman in the first pew stumbled to her feet, then turned and ran down the aisle, breaking the spell that had pinned them in their pews. The crowd panicked, pushing, shoving, clawing—anything to get away from the man and the knife and the corpse. Nic and Leif were trying, and failing, to fight their way forward, calling repeatedly for the man to drop the knife. Allison, Marshall, and Lindsay stayed frozen where they were, an island of calm in a river of chaos.

The next second, the man drew the knife across his throat, the white skin parting before it, the red blood streaming after. Crimson drops rained down on the white satin, as well as on Cassidy's face and hair. It seemed to Allison that every woman in the crowd was screaming, every man shouting, but the man with the knife appeared to hear nothing as the drops became a trickle, and the trickle a flood.

He pursed his lips and leaned down, as if he were the prince whose kiss could wake up the enchanted sleeper. But his face was pale, and his head suddenly seemed too heavy, drooping forward like a flower. The microphone slipped from his fingers and landed on the floor with a loud thump and whine that made people cry out even louder. It was followed by the knife.

And then the man collapsed on top of Cassidy's body.

CHAPTER 18

Any remaining decorum was shattered. The aisles flooded with people shoving and shouting, desperate to get safely outside, away from the atrocity behind them. Away from the blood. Away from the corpse. Away from the man with the knife who, they all knew from horror movies, despite collapsing might prove not to be quite so dead after all.

Nic staggered as a man elbowed her. A young woman bulldozed her with a shoulder, nearly knocking her off her feet. Then Leif grabbed her hand and yanked her back into the safety of their pew.

Why had the guy asked for Cassidy's forgiveness? What did he know?

Nic tried to see him through the crowd, but after collapsing on top of Cassidy he had fallen to his knees and then crashed to the floor. Now all she could glimpse were his feet in dark dress shoes and white tube socks. Was he still alive? Nic stepped up on the pew to raise herself above the crowd. The man lay in a rapidly spreading pool of bright scarlet, curled on his side, his face turned away from her, one arm outstretched.

As she watched, his fingers twitched.

Even standing on the pew, Nic wasn't that much taller than Leif. She leaned down and put her mouth next to his ear. "I'm going to try to help him."

Before she left home she had stuffed a shawl in her purse, thinking—or hoping—that the chapel might be chilly. Now she yanked
it out. But how could she reach him? The aisles were clogged with
desperate people. There was no way she could swim upstream.

But the pews—the pews were now half empty. Nic draped the
scarf around her neck, then leaned forward and grabbed the back of
the pew in front of her. Slinging one leg over, she scissored the second
to join the first. As fast as possible, she repeated the process, over and
over. Leif followed her, and a couple of pews behind so did Allison,
not quite as nimbly. Some of the remaining mourners, taking a hint
from Nic, began clambering over the pews in the opposite direction.
Toward the exits.

Finally Nic reached the first pew. She kicked the knife out of
reach and then dropped to the floor beside the man who lay next to
Cassidy's open coffin. Her hand slipped in the pool of warm blood,
and she landed on him, his shoulder painfully bruising her ribs. Her
nose was filled with a rich, meaty stink. Gagging, she pushed herself
upright. After tucking one corner of the scarf under his neck, she
rolled him onto his back. The blood was coming so fast she didn't see
how much longer he could live, but it wasn't spurting. By sheer dumb
luck he seemed to have missed any arteries or a jugular vein, but that
didn't mean he couldn't die right here, just as he had wished.

Keeping her back to the coffin and Cassidy's corpse, only a few
inches away, Nic sat on the floor in the middle of the mess. She
propped the man's head on her right thigh so that the cut closed its
gaping mouth and was at least a few inches above his heart. His face
was so white against her black pants, his lips a pale violet. She pulled
both ends of the scarf tight and then cupped her right hand and
pressed it against the cloth over the wound while she supported his
neck with her left hand.

His life pulsed under her fingers. Tony had said that Cassidy's killer had felt her die. Nic didn't want the same experience. She had to stop the bleeding. Obviously she couldn't apply a tourniquet or press so hard that she closed off his airway, but she didn't know where that line lay or how she would know if she crossed it. Rivulets of hot blood ran down her hand and dripped off her wrist. She pressed harder.

Leif crouched beside her. "The ambulance is on its way."

Allison leaned over them, her hand across her mouth.

"Do either of you recognize him?" Nic asked.

A voice she didn't expect answered her. "It's that guy. That Roland Baxter. The one who was stalking her."

Nic craned her neck to look over her shoulder. The speaker was Brad Buffett. And behind him was Andy, the cameraman Cassidy had worked with most, the one who had been stationed in a back corner of the chapel.

And Andy was filming.

It was this side of the news that Nicole hated. Voyeuristic. Media people who would film an atrocity rather than stop to help. "Get that camera out of here," she snapped.

Andy didn't move.

Leif stepped in front of the lens, towering over Andy. "You heard the lady. Turn that off and take it outside. Now move."

With a put-upon sigh, Andy let the camera drop to his side and slowly turned away.

"You too." Leif pointed at Brad.

Brad looked peeved, but he didn't argue, which made Nic wonder if he figured they already had enough for the nightly news. The chapel, she realized, was now nearly empty. Lindsay and Marshall were still in the same pew they had been in when the whole thing started. But Lindsay was doubled over, weeping, and Marshall had his arm around her.

"Marshall," Allison called out. "Could you take Lindsay home, and I'll meet up with you later?"

"Okay." Marshall's face looked a little green.

Nic started when a hand rose from the floor and grabbed her right wrist.

It was Roland. "Just let me die," he whispered.

"No." Her right hand was cramping.

Roland's lips moved again. Nic leaned closer.

"It's my fault she's dead. All my fault."

"Don't talk," she said, even though she wanted to shake him and ask exactly what he meant.

The sound of sirens filled the chapel, and then two paramedics burst in through the rear doors on the run, carrying bags of equipment and pushing a portable gurney. In a few seconds Roland was being strapped down while one of them applied steady pressure onto the wide white gauze wrapped around his throat.

"Are you taking him to OHSU or Portland General?" Nic asked as she got to her feet. Both were Level I trauma centers.

"Portland General," the second paramedic answered, not looking up from where he was threading a needle into Roland's arm. A moment later the gurney was rattling down the now empty aisle and out the doors, its wheels leaving bloody tracks.

Now it was just Nic and Leif and Allison. And Cassidy, her hair now matted with blood, her white dress covered with scarlet splashes and drips like a monochromatic Jackson Pollack painting. If her family had hoped to leave mourners with one last memory, it certainly wasn't this.

Nic swayed. She was, she realized distantly, about to pass out.

Leif put his arm around her and turned her so she faced the doors. "Let's get you out of here."

"Wait," Nic said. "Did you hear what Roland said? He said it was all his fault that Cassidy was dead."

"That's because he's crazy." Allison looked nearly as pale as Roland had. "He also thought he could spend eternity with Cassidy if he killed himself over her coffin."

"But why would he think her death is his fault?" Nic couldn't shake the guilt she had seen in his eyes. "Maybe he knows something." She thought of Rick's claims that he couldn't remember harming Cassidy. "Maybe he even *did* something. We need to make sure that knife gets processed as potential evidence."

Leif looked dubious. "He wasn't thinking straight."

"But, Allison, remember what Jensen said? About that voice mail Roland left her?"

Allison looked up, thinking. "Roland said that he loved Cassidy no matter what, but she needed to be true to him."

"Right. What made him think Cassidy was 'cheating' on him? Maybe he saw Rick with her that night. We have to talk to him."

"First things first, Nic." Leif gave her shoulder a squeeze. "Let's get you cleaned up. You can't go anyplace like that or people will be calling 9-1-1 for you."

She looked down. Her hands and forearms were tacky with already drying blood. Her pants were sodden. "I'm going to have to go home to change. And I just hope you have something I can sit on."

"Don't worry, there's a tarp in my trunk with your name on it," Leif said. "And there's no point in hurrying. We won't be able to talk to Roland until after they stitch him up."

Nic had taken her memories of Portland General and put them in a box, and put the box in a closet, and then locked the closet door and thrown away the key. But here she was, less than a year later, smelling that sickeningly familiar mix of urine and industrial antiseptic, and the memories were threatening to bust the closet and the box wide open, key or no key.

The girl behind the information desk wore a blue polyester uniform blouse and a gold name tag that read *Kenya*. Her relaxed hair was pulled back into a stubby ponytail. She didn't look much older than Makayla, and suddenly Nic missed her daughter, missed her fiercely. When she was fighting cancer, it had been the thought of leaving Makayla alone that had frightened her the most.

"We're here to see Roland Baxter." Nic's voice sounded normal, and she was proud of that.

Kenya typed into her computer, then looked up at the three of them. "He's on 3NW. But he's not allowed any visitors."

"We're not visitors," Nic said, showing her badge. "We're with the FBI."

"Oh." Kenya's eyes got wide. "Okay."

In her head Nic heard Bond's voice. *Don't be a distraction, Hedges. Don't be a liability.*

But she couldn't let this go. She just hoped this visit wouldn't get back to Bond, that she wouldn't end up in Butte with her career in the toilet.

As they walked toward the elevators, Leif touched her arm, and she jumped. "What?"

"Nic. Don't forget to breathe."

Obediently, she sucked in a breath.

"From the abdomen," he reminded her.

She let her belly expand and felt how it loosened even her shoulders.

They found Roland's room. There was only one woman at the

nurses' station, and she had her back to them. In a second, the three of them had slipped inside his door.

Nic couldn't tell if Roland was asleep or unconscious. He was on his back with his arms by his sides, nearly as pale as the white sheet on which they lay. They looked posed. Other than the thick bandage around his throat, he was an eerie echo of Cassidy.

She and Allison went over to the bed, while Leif stayed by the door, ready to alert them if someone came. Roland's lips were still that odd shade of pale violet, and his skin looked almost translucent.

His eyes opened. He focused on Nic, blinked a few times, and then looked at Allison. In a raspy whisper, he said, "You two. You're Cassidy's friends."

Nic jerked her head back. "How do you know that?"

"I've seen you with her. Usually eating."

A tiny laugh escaped her, even though it was creepy. How many times had he been lurking in the background as they'd gone about their lives unaware?

"Why did you say her death was your fault?" she asked. "Did you hurt Cassidy? Is that what you meant?"

"I would never hurt her." He grimaced. "Cassidy and I had a secret understanding. Just between us."

"What kind of an understanding?" Nic asked, keeping her expression neutral.

"She sent me messages through the color of the blouse she wore on air. She had communicated to me mentally that she wanted me to be the father of her children."

"Really?" Allison said in a noncommittal voice. "So why do you feel guilty?"

"Because I didn't protect her, even though I was there." He swallowed, grimacing again. "The night she was killed, I followed her home. I just liked to look up at her and imagine what it was going to be like when she could reveal our love to the world."

"Look up at her from where?" Nic asked.

"There's a Dumpster across the street. If you stand behind it at just the right spot, you can see straight into her windows. Wednesday night, after she came home, I watched for a while, but I didn't see her. I was just about to leave when she appeared. She was facing the window. There was a man behind her. His hands"—Roland's voice broke—"his hands were on her shoulders."

Roland lifted his own hands and gingerly rested them on either side of the bandages, where his neck met his shoulders. "It looked like he was whispering in her ear. I couldn't believe she would cheat on me like that. When he pulled her away from the window, I left." He hesitated, his voice shaking. "But now I know that he wasn't her lover. He was her killer. I saw it happening, and I just walked away."

"What did he look like?" Allison asked. All three of them were staring at Roland, waiting to hear him describe Rick.

"Tall. Cassidy is five foot five"—he was right, which made Nic wonder exactly how obsessive he was—"so he had to have been about six one or two. He was thin. And bald. And there was something . . . off about his face. Like it was lopsided."

Nic and Allison looked at each other, wide-eyed. Rick was five foot eleven, stocky, and had brown hair so thick it looked like a pelt.

"That's not Rick," Nic said. In fact, she couldn't think of a single guy Cassidy had dated who met the description. "Why didn't you come forward when you heard she'd been murdered?"

"Do you think the police are going to listen to me? And going to them couldn't bring her back."

"But when they arrested Rick McEwan, you could have said you saw her with someone else," Allison said.

Roland shook his head. "I figured that Rick guy hurt her before and didn't get in trouble then, so this was only fair. And meanwhile, I decided to join Cassidy. Or I was going to, until you stopped me."

Nic heard his words, but she had stopped paying attention.

They had an eyewitness who might have seen the beginning of Cassidy's murder.

Only the killer hadn't been Rick McEwan.

CHAPTER 19

What are you doing in here?" a voice behind them demanded. Allison turned. It was a middle-aged nurse dressed in pink scrubs, her hands on her ample hips. "This man is not allowed any visitors. He needs to rest."

"Sorry," Leif said, and jerked his head for the other two to follow him. "We made a mistake." He pressed past her, with Allison and Nicole right on his heels.

"A mistake is right," Allison said when they were safely around the corner. She was still in shock. "Whoever Roland saw, it wasn't Rick."

Nicole made a huffing noise. She was walking so fast that Allison had to hurry to keep up with her. "That's just what Roland says. But think about it. What are the chances what he said is true? We don't even know if he was really there. Maybe he only wishes he had been so he could still be central to the story. After all, this is the same guy who thinks he and Cassidy are soul mates and that she sends him messages by what she wears on the air. Just because Roland Baxter thinks he saw some guy with his hands around Cassidy's throat doesn't mean that he did."

"He may be crazy," Allison said as she pushed the elevator button with a shaking hand, "but even crazy people sometimes tell the truth."

"But who will believe him?" Nicole said. The elevator doors

opened, and the three of them got on. "Not when it's obvious to any-one how mentally ill he is."

Allison pushed the button for the ground floor. The truth was getting complicated. "Rick says he doesn't remember being there that night. And now we have someone who saw a different man with her. Who maybe even saw Cassidy being attacked. We have to find out the truth."

"There's one thing you two are overlooking," Leif said. "You both have been warned to stay out of this. If you keep asking questions, you're putting your careers on the line."

Nicole stepped out on the ground floor, then whipped around to face him with eyes blazing. "Are you saying we just let this go? Don't we owe it to Cassidy to figure out what really happened?"

Allison was glad she wasn't on the other side of that look, but Leif's words were as mild as Nicole's were fraught.

"I'm not saying you should let it go. I'm saying you need to get someone else to put the pieces together."

Nicole put her hands on her hips. "And just who would that be?"

Allison held the elevator door for a couple in their midsixties. The woman had wet cheeks and red-rimmed eyes. After they stepped inside, Allison followed Nicole and Leif down the hall.

"I've been thinking about that PI I was telling you about, Nic," Leif said. He turned to Allison. "Her name's Ophelia Moyer. I met her when we were tracking a girl we thought might be a kidnapping victim. It turned out she was really on the run from her father, and for good reason. Ophelia helped her stay gone and safe. Ophelia's a little odd, a little intense, but she's also very competent and very dis-creet. And she can do things that the three of us couldn't do."

"So . . . what?" Allison asked. "We just ask this Ophelia to take this on? Even assuming she says yes, how much would it cost?" She imagined trying to explain the sudden expense to Marshall. She was already risking their finances by cosigning Lindsay's loan.

"That's the thing," Leif said. "Ophelia doesn't charge." He held up a hand as both Allison and Nicole began to speak. "I know it sounds crazy, but she doesn't need the money. She came into a trust fund from her grandmother when she turned twenty-one, and in three years she's made a killing in the stock market. But she only takes on cases she wants."

"Wait a minute. She's twenty-four?" Nicole's voice and expression left no doubt as to what she thought of Leif's suggestion. "She's just a baby."

"Well, even babies can bite." Leif grinned. "And they have sharp little teeth."

Leif made arrangements for the three women to meet for brunch the next day. When Allison got to Mother's Bistro, she found Nicole pacing on the sidewalk out front.

Nicole said fiercely, "I don't know about this. I just don't know."

"We have to wait and see," Allison said, although she had her own doubts. "If she doesn't seem like she can get to the bottom of things, then we'll walk away and keep looking into it ourselves."

A young woman walked up to them. "Allison Pierce? Nicole Hedges?"

When they nodded, she said, "I'm Ophelia Moyer." She winced when they shook her hand.

For Allison, the name Ophelia had conjured up an image of a girl dressed in white, flowers twined in her hair. Not this skinny girl wearing black-framed glasses, a tank top, and cargo shorts. Her dark-blond hair was pulled back in a ponytail.

"Ophelia, huh?" Nicole said. "Didn't Ophelia fall in love with Hamlet and drown herself?"

This Ophelia's response was flat, her face expressionless. "Ophelia is Greek for 'aid' or 'help.' And that's what I am. As for the Ophelia in *Hamlet*, a witness said that she was in a tree when a branch broke and she fell into the water. Does that sound like the action of a woman who wanted to kill herself?"

"Good point," Nicole said, her face deadpan. When Ophelia turned to go in the restaurant, she shot Allison a look.

In the high-ceilinged restaurant, the hostess showed them to their table. Ophelia chose the chair that would keep her back to the room. She licked her fingers and then pinched the flame of the tea candle that had been flickering in the middle of the table. "Sorry. That smell is nauseating."

"No problem," Allison said, thinking that Leif's description of Ophelia as "a little odd, a little intense" hadn't exactly covered it.

Before she opened her menu, Ophelia took a moment to straighten her silverware, nudging the spoon until it lined up exactly with the knife. When the waitress came, she ordered biscuits and gravy, while Nicole got the pork sausage and cheddar cheese scramble, and Allison went with the Greek frittata.

As Allison looked at the brick walls, the white gauzy curtains, the clear glass chandeliers hanging from long cords, she tried to remember when they had last eaten here with Cassidy. It had been at least a couple of years, and she was pretty sure it had been dinner, not brunch. Still, she could picture Cassidy laughing, her head tilted back to expose the long column of her throat. Allison didn't know if it was a real memory or one she had assembled from the thousands of hours of memories she had stored up over the last six years. Sadness washed over her. Would it have been better to pick a

place with no history, or was it okay to be reminded afresh of what
they had lost?

She took a deep breath, trying to focus on the here and now. "So
Leif Larson told us you might be able to help us figure out what really
happened to Cassidy Shaw."

"Leif said the three of you were friends in high school?" Ophelia's
question was direct, but her eyes slid away from Allison's gaze as
though their eyes were magnets of the same polarity, repelling instead
of attracting.

Something about Ophelia inspired a reciprocal blunt honesty.
"Not then, actually, no," Allison said. "We were too different. But at
our ten-year high school reunion we realized we were all involved in
bringing criminals to justice."

"And that's when we started to be friends," Nicole added. "I was
still working at the Denver field office then."

Allison picked up the story. "Then Nicole got transferred back to
Portland, and the three of us got together for dinner at Jake's." She
remembered the way Cassidy had squealed when she spied a partic-
ular dish on the dessert menu. "We ended up splitting this dessert
called Triple Threat Chocolate Cake. The first time we did it, it was to
save on calories. But we started joking about it, and we ended up calling ourselves the Triple Threat. And after a while we realized it was
true. Each one of us has—had—resources the others didn't. And from
that first night on, we always split the richest dessert on the menu."

Ophelia hunched her shoulders. "Did you all use the same fork?"

"What?" Allison said, thrown off her stride and out of her
memory. "No. Different forks."

Ophelia still looked troubled. "That kind of communal eating
would challenge the immune system. What if one of you had a cold?
What did you do then?"

Nicole made an exasperated noise. "Look, don't get fixated on the details. That story isn't about the forks, it's about the friendship. Cassidy Shaw was our friend, and she was murdered, and we want to be sure that her killer is brought to justice."

Ophelia nodded, then said, "I've been reading about what happened. Which is why I don't understand why you are concerned." She held up one finger. "Number one. The accused, Rick McEwan, used to date Cassidy Shaw." She added a second finger. "Number two. Their relationship became abusive. Number three. She broke up with him and charged him with assault, and even though questions were raised, he was never punished. Number four. Now, a year later, she has been murdered, and McEwan's prints are on the murder weapon. And most recently, number five. He's been arrested." She closed her fingers and made a fist. "So what is there to investigate?"

Allison and Nicole looked at each other. How could they best explain things to this girl who only seemed to see things in black and white? Their food came, and for a moment they were quiet as they lifted their forks and took their first bites.

Then Allison said, "Rick claims that he has been having blackouts. He told us that he has no memory of being there that night. I've never liked Rick, but there was something about the way he said it that made me believe it. We've also found an eyewitness who saw Cassidy in her condo with a different man—an unknown man—that night." She didn't mention that the witness was mentally ill. No need to bring that up yet. "It's possible this witness even saw Cassidy being attacked. We need to know if someone else other than Rick killed Cassidy."

Ophelia waited an uncomfortably long time before she finally said, "My stepfather beat my mother and he beat me. Beat us and worse." She paused. "She's dead now."

"I'm sorry," Allison said.

"I'm not," Ophelia said flatly.

Nicole blinked.

Ophelia shrugged, her face impassive. "My mother wouldn't leave him. He did terrible things to her. If she wouldn't leave, then death was a better option." She held out her left hand, which until now had been tucked under the table. "See my pinky finger?"

It was crooked, splayed out from the others.

"One summer my stepfather broke it, and then he wouldn't allow my mother to take me to the doctor. He was afraid people would ask questions. All she could do was tape my fingers together. It didn't heal correctly." She put her hand back in her lap. "I could get it broken and reset now, but I won't. It reminds me that there is evil in the world." Ophelia leaned forward. "So why should I care about a man who beat his girlfriend?"

"Beating is one thing," Nicole said. "Killing is another."

"Is it?" Ophelia asked. "Is it really?"

Had her stepfather killed something in Ophelia? It would explain why her affect was so flat and emotionless.

"Besides . . ." Allison leaned forward, trying to catch Ophelia's blue eyes. "If Rick goes to prison for a murder he didn't commit while the real killer roams around free, that's not justice."

At the word *justice*, something in Ophelia's expression shifted. "I have three special interests," she said, which at first seemed a non sequitur. "They are cats, the stock market, and helping other women get justice. Do you know what a skip tracer is?"

"Skip tracers find people who don't want to be found," Allison said, trying to keep up.

Nicole was watching Ophelia, with her head tilted and one eyebrow raised. "Usually people who owe money," she said.

"Correct. I'm like a skip tracer in reverse. I often help women get lost and stay lost. Only it's not women who owe money. Well, I should be honest and say not usually. I did help a woman once who owed money to the mob. But to generalize, I help women and girls who are in untenable situations make new lives for themselves. I'm very interested in helping them find justice that may not be available under the traditional court system."

"You do know that's what we represent, right?" Nicole said. "The traditional court system?"

"So? It's not perfect," Ophelia countered. "Nothing is. If it were, then I wouldn't have people seeking me out for help. And if it were, something would have been done about Rick McEwan assaulting your friend. Instead he got away with it."

"But if Rick goes to prison—or is even executed—for a crime he didn't commit, then that's not justice either," Allison said passionately. "Justice has to be fair for it to be justice. That's why we need to be sure that Rick is really the one who killed Cassidy."

Ophelia closed her eyes and was silent for a long time. Finally she sighed and said, "Okay."

Allison wasn't sure exactly what the girl was agreeing to, but she wasn't about to interrupt.

Ophelia opened her eyes. "Tell me exactly what happened the night that Cassidy Shaw died," she said. "And don't leave anything out."

CHAPTER 20

Allison's head ached as she drove home from the meeting with Ophelia. Were they making a mistake by asking her to help? Ophelia had listened closely to every word she and Nicole spoke, asked a thousand questions, then finally said that she would try to uncover the truth.

As she pulled into her driveway, Allison couldn't wait to go upstairs, kick off her shoes, turn on the air conditioner, and lie on the floor directly in front of it. Maybe the white noise would block out everything that had happened in the last day, the last week. She wanted to stop thinking. Stop remembering what Cassidy had looked like. Stop wondering if Rick had really killed her and why. Stop reliving the awful scene at the funeral. Stop speculating what Roland had actually seen.

But as soon as Allison opened the door, Lindsay hurried into the living room. She was wearing a navy tank top and shorts, an outfit that had once belonged to Allison. Now that Lindsay had finally stopped smoking, the sisters were about the same weight. The yellow nicotine stains were gone from Lindsay's fingers, although Allison had noticed her inhaling wistfully whenever they passed through a cloud of cigarette smoke outside a shopping mall or restaurant.

In the months she had spent with Allison and Marshall, Lindsay had seemed to shed years as well as bad habits. With her face filled out and a healthy color in her cheeks, people no longer looked surprised when Allison introduced Lindsay as her younger sister. But today something else was different about her, something new.

"Are you ready?" Lindsay asked.

Allison didn't answer. She was still trying to figure out what had changed. Then she realized it wasn't something new, but something old. Lindsay's hair was once again dark brown all over, without a single pink shock.

"Lindsay!" She put her hand up to her own hair. "Your streaks! They're gone."

Lindsay ducked her head and shrugged one shoulder. "I figured it was time for me to start looking like a grown-up." She suddenly looked very young. "I did it while you were at brunch. I've also been practicing making flowers and hearts in my lattes. Everything has to be just the right temperature, and the milk has to be poured just the right distance from the cup. It felt wasteful to dump the mistakes. So I drank them." Her words came out rapid-fire. "Only I think I drank way too much. Occupational hazard, I guess."

"Why didn't you use decaf?" Sometimes it seemed that Lindsay had just exchanged one addiction for another. Maybe once you were an addict, you always were.

"Oh." Lindsay's smile was rueful. "You're right, I should have thought of that. I can't wait until I can get my real machine. I mean, yours is cool, but the professional models are so much more powerful." She bounced on her toes. "So are you ready?" she asked again.

Allison rubbed her temple. "Ready for what?"

"You said we could practice." Seeing Allison's blank look, Lindsay added, "For the meeting tomorrow with the loan officer?"

"What? Ohhh." Comprehension dawned. It was the last thing she wanted to do, but Lindsay was right, she had promised. "Okay."

Lindsay had tried for months to get a job, but in the down economy no one wanted to hire someone who had dropped out of high school. Not to mention someone who had a criminal record that included arrests for theft, prostitution, drug dealing, and drunken driving. The only alternative was to create her own job.

"All right, now just sit at the dining room table," Lindsay directed. "We'll pretend that's the desk." She went over to the coffee table and picked up a stack of printouts.

When was the last time they had played pretend? It had probably been twenty-five years.

Allison sat in a chair, straightened imaginary papers in front of her, then half rose from her seat, leaning forward and extending her hand. "I'm Annie Botinelli," she said, using the name of the loan officer they were to meet with the next day.

"Lindsay Mitchell." Her hand was slightly sweaty. She squeezed Allison's hand firmly. Breaking character, she whispered, "Is that the right amount of pressure?"

"It's fine, Lindsay. Your handshake feels like you mean business."

So many niceties were foreign to her sister. She had sold drugs, sold her body, but back then her business partners had been judged under the light of a streetlamp and by the color of their cash. Handshakes had no part of that world, unless it was as a cover to pass drugs or money.

"Nice to meet you, Lindsay."

"Thank you so much for meeting with us today to talk about the coffee cart I want to open," Lindsay said rapidly as they both sat down. "I've brought you my business plan."

She handed Allison the sheaf of papers they had been working on for weeks. In some ways, the business plan was a formality. Allison's credit was good enough that pretty much anything for which she was willing to cosign a loan would be approved. But making the plan had helped Lindsay think through what she could afford to do, what she could offer that would set her cart apart, and what she would do when the rains came and food carts weren't as appealing.

Allison looked down at the business plan and then back up at Lindsay. "Why don't you just tell me more about the cart?"

"Oh, um, okay." She bit her lip. "My idea is to open a cart called Lindsay's Lattes and More that sells coffee and cookies. I've already talked to the owner of a food cart pod near Portland State, and there's space available. He has seventeen carts there, but right now none of them offers coffee and only a few have baked goods. The customers would be students and people who work downtown." Lindsay was speaking in a slight singsong. She took a gulping breath. "Everyone needs coffee. Especially in Portland. This city runs on coffee. Well, coffee and beer, but I can't be around that." She colored. "Oh, shoot. I won't say that last part."

Allison nodded encouragingly, then prompted Lindsay to unleash her secret weapon. "Even if there isn't another coffee cart in the pod, how are you going to compete with the larger coffee shops in the neighborhood?"

"What will make me stand out are my cookies." She jumped up and ran into the kitchen and returned with a plate that held a peanut butter cookie, a molasses cookie, and her secret weapon, a cookie that she called Lindsay's Special. It had chocolate chips, oatmeal, and coarsely chopped walnuts, and was absolutely delicious.

Tomorrow Lindsay would pack up more sample cookies and bring them with her on the bus. They would serve as an extra inducement for the loan officer to say yes.

"Not only will I give out free samples, but I'm also going to bring free cookies and coffee drinks to the people in the other carts so they'll want to recommend me to their customers."

They had already gone through the hoops to get a home-certi-
fied kitchen. As part of that process, the county declared that their
kitchen would have to have operating hours, and during those hours
Allison and Marshall were not to be allowed in. Even if it was their
own kitchen. They had also purchased a dorm-sized refrigerator for
the butter, cream, and milk Lindsay used in recipes, since she wasn't
allowed to store perishables alongside their own food.

Allison picked up the Lindsay's Special and took a bite. The house
was so warm that the chocolate chips were still soft. "Mmm," she said,
keeping in character. "Why don't you tell me about the start-up costs?"

She barely heard Lindsay as she began going over the numbers
that Allison already knew by heart. Opening a coffee cart was an
expensive proposition. An eight-by-sixteen-foot food cart cost at least
ten thousand. A professional espresso machine cost eleven thousand.
It would take another fifteen hundred for a coffee grinder. And rent
would be at least five hundred a month. Added all up, it was still
going to cost something close to the cost of a car. But as Lindsay put
it, "A car won't make me money. In order to make money, I need to
invest in this business first."

Only it wasn't Lindsay's money, was it? For a second, Allison
sucked on the thought like a sourball. Sure, Lindsay's name would be
on the loan, but so would Allison's. And even if Marshall wasn't sign-
ing it, it would still affect him if Lindsay defaulted. Something like
85 percent of small businesses went under during the first year. But
Marshall had looked over all of Lindsay's carefully drawn-up plans
and projections and ultimately given his blessing. Lindsay had been
sober for a year. She had attended NA—Narcotics Anonymous—
meetings nearly every day, pulled herself out of her funk, and found
there were reasons to live even when she wasn't high.

And this was Lindsay's dream, and she hadn't had a dream for a long time. Years. Allison guessed she had stopped dreaming when she was thirteen and their dad died from a heart attack.

That terrible day was lodged in her memory. But as bad as it had been for Allison, it had been worse for Lindsay. She had cried so hard she'd thrown up. Allison could still picture Lindsay weeping, gagging, and moaning, "Daddy, Daddy, Daddy," her face red and sweaty and indescribably bereft as she lay curled on the bathroom floor. She had been going through a phase where she claimed to hate their father and had fought with him the night before he died. His death meant that they had never had a chance to reconnect. Allison suspected that Lindsay had never forgiven herself.

Afterward, Lindsay had embraced chaos as Allison embraced order. Two years later, when Allison went off to college, she had been glad to leave her troubled family behind. Out of sight, out of mind. College had let Allison be a kid again, instead of trying to parent her own mother and sister, to save one from drinking and the other from drugs. She had been happy to live in a dorm, happy to follow the rules, happy to push her tray down the cafeteria line, happy to scoop up bland food she hadn't had to shop for and prepare. During those four years of college, Allison's mother got sober, and her sister was sentenced to her first correctional facility.

Belatedly realizing that Lindsay had fallen silent, Allison looked up.

"Allison, you're not even paying attention!"

In her sister's voice she heard echoes of plaintive cries from their childhood.

"I'm sorry. I've got a lot on my mind."

Lindsay surprised her by squeezing her hand. "I'm the one who should be sorry, Ally. Yesterday was awful. Cassidy dead and then that man cutting his throat in front of everyone."

"That's why Nicole and I met with that woman today, because of what he said about seeing someone else at Cassidy's place that night. I'm hoping she can figure out if Rick really killed Cassidy."

Lindsay hesitated and then spoke in a rush. "But he probably did, Allison. I know you want it to be different. I know you don't want her to have died because Rick got drunk at a strip club and decided to get back at her. You don't want it to be because of something stupid. But I've seen people killed before, and it pretty much always involves somebody getting drunk or high and doing something stupid. Even if you find out the answer, I don't know if it will make you feel any better."

CHAPTER 21

If someone were to custom-design a place to drive her insane, Ophelia thought, it would closely resemble Diamonds. It assaulted her senses. The music was so loud she could feel the bass thumping in her rib cage. Underneath her elbows, the polished wood of the bar felt greasy. But worst of all were the smells. Diamonds reeked of stale sweat, mildew, perfume, cigarette smoke, industrial cleanser, and chicken wings.

A tonic water with lime, a file folder, and her wallet rested in front of Ophelia, who had taken a seat along the main stage. She was dressed in the same outfit she had worn to brunch: a comfortable old tank top, a pair of cargo shorts, white socks, and Vans. Her clothes were worn and soft, just the way she liked them. The only other women in the bar wore tiny pieces of spandex and were perched on cheap plastic heels.

Ophelia knew that while women did occasionally go to strip clubs, it was usually with a boyfriend or a rowdy group of women celebrating a birthday or a bachelorette party. As a woman alone, she had attracted more than a few looks when she walked in. But she figured Diamonds was in no position to get picky. There were only a half-dozen other customers present. Sunday night was clearly not prime time.

Rick McEwan had told Allison and Nicole that he had been at Diamonds after his shift ended on the night Cassidy was killed. Day shift for the Portland Police Bureau ended at four. That would have given Rick plenty of time to visit the strip club and still kill Cassidy before Allison and Nicole discovered her body.

Ophelia knew she had upset the two women earlier, although she wasn't sure how. Maybe it was because she had asked so many questions about the condition of Cassidy's body. Regular people—or *neurotypicals*, as they were called on the websites she liked to visit—had so many rules, rules they didn't even know they had. You weren't supposed to stand too close. You weren't supposed to stare. You were supposed to take turns.

Death was one of the big conversational no-nos, along with sex, surgery, and anything that happened in the bathroom.

Taboos made no logical sense, but neurotypicals were oddly sensitive to them, the way Ophelia couldn't stand the sound of a leaf blower or the scratch of a clothing tag.

The girl on the stage wore a blank expression as she slowly gyrated to the grinding beat of the music. She was dressed in an abbreviated white nurse's uniform, complete with a cap, an outfit that Ophelia only recognized from old movies. She supposed the more current look of baggy printed scrubs wouldn't be as appealing a fantasy. Now the girl took the cap off and tossed it backstage, then unpinned her long brown hair.

Over the girl's head, a tiny movement caught Ophelia's eye. A camera on the ceiling was panning the room. She tracked its path, wondered how long they kept the tapes.

High-stepping in blue platform boots, a girl walked up behind her. Her blue Afro wig, Ophelia estimated, was eighteen inches in diameter. Her tiny blue outfit was set off by a silver garter belt.

She batted long tinsel eyelashes at Ophelia. If one fell in her eye, it seemed likely that it would cause damage. "My name's Velvet," she said. "Can you buy me a drink?"

"Sure." Ophelia pulled out a twenty, letting the girl see that there were many more. Money always talked to neurotypicals.

The girl murmured to the bartender, then turned back to Ophelia. "Are you thinking of being a dancer?" She looked her up and down.

"No." Ophelia took another sip of her Coke.

Velvet tilted her head. "You're a lesbian, then?"

"No."

"Then why are you here?"

The bartender handed the girl her drink. It sported not one but two paper umbrellas.

Ophelia appreciated the girl's direct questions. So many neurotypicals communicated with body language or other nonverbal signs instead of simply saying what they meant.

"Just trying to figure a few things out." Ophelia gestured at the ceiling. "Is there someone I can talk to about seeing older tapes from that video camera?"

A corner of Velvet's mouth quirked in what Ophelia recognized as amusement. "That's not a real camera. It's just for show, to keep people from getting rowdy. If someone starts acting up, the bartender points to it and threatens to turn the tape over to the cops. Only there is no tape."

Undeterred, Ophelia took a photo of Rick from the folder and slid it over. "I'm interested in whether anyone here knows this guy." In the purple glow of what passed for mood lighting, his gray eyes shone silver, like a wolf's.

A flicker ran across Velvet's face. "So you're a cop?"

"No. I am not a cop." Although if Ophelia were a cop, it would have been legal for her to lie about being one. Not that she would. She found it hard to say one thing and mean another.

"Then what are you?"

"Just someone who's trying to figure out if this guy was in here last Wednesday night, what kind of mood he was in, how long he stayed . . ."

"I've seen him on TV," Velvet offered. "He's the one who killed that lady, right? The TV crime reporter?"

"That's what they're saying," Ophelia said. "Her friends have asked me to find out more about what happened. So have you seen him here? I've heard he might be a regular customer."

"I've seen him. But I've never said more than a few words to him. I don't think I'm his type." Velvet shuddered. "Maybe that's a good thing, huh?"

"Do you think you could find me someone who knows him better?" She tapped her wallet. "I can make it worth your while."

Velvet considered this. She looked at the wallet, then up at Ophelia, then back at the wallet.

"It's for that girl's friends, you said?"

Ophelia nodded.

Velvet seemed to come to a decision. "Come on. I'll take you upstairs to the dressing room, and you can talk to the girls there."

As Ophelia followed her, Velvet said over her shoulder, "Besides, you're making people in here nervous. You don't fit, and they don't like that. Customers come here because they know what to expect, you know what I mean?"

"No," Ophelia answered honestly as she followed Velvet down a narrow hall. No purple mood lighting here, just flat fluorescent.

Velvet started to laugh. But when she turned back again, she must have seen something in Ophelia's eyes. She stopped. "Look, the reason guys come here is because they know exactly what to expect. They know no girl here will reject them. If a guy meets a regular girl out in the real world, he doesn't know how she'll react if he talks to her. But here, girls are always interested in him. For as long as his money holds out, anyway."

In her own way, Ophelia understood what Velvet was saying. The men who came here were people who longed for closeness, but had no idea how to achieve it.

If Ophelia had thought that being in Diamonds was bad, being in the upstairs dressing room was much, much worse. It was crowded with five girls, five suitcases, drinks, hot curling irons, cans of hairspray, and tubes of body glitter and mascara. Cell phones were ringing, two girls were arguing over a missing bikini top, and in the corner a TV was blaring away. It was showing a silly program all about relationships, supposedly a comedy. It was a very neurotypical show.

Lockers lined two of the walls. The other two had worn wooden benches facing white Formica counters topped with long mirrors. Above the mirrors, white lightbulbs were spaced every six inches. This might have looked glamorous, like something out of Hollywood, if a third of the lights, by Ophelia's estimate, were not burned out.

A tall brunette wearing nothing but a G-string looked at Ophelia curiously. She was brushing her teeth. A redhead wearing a thong and matching tiny bikini top was ironing the wrinkles from a satin ball gown.

Velvet clapped her hands. "Okay, girls, this nice lady wants to know if any of us have recently talked with that customer who killed the blond TV reporter woman. You know, the one who's been all over the news? She was this lady's friend."

Ophelia bit her lip so she wouldn't correct Velvet, and instead held up photos of Rick and Cassidy. Neurotypicals liked to help. And they would want to help a friend of the dead woman.

One by one, the girls came over to talk to her.

"That guy Rick comes in alone, he drinks, he gets a little drunk, he leaves," the brunette said. "He's looking for someone to listen to him while he goes on and on about how nobody appreciates him."

"And do you?" Ophelia asked. "Listen?"

She shrugged. "Until someone who's a bigger spender shows up. But I wasn't working that night."

The redhead said, "Sure. I remember that guy being in on Wednesday. He was saying things like, 'You don't know what kind of day I had.' "

Ophelia straightened up. "What time was this?" If it had been after Cassidy was killed, Rick might have come in trying to establish an alibi.

The girl shook her head. She wasn't looking at Ophelia, but rather at the TV behind her. "I don't remember. When I walk out of here, I wipe my mind clean, just like pressing Control and Z on the computer." She smiled broadly, which was confusing.

But then Ophelia followed the girl's gaze. She was unconsciously mimicking the smiling face of the actress on the screen. When the actress raised her hands to her mouth, the redhead made an abbreviated version of the gesture.

Monkey see, monkey do. Evolutionarily, it must have been a useful trait at some point.

The last girl to talk to Ophelia wore a platinum wig and white angel wings made of feathers. "My name's Angel."

"How apropos."

Angel shrugged, and Ophelia wondered if she knew the word.

"I saw Rick that night. That Wednesday. He comes in here two or

three times a week, and if I'm working he always wants me to sit with him and listen to him talk. Of all the girls, I probably spent the most time with him."

"Did he ever get angry with you? Or even hurt you?"

Angel reared back. "No. That's why it's so hard to believe what happened. He was basically nice."

"Really?"

She hesitated. "He did get jealous if I talked to other customers." Tugging off her wig, she rubbed the fingers of her free hand over her scalp.

Ophelia narrowed her eyes. The girl had a dark-blond shoulder-length bob and a turned-up nose. She didn't need to look at the photo again to know that Angel looked a lot like Cassidy Shaw. "Do you always wear that wig?" she asked.

"No." Angel's voice dwindled. "I look like her, don't I?"

"There's a resemblance."

"He even told me one time that I looked like his old girlfriend." She shuddered. "Now I guess I know how creepy that is. And I thought I had pretty good intuition about people."

"So what time was Rick here on that Wednesday? What did you talk about?"

"It was late afternoon. He was upset. Talking about having a bad day, but I didn't ask the details. I tried to take his mind off things. The only time he really lightened up was when his friend came in."

"Friend?"

"I don't know his name. He's got a weird vibe, so I stay away from him. I think he and Rick met here at the club. He's tall and thin. And there's something wrong with the left side of his face." She put her fingers on her cheek and dragged it down. "Like he was in an accident or something. Oh, and he's bald."

Bald. Ophelia remembered what Nicole and Allison had told her about the bald man Roland Baxter had seen with Cassidy the night she died. Had Rick and his bald friend gone over there together and killed her? Maybe they were both cops trying to cover up the truth about the planted gun.

"So he's a cop like Rick?"

Angel shook her head. "I don't think so. He doesn't seem like one."

"And he's a regular customer?"

"He's been coming in for a week or two. But I haven't seen him in the last few days. The first time I saw him, I tried to get him to buy me a drink, but he brushed me—and every other girl—off. It wasn't like he was gay. It was more like we were beneath him." Angel opened her eyes wide. "When, hello, he's at Diamonds. He's got these really intense eyes, but when he looks at you, it's like he's looking right through you. Like you're nothing. But for some reason, he likes Rick. And Rick loves to talk about being a cop. The first night they started talking, Rick ended up telling all these stories. He was really chatty. But then all of a sudden he was wasted, even though he was only on his third drink. He could hardly walk. That's not like him, but I figured he might have been drinking before he got here. A little party before the party, and the drinks don't cost ten bucks."

"What happened then?"

"I had to go back onstage, but the bald dude took Rick's keys away and told me he would help him get home."

Ophelia leaned forward. "And all this happened on Wednesday?"

"No. It was a few days before."

"Oh." So much for the idea that had glimmered in front of her for a moment.

"But on Wednesday, Rick got pretty drunk again. I was onstage, and he and that bald dude were talking, but when I came down again, the bald dude was gone and Rick was already slurring his words. He must have had a couple of drinks while I was up there." She grimaced. "Maybe he was just trying to work up his courage to do what he—to do what he did."

The idea was back. "Have you ever seen someone who's been given a roofie?"

"What? Like the date rape drug?"

Ophelia nodded. Flunitrazepam, nicknamed roofie because its trade name was Rohypnol, could induce short-term amnesia in sufficient doses. Someone given a roofie would be unable to remember events they experienced while they were under its influence. It could explain Rick's sudden drunkenness. And Allison and Nicole had told her that he claimed to have been having trouble with blackouts.

"Once," Angel said. "Some creepy customer slipped it in the drink of this girl, Cinnamon, but we always watch each other's backs. When she started staggering we got her off the floor and away from him." Angel's expression changed. "Wait—are you thinking this bald dude slipped Rick one?" She narrowed her eyes, considering. "You know what? You might just be right. But why . . ." She let her voice trail off.

Ophelia didn't answer. She was still turning things over. What if the bald man had drugged Rick and then manipulated him to be on the scene when Cassidy was killed? Maybe even held Cassidy while urging Rick to stab her? That could explain why she had been both strangled and stabbed.

"Would you be willing to testify about this to a grand jury?"

Angel's eyes widened. "I don't really want to get involved. Especially not when there are cops. They have ways of getting back at you."

"Just think about it, okay?"

Instead of answering, Angel said, "I am dying for a cigarette." She went to one of the lockers, spun the combination, and pulled out her purse. "We can't smoke in here. I'll be right back."

Ophelia considered offering to go with her, but the thought of cigarette smoke made her gag. Instead she sat with her eyes closed, rubbing her temples and trying to block out all the sensations. She needed to get home where she could be alone. Too many people, too much noise, too many expressions she couldn't read, too many comments that weren't plain.

Ophelia waited five minutes, ten. It was only after twenty minutes that she realized the girl wasn't coming back.

Angel was gone. Probably for good.

CHAPTER 22

When Nic got up, she found an e-mail summarizing Ophelia's evening at Diamonds. A dancer had seen Rick with a man at the club late in the afternoon the day Cassidy was killed. While the description was vague—"bald," "intense eyes," "droop on the left side of his face"—it still sounded eerily like the same man Roland had seen Cassidy with later that evening. One theory Ophelia had was that the bald man was another cop, and that together he and Rick had gone after Cassidy once she started asking about a throw-down gun.

Ophelia also had another theory. The dancer had reported that on Wednesday evening, as well as on an earlier one, Rick had become unusually inebriated. Ophelia wondered if someone had slipped him roofies.

That could explain Rick's blackouts. Nic had even heard stories of criminals who took roofies before committing a big crime, craving the calm it gave them, as well as the chemical blankness that would swallow any memory of what they had done so they couldn't give themselves away when questioned about it later.

On her way to work, Nic kept turning over the new pieces of information. Maybe they didn't mean anything. The connections were tenuous. Eyewitnesses were often wrong. She kept coming back to one certainty. Bald man or no bald man, roofies or no roofies, one thing was for sure. Rick had been the one who stabbed Cassidy.

Did the bald man even matter?

But of course he did. Nothing could take away Rick's culpability, but that didn't mean the bald man might not also bear some responsibility for what had happened.

By midmorning Nic couldn't take her seesawing thoughts any longer. She picked up her cell phone and called Jensen.

"It's Nicole Hedges."

"Yes?" His voice was edged with suspicion.

"Look, can I come talk to you?"

There was a long pause. "What? Why do you even think I would say yes?"

"There're a few things you should know."

"Sorry. I don't think I'm interested."

"Look, I'm sorry for getting off on the wrong foot with you, all right? But what I've learned could change things. Maybe even help your friend." Nic wasn't going to say Cassidy's or Rick's name out loud, not in her open-air cubicle, not when she had specifically been warned off the case. But then again, Bond would want to see justice done. If she had to, Nicole could always fall back on that as a defense.

"I'll give you five minutes," Jensen said grudgingly. "No more. And this had better be good."

Fifteen minutes later the detective sat with arms folded while Nic told him about Roland Baxter. He had seen Roland cut his throat at Cassidy's funeral.

What Jensen didn't know about was the bald man Roland had seen with Cassidy and the stripper had seen with Rick. As he listened to Nic, Jensen's arms loosened. He put his hands on his thighs and leaned forward.

"What if the two of them acted together?" Nic said. "Did the lab find anyone's fingerprints on the knife besides Rick's?"

"On the murder weapon, they just found partial prints from Rick. No one else. The knife even matches ones from his apartment. Hers are Wüsthofs, and his was one of those J. A. Henckels."

"Wait—so Rick brought the knife with him?"

Jensen nodded.

Nic tried to imagine how that had worked. Earlier she had thought that if the knife proved to be Rick's it would show premeditation, but now she thought of another consideration. "It's a hundred degrees. People are wearing as little as they can get away with. It's not like he could have hidden it inside a coat."

"He could have carried it inside something," Jensen said. "A backpack or even a grocery bag."

"Where else were Rick's fingerprints found?"

"They weren't. Not really. On a drinking glass next to the sink and the murder weapon. That's it."

Nic thought back to the scene. "What about the garbage can that was sitting in the middle of the kitchen floor? Whose prints were on that?"

Opening up a file drawer, Jensen pulled out a fat blue binder. Nic recognized it as the murder book—a record of the investigation of Cassidy's death that would include crime scene photographs and sketches, evidence documentation, the autopsy report, transcripts of the investigators' notes, and witness interviews. Basically, it was a complete paper trail of a murder investigation.

Jensen leafed through it. "The only prints on the garbage can belonged to Cassidy."

"No one else? Even someone you can't identify?"

"No." He tapped his index finger against his lips.

"Okay," she said, thinking out loud. "Say Rick acted alone and not under the influence of anything but alcohol. Rick goes to Diamonds, then he goes home, then he decides to visit Cassidy and bring his own knife with him. Which means the murder was not a spur-of-the-moment thing."

Jensen didn't agree or disagree, just watched her with hooded eyes.

"Sometime that night, before he stuffs Cassidy's body under the sink, Rick moves the garbage can, but he's careful not to leave prints on it. Or on the doors or windowsills or cupboard knobs or anything else in her condo but a single glass. Which means he was more than likely wearing gloves. Again that points to premeditation."

Jensen's mouth opened, but Nic didn't let him speak.

"Except there's one problem with that scenario. Why did Rick stab her without gloves? Why did he leave the knife right next to her body? Those are the actions of someone panicking. Who doesn't have any plan." Nic shook her head. "It would make sense if Rick wore the gloves the whole time, or if he never wore them. Discarding them only for the moment when he murdered her makes no sense. No sense at all."

"Maybe we just haven't thought of the right explanation," Jensen said.

"Even if this bald guy went over there with him and they acted together, it still doesn't explain the evidence. Rick should have touched more things or none at all." She pointed at the binder. "Can I look?"

When he nodded, she stood and looked over Jensen's shoulder as he paged past the crime scene photos, first the establishing photos of various rooms of the condo, then the closeups of various pieces of evidence.

Nic put out her hand. "Wait. Go back through the photos of the drinking glasses again."

There were six in the book. All tall, all made of clear glass, a common style you would see in anyone's kitchen.

She pointed at the third one. "And this is the one that showed Rick's fingerprints, right?"

He looked at her, at the glass, back at her. "Yeah."

"Look at them again."

Jensen's eyes narrowed. He paged back and forth until he spotted the difference. "The bottom of the glass with Rick's print is a lot thicker than the others."

"It could be a coincidence." She played devil's advocate. "We all break glasses and replace them with glasses that look similar but may not be identical."

"Yeah, but remember that case in New York about twenty years ago? Where the trooper lifted fingerprints from the interrogation room and then put them on evidence cards and claimed they came from the scene of the murder?" Something like hope sparked in Jensen's voice. Flipping past other photographs of evidence, he paged ahead to the fingerprint section. Cassidy's prints were in there—taken at the autopsy—as well as Nic's and Allison's. All as elimination prints. There was also a card with Rick's prints.

Each item that had been dusted had then been photographed before the lift tape was applied. After the tape lifted the print, it had been placed on a lift card. The criminalist had then drawn a picture on the other side of the lift card to show orientation, and the card was marked on the print side as to which side was up.

Nic bent over Jensen's shoulder as he compared the prints taken from the glass with Rick's prints. She wasn't a fingerprint examiner, but she did have a trained eye, and she couldn't see any difference. The prints on the glass seemed to belong to Rick. If they had been faked somehow, whoever had done it hadn't left behind any clues.

Jensen lifted his head with a sigh.

"What about the knife?" Nic asked.

He turned back. The black smooth polymer handle of the knife had been dusted with silver powder so that the prints would show up against the surface. The partial fingerprints were on the right-hand side of the knife, if the knife was pointing up and away from the viewer.

Nic knew that the prints had been scanned and inputted into IAFIS, the Integrated Automated Fingerprint Identification System, which could compare them to the fingerprints of the nearly seventy million people in its database. However, the system was not as auto-mated as it appeared on TV. Instead of spitting out an instant match, once the prints on the knife had been scanned, IAFIS would have provided a human print examiner with a list of candidates whose fingerprints were the closest matches to the latent prints on the knife. The latent examiner would then compare the two images on-screen and decide if there really was a match.

The prints had matched, but still something seemed off to Nic. She made a fist, looked down at her hand, twisted it back and forth, looked back up. "Is there a kitchen around here?"

Back out in her car, Nic called Allison. "Do you have a minute? I want to come by and show you something."

"I have a few minutes but then I have to leave for an appointment. Can't you just tell me on the phone?"

"It won't take very long." Nic could feel her heart beating in her ears. "But it's important. And you'll understand better if I can show you in person."

Ten minutes later Nic was in Allison's office and pulling

something from her purse. She didn't know if she would have been able to get it past the security guards and the metal detector if she hadn't been an FBI agent. As it was, it had taken a bit of talking.

"What is that?"

"It's a knife."

Allison's brow creased. "It's a table knife."

It was a battered stainless steel piece of silverware Nic had found in the police break room. "It doesn't matter what kind of knife it is. The principle is the same." She handed it to Allison. "Now stand up and hold it like you're going to stab me in the belly."

Allison winced, but did as she was told. She gripped the knife so that the sharp side was pointing up and so were her fingers. Her thumb rested on the thick heel at the bottom. She looked up at Nic with wide eyes. "Okay."

"Look down and remember exactly where your fingertips are on the handle. Now hold the knife as if you're going to chop onions."

Turning the knife over, Allison shifted her grip so that her fingers were pointing down and her thumb rested on top of the handle. She turned it back and forth, holding it both ways. "My fingers end up on the other side of the handle. But what if he stabbed down with the knife?"

"The only way he could reach her heart was to thrust it up." Nic pushed her fingers into her abdomen, just below the ribs. "But it doesn't matter anyway. Try it."

Allison raised the knife as if she was going to stab down with it, but she had to flip the knife, placing her pinky finger where her index had been. "Okay, we've established that each way of holding the knife is different." She looked from the knife to Nic. "But why does it matter?"

"I went to talk to Jensen about the bald man, and we ended

up looking at the murder book. The prints on the knife are Rick's. But he couldn't have made them holding the knife when it stabbed Cassidy. It looks like he was using the knife as it was intended—to chop vegetables."

"How come no one else figured this out before?"

"It's the print examiner's job to match the prints on the knife with the prints on the card. And they do match. But they're only partials, so it wasn't immediately obvious that they were on the wrong side of the handle. Jensen and I only noticed it today. And the knife itself doesn't match Cassidy's knives. But it does match Rick's. So it was brought there."

Allison's brow creased. "Someone planted the knife?"

"More than that. It really was used to kill her. It has Cassidy's blood on it. And it matches the wound they saw on the autopsy. I think someone took Rick's knife from his kitchen and used it to kill her. That's probably why she was strangled and only stabbed when she was dying or dead. When I first heard it, I thought it was overkill. That Rick was so angry he needed to kill her twice. But now I think the only reason she was stabbed was to frame Rick for the crime. That's why the prints are only partials. The real murderer took Rick's knife and then used it when he was wearing gloves."

"The real murderer?" Allison asked.

"The bald guy."

CHAPTER 23

Allison parked in front of Oregon Federal, her mind whirling. Was Rick really innocent? She had hated to leave Nicole, but she was already late for the meeting with Lindsay and the loan officer.

She saw that Lindsay was waiting for her, peering out the floor-to-ceiling window of the lobby, her hand shading her eyes. It was time for Allison to be the big sister. The mystery of what had happened to Cassidy could, sadly, wait.

Part of Allison had been afraid that Lindsay would be a no-show, nap through it, miss the bus. Part of her had even been afraid that Lindsay would snap under all the expectations being piled on her—by Lindsay herself, most of all—and she would disappear again into the streets. It wouldn't be the first time she had left behind shattered dreams and broken promises.

Now Lindsay smiled, lifted her hand away from her eyes, and gave her a little wave. Looking a little relieved herself, as if she'd had her own doubts about whether Allison would show.

The air inside the bank was a good thirty degrees cooler than it was outside. It felt good to shiver. Walking past the two people waiting in the teller line, Allison joined Lindsay in the small waiting area separating the teller area from four desks that sat, evenly spaced, on the flat blue carpet. One loan officer was on the phone, while the other three were talking to customers.

"That's our person," Lindsay said in a stage whisper as she and Allison sat down. "That Annie Botinelli you made the appointment with. She's the one who's on the phone."

"Nervous?" Allison asked.

Lindsay's smile was tremulous. "Sometimes I can't believe this is really happening. I mean, I'm going to have my own business. I'm going to call all the shots."

"And pull them too," Allison said, making a joke about the espresso machine that cost as much as a used car.

Lindsay swatted her shoulder playfully. "Ouch! You never could resist a bad pun."

"Sorry," Allison lied, hiding a smile. The world was finally opening up to Lindsay, eighteen years after their father's death had nearly shut down her heart.

"That's okay. You can make all the bad puns you want. There's no way I'd get this loan on my own. I'd be lucky if I could get someone to loan me a quarter for the vending machine."

It was a big risk. If Lindsay got lured back into the street life—and she would be right in the middle of it with her cart . . .

"You're my sister," Allison said simply. Her heart was full of memories of the kid sister who had always tagged along, wanting to do whatever Allison was doing, see what she was seeing, wear what she was wearing, play with whatever she had in her hands.

She had spent thirteen years with Lindsay looking up to her. Thirteen years fending her off with annoyance, more often than not. Then, after their dad died, Lindsay had spun out of Allison's orbit, sucked into a black hole of destruction.

Finally she had her sister back.

Lindsay must have been thinking along the same lines. "You've always been a good sister to me, Allison."

"Thanks," she said softly, wondering if she really had been.

"Look, I know you thought I would never get my act together." Lindsay sighed. "To be honest, there were days—heck, whole years— when I thought the same thing."

"But you did." Allison squeezed her hand and let it go. "And look at you now."

Lindsay looked down at her lap. "I keep feeling like someone is going to jump up and snatch it all away. Like I'm a fraud. A fake."

"You know what, Linds? That's normal. Everyone feels that way, at least at first. I think it took a couple of years before I stopped feeling stupid introducing myself as a lawyer. It was like—who am I kidding?"

Allison and Lindsay had been so busy talking that they hadn't noticed the loan officer hanging up her phone. Now she beckoned to them. She was a tall, athletic-looking woman in her late thirties with a curly, blond-streaked bob.

Taking a deep, shaky breath, Lindsay stood and collected the box of cookies and her business plan. Allison followed her.

The loan officer stood up and offered her hand. "I'm Annie Botinelli."

Lindsay and Allison introduced themselves.

"Wow!" The loan officer looked from Allison's face to Lindsay's and back again. "You guys look so much alike."

"Thank you," Lindsay said, and winked at Allison with the eye the other woman couldn't see.

One reason they looked so much alike was that this morning Allison had done Lindsay's hair and makeup, loaned her a pair of earrings as well as a dark blue suit. Even the shoes Lindsay was wearing were Allison's. At first Lindsay had wanted to wear a shorter skirt and higher heels, an outfit Allison would only wear to a night out on the town. Lindsay was still getting the hang of dressing like a business-woman. But the suit, which Allison had worn to court many times, said that Lindsay was serious, that she was mature. Just the look her sister needed to project today.

"I brought a copy of my business plan." Lindsay bit her lip, as if Annie might refuse it. Instead the loan officer held out her hand.

As Annie started leafing through the pages, Allison realized she had to go to the bathroom. Again. She had been drinking so much water lately, trying to stay hydrated in the heat. "Excuse me. Do you have a restroom?" she asked.

Lindsay gave her a slightly panicked look, but they had rehearsed this so many times. Sometime she was going to have to learn how to play grown-up all by herself. And Allison really had to go. As she stood, Allison whispered into Lindsay's ear, "Don't forget the cookies."

Annie had pointed at a swinging door at the back of the carpeted area. A small square window was set at eye level. When she pushed open the door, Allison found a door for the men's on the right, a door for the women's on the left, and an unmarked door at the back.

In the empty women's room, she took the second of the two stalls. As Allison pulled up her panties a minute later, she had a sudden realization. She counted in her head. She was late. Could it be?

No.

Yes?

No.

What had she been thinking, risking it?

The year before, she had lost a pregnancy in her thirteenth week. They hadn't known why, not in a medical sense. Not even in a spiritual sense.

She remembered how she had thrown up Thursday night. How lately smells had seemed so, well, smelly.

Could she be?

And if she was, could she stand to lose a baby again? Could they?

Since the miscarriage, she and Marshall had been in something of a holding pattern. They seldom talked about what had happened, but Allison suspected Marshall thought about the lost child as much as she did.

It had to be a false alarm. The last week had been horrible. The stress of Cassidy's death and everything that followed had probably thrown off her cycle. No point in dwelling on the hope or the fear. Both would prove to be misplaced. No point in giving it a second thought.

In the mirror, Allison stared at her own reflection as if it belonged to a stranger, a young woman with her dark hair pinned up and a faint flush staining her cheeks. Her hand shook a little as she reached for the faucet.

As she started to twist it, she heard three loud bangs, one right after another.

Gunshots.

Her heart seized.

The shots had come from inside the bank.

Allison turned off the water. What should she do? Her gaze pinged from one corner of the room to the other. She was trapped in here, trapped in a tiled box without even a window. The space under the sinks was open. There were no cupboards or closets. There was no place to hide.

On tiptoe she took two steps and stood next to the restroom door. But she was too afraid to open it.

Over a frantic murmur of voices, a man was yelling, "No alarms, no dye packs, and no tracers, or you all die!"

Allison stepped back and looked at the door. Looked for what wasn't there. There was no way to lock it.

She remembered the unmarked door at the end of the hall-way. But to get to it, she would have to leave the restroom and go back out into the hall. The hall that was separated from the bank by only a swinging door with a small window anyone could look through.

Allison jumped as a woman inside the bank began screaming. She didn't think it was Lindsay, but she couldn't be certain. *Oh, God, help us.* What should she do, what should she do?

One of the tellers should already have triggered a silent alarm. *Should* was the operative word. What if they had been surprised? What if the tellers had decided to obey the robbers' commands?

Allison pressed herself into the corner on the back side of the door, grabbed her cell phone, and pushed a couple of buttons.

"Hey, Allison."

She blessed caller ID for saving her precious seconds. Keeping her voice as close to a whisper as she could, she said, "Nicole—listen. I'm at Oregon Federal on Seventh and it's being robbed. I was in the bathroom when I heard three shots fired and a man yelling about no dye packs and no alarms."

"Where are you now?"

"I'm hiding in the bathroom, but, Nic, hurry, get people here, a woman in the bank won't stop screaming."

"How many men? What kind of weapons do they have?"

"I think at least two guys, and I don't know."

"Is anyone hurt?"

"I don't know," Allison said again. "Maybe." She didn't know anything. Other than that she was paralyzed thinking that at any moment a man might come crashing through the door and shoot her. Shoot her in the belly. She realized her free hand was shielding her flat abdomen and whatever it did—or didn't—contain.

"Just hold on a second." Allison heard Nicole relaying information. Part of her dared hope. Nicole would move heaven and earth to help her.

Then she was back on the line. "Is there any place you can go that's safe?"

"I can't lock the bathroom door. It's in a short hall and there's a men's bathroom on the other side. There's another door at the end, but I don't know if it's locked, and in the door to the hallway there's a window they could see me through."

"Don't chance it. Just stay where you are. Get in a stall, close the door, and stand on the seat. With luck, they'll be too busy getting out with the cash to go looking for anyone. The cops are on their way."

Before Allison could move, the noise from the bank suddenly escalated.

She heard a man shout, "Why are you looking at me? I told you not to look at me!"

A woman screamed back, "No, I'm not, no, please, what are you—"

And then another shot. And more shrieks, more shouts.

But the woman whose pleading had just been abruptly silenced.

Allison would know that voice anywhere.

It was Lindsay.

Her little sister.

"I have to go, Nicole. Something bad's happening."

"No, Allison! Stay where you are. The cops are coming."

Barely hearing Nicole's words, Allison disconnected the call and set the phone on the counter. She wanted both hands free.

She took a deep breath, bent down to provide as small a target as possible, and yanked opened the restroom door.

As soon as she had understood what was going on, Nic had burst from her cubicle and alerted Martin Buckley, relaying the little that Allison knew. A Portland cop, Martin was permanently assigned to work alongside the FBI's own bank robbery squad.

He sprang into action, putting the scant information out over the radio on both the police and FBI frequencies. And he also requested that EMS—emergency medical services—respond.

By the time Allison broke the connection, the guys on the bank robbery squad were already hustling out the door. Nearly all bank robberies were note jobs, the work of a lone guy with a habit. A robbery with more than one robber and shots fired was already an anomaly. The authorities would be considering a dozen questions: Were there injured or dead? Would it become a hostage situation? If the robbers felt there was no way out, would they try to provoke law enforcement into killing them? Or did they already want to kill a few cops or agents themselves?

But all Nic could think was, *Allison, Allison, Allison.*

She jumped when Leif touched her shoulder. "Let's go," he said. The keys were already in his hand. "I'm driving."

Just as they pushed open the door, Nic saw Bond coming out of his office. She thought he might be saying her name, but she kept on walking. She had no ears to hear him and no time to stop and explain. Not when Allison might be in trouble. It was better to beg forgiveness than to ask permission. Besides, nothing in the FBI's rules and regulations prohibited those who weren't on the squad from responding to a bank robbery.

As they ran for Leif's car, Nic replayed her conversation with Allison. *"I have to go, Nicole. Something bad's happening."* Would those be the last words she ever heard from her friend? In the background, Nic had heard garbled noises—shouts, screams, what could even have been another gunshot—and then the connection had been severed.

Had the robbers figured out that Allison was hiding in the bathroom? In her mind's eye, Nic saw a masked man kicking open the door, the barrel of his gun the first thing across the threshold. And Allison with no place to go. She saw Allison with her hands up, her back against the white wall, her mouth pleading. But the only response might be a bullet to her chest, the sound reverberating in the small space as she slid to the floor, leaving a bloody smear on the wall behind her.

No! Nic threw herself into the passenger seat and yanked the door closed. Allison couldn't be dead. Not Allison and Cassidy both. The world could not be such a cruel place. Wordlessly she bargained with and prayed to what she could not yet bring herself to call God. Allison was a good person. The best person Nic knew. She didn't deserve to die.

Leif drove fast, with lights on but no sirens. No need to spook the bank robbers by letting them hear the cops approaching. You didn't want to have them decide to take a hostage along in the getaway car or, worse yet, to hunker down with a whole bank full of them. The robbers would want to get out of the bank, and the police would want exactly the same thing, so that they could deal with them without putting civilians at risk.

To law enforcement, the money taken in a bank robbery had no value. It was insured by the FDIC, which would print more of it before an agent even finished writing his report. The only thing that mattered was protecting the lives of the innocent people inside the bank and the lives of the people responding.

The radio crackled with cops and agents giving their locations and quickly drawing up a plan in case the bank robbers were still on-site when they arrived. Routine note-job bank robberies occurred so frequently in Portland that uniformed officers and agents were used to responding and working together. Nic knew that the dispatch center would be contacting the bank by phone to determine if the robbery was real—which she already knew was true—and if the suspects had left. If so, the manager would come outside to meet the cops and agents so law enforcement could ensure that he or she wasn't being forced to lie about what was happening.

Nic was sitting on the edge of her seat, as if the extra six inches put her closer to Allison. Traffic was so thick! She could get out of the car and run to the bank faster than they were moving.

Leif glanced over at her. "Put on your seat belt."

It seemed silly. Inconsequential. Who cared what happened to her when Allison was in trouble? Still, she found herself scooting back and complying.

"Now what exactly did Allison say?" he asked, cutting through the narrow streets.

Nic repeated the conversation as best she could, then said, "Right before the line went dead, I thought I heard a gunshot. Oh, Leif, what if she's—"

He touched her knee for a second and then put his hand back on the wheel and zipped between a Pathfinder and a Subaru. "Don't say it. You don't know what's happening, and we won't know until we get there."

Leif was forced to weave around a panicked driver in an old green Malibu who had simply stopped in the middle of an intersection instead of pulling over. The closer they got to the bank, the worse the traffic became. Leif squeezed through spaces, darted around cars, and managed to keep making progress. But he couldn't go fast enough, not as far as Nic was concerned.

Since a police uniform car was likely to be closer, she knew that the cops would probably be the first on the scene no matter how fast he drove. But even if a cop had happened to be driving right by the bank when the call came in, he or she would be trained to keep driving until it was possible to turn into the driveway of a business that was far enough away to appear routine. Again, the cops wanted the robbers out of the bank before they confronted them.

On the radio, the dispatcher called out one of the unit numbers. "Dispatch, six-seven. Update."

Update? Nic waited for the latest news, not even daring to breathe.

"Six-seven," the cop in Unit 67 responded.

"Manager reports shots fired, one down. Suspects fled."

One down! Nic's heart was a big bird in a too-small cage. What did that mean? Down could be anything from being grazed to dead.

"Ten-four. Direction of travel?"

"Manager states unknown." A brief pause, then, "Second call received. Witness reports two white males running from the bank. Both seen getting into a late-model green or blue four-door compact car, unknown make, driven by a third person. Direction of travel south through the parking lot onto eastbound Market Street."

"Copy. License number?"

"No plate seen."

"Six-seven copy. Arriving on scene."

"Ten-four, six-seven." The dispatcher then began to call out the other unit numbers to make sure they had received the same information. "Four-five, copy?"

"Four-five, copy."

Nic barely heard the other units chiming in. "Dispatch said one down, Leif. You heard her. One down."

"Don't go borrowing trouble, Nic. We won't know until we get there."

Still, when he found the street they needed to take clogged by traffic, Leif yanked the wheel until with a bump and a shudder the car was suddenly on the sidewalk. The parking meters whizzed by just an inch from his side-view mirror and then with a clunk they were back on the street again, having circumvented the knot.

Two minutes later they arrived at the bank and jumped out of the car. The parking lot was filled with cop cars and unmarked cars, with more still arriving, but Nic had tunnel vision. All she could focus on was what lay past the bank's windows and glass doors. She saw people milling around, but no Allison.

At the door, Leif held up his badge, and a uniformed officer unlocked it. Nic pushed past him, nearly running. She had to find Allison. Looking for that familiar dark head, her eyes scanned the ever-growing crowd of customers, employees, cops, and agents. Her ears strained to pick out Allison's low voice among the babble of people crying, yelling, explaining, and barking orders. Then she stopped so fast that her feet nearly slid out from under her. A body, covered by a white sheet, lay on the carpeted area between two desks. A woman's body, lying on its back. Through the sheet, Nic could make out the fine-boned contours of the face, the slender arms and legs. Over the heart a poppy-red flower of blood was growing as it wicked up blood from the corpse.

No. Please, no.

Behind Nic, a woman's nasal voice said, "And the guy was yelling something like, 'Don't look at me, I told you not to look at me!' And he hadn't said one thing before that about not looking at him. He was wearing a mask, so what difference did it make if she looked at him?"

A young patrol officer standing near the body took in the FBI badge on Nic's belt and misunderstood her stare. "One of the tellers wouldn't stop screaming and pointing, so we covered the victim. Don't worry, it's one of those sterile sheets the medical examiner has us carry."

The woman witness continued, "And then he shot her in the chest. He just shot her!"

Nic barely heard her or the patrol officer. All she could do was focus on the shoes protruding from under the white sheet.

The woman said, "And she fell back, but the poor thing was still holding herself up with her hands and staring at her chest. It was like she couldn't believe it was happening. And then he walked right up to her and leaned down and said something and he shot her again. He shot her again!"

Leif grabbed Nic's arm and tried to pull her back. She shook him off as the patrol officer stared.

Nic knew those shoes nearly as well as she knew her own. She had been with Allison one Saturday afternoon when she purchased them at Nordstrom. Allison had declared them perfect for court. Two-inch heels, slightly rounded toe, a basic pump that did not call any attention to itself. The last thing you wanted to be in court was flashy, Allison had said, especially if you were representing the United States government. More times than Nic could count, those shoes had rested next to her sensible flats under the prosecutor's table.

And now those shoes were on a dead woman's feet.

"Do you know who it is?" asked the young officer. His Adam's apple bobbed as he looked from the body back to Nic.

"It's Allison Pierce. She's a federal prosecutor." Nic heard her own voice as if it were coming from somewhere far, far away. "She called and told me there was a bank robbery in progress. She said things were getting bad and then the line was cut off."

"I'm—I'm sorry," he stammered.

Nic fell to her knees, not caring how weak it might make her look. She *was* weak. Too weak to stand. Too weak, almost, to draw another breath.

Nic had never told Allison how much she loved her. Not even after Cassidy died. And now Allison was gone too. And Nic was all alone.

With one finger she touched the slender ankle. Still warm. Her friend's body hadn't even had time to figure out that it was dead.

A sob ripped through her. She saw heads turn as coworkers and cops took in the sight of FBI Special Agent Nicole Hedges falling apart and then courteously looked away.

All her friends were dead. She was the only one of the three who would remember all those meals, all that laughter, all those conversations, all the chocolate and butter and sugar and whipped cream they had shared.

The Triple Threat was now no threat at all.

Nic was still in the same position, bowed over Allison's shoes, her mouth open as her chest heaved, when a touch on her shoulder made her slowly raise her head.

And then Nic's heart cracked.

Cracked wide open.

CHAPTER 25

Nic stared up at the woman who was touching her shoulder. It was Allison. Allison!

"You're–you're alive!"

Allison nodded. The fingers of her other hand were pressed against her lips. Her face was as white as the sheet that covered the body. The body of the woman wearing Allison's shoes.

Nic jumped up and hugged her. Hugged her hard. It was like embracing a stiff plastic mannequin. Allison kept one hand across her mouth, the other limp at her side. She smelled sour and metallic, like sweat and vomit and blood. It was the sweetest scent Nic had ever smelled.

Finally Nic pulled back. Instead of looking at her, Allison continued to stare down at the covered body.

But if Allison was alive, then who was under the sheet from the medical examiner's office, wearing Allison's shoes? Nic leaned down and twitched back the cloth to reveal the face of the dead woman.

At first she thought she was seeing double. Could the Allison standing behind her be a ghost? A figment of her freaked-out imagination?

And then everything shifted and fell into place. Lindsay. It was Lindsay, with her hair all dyed one color. The last time Nic had

seen her, Lindsay's hair had been streaked with pink. But the star-
tling resemblance to Allison was more than that. The earrings, the
makeup, even the way Lindsay's hair was pinned up made her look
like Allison.

Nic let the sheet drop. "Oh, Allison," she said.

Allison did not move or even change expression.

"She's in shock," Leif said in her ear. "Take her over in the corner
and keep her back to the body."

Nic took her friend's cold hand and drew her, unresisting, over to
the far corner of the bank.

"I thought it was you, Ally." Nic had never called Allison *Ally* in
her life. "I thought it was you."

Allison said nothing. Her gaze was unfocused. But bright blood
was smeared around the cross she wore around her neck.

When Nic noticed the blood, her heart jumped. Her thoughts
flashed back to Cassidy and the blood that had soaked the front of
her jacket. "Are you hurt?" With a trembling finger she touched the
blood, trying to see where it was coming from.

"What?" Allison said vaguely. "No, that's from Lindsay. I tried to
help her, but she died in my arms."

"I don't understand. Why were you both here?"

"I was cosigning the loan for Lindsay's coffee cart."

Allison hadn't said where Lindsay was going to get the money
for the cart, and Nic hadn't asked. Now she understood. Allison had
remade her sister in her own image, helped her to look like a successful businesswoman instead of an addict who had spent years on
the streets. But the transformation hadn't reached as far as her credit
score, so Lindsay had needed a cosigner.

"And now Lindsay's dead," Allison said, "and it's all my fault."

This made no sense, but her friend was in shock.

"Allison, it was a bank robbery. Whoever shot your sister must have panicked."

A muscle under Allison's eye spasmed. "That's what they want you to think."

They. She had clearly slipped off the edge of sanity. Two murders in one week were more than she could bear.

"That's what who wants me to think?" Nic tried to keep her expression neutral, as if Allison were talking some kind of sense.

"I came out of the bathroom when I heard her scream. The robbers were running out the door. I tried to help her, but it was already too late. She was bleeding, and I tried to press on it, to keep the blood from coming out. I told her not to talk." Allison's voice was flat. "But she kept trying to tell me. She said the man who shot her called her Allison. And he told her to say hello to Cassidy. And then he shot her a second time."

Nic thought of the witness she had heard describing how the robber accused Lindsay of looking at him, of how bizarre the woman had found the charge. Had his words been just a cover? Had the bank robbery itself been a cover?

Allison must have been thinking the same thing. "Whoever did this—I think he must be the one who killed Cassidy too. Killed her and found a way to frame Rick for it." Finally, a spark of life appeared in her eyes. She looked at Nic. "Why would someone hate me and Cassidy that much?"

Nic didn't answer. She was too confused. Nothing was as it seemed. Allison wasn't dead, and Lindsay really was. And there was a cop who couldn't remember. A crazy guy who said he had seen a bald man with a murder victim. A knife with upside-down prints. A bank robber who really wanted to kill.

Something was going on. Something bigger than Cassidy. Bigger than Lindsay. Two women had died. And right now, as far as Lindsay's killer knew, Nic was the last of the Triple Threat standing.

Allison grabbed her wrist. "They'll come for you now, Nic. They'll come for you."

"You're just guessing. We don't know that," Nic said, even though part of her did know. "But what we do know is that if they figure out they killed the wrong person, they'll come back for you and finish what they started." She looked past Allison at the people milling about the room. Who had seen Allison talking to Nic? More importantly, who had seen Allison who would recognize her?

Only a minute or two had passed since Nic came into the bank. She had to hurry. And pray. Nic finally called it what it was. Prayer. *God, help me to keep Allison safe.*

She caught Leif's eye, and something in her expression must have tipped him off, because he was with her in a few long strides.

"Leif, we have to get her out of here. This wasn't a bank robbery, it was a hit on Allison. Only they goofed and shot her sister. We have to make sure they still think she's dead before they come back and fix their mistake." Her thoughts were racing faster than she could spit them out. "Before I knew the truth I told one of the uniform officers that it was Allison under the sheet. Now we need everyone else to think that."

Even though he looked like he wasn't following all of it, Leif seemed to be willing to take her word. "How are we going to clear this with the Bureau?"

"I don't think that's an option, at least not right now." Nic knew that she might be torpedoing her own career. "By the time we explained everything it would be too late and too many people would know that the wrong woman got killed here. We'd never keep it quiet. We can figure out how to explain it later, but for right now, we've got to get her out of here."

Leif's expression was unreadable.

"Maybe you should just stay out of it," she said. "I'm willing to put my career on the line, but not yours."

He didn't hesitate. "No. I'll help."

Allison seemed to be tracking better. "I won't let you get in trouble, Nicole."

Nic wagged her finger. "You don't have a choice," she whispered urgently. "Because your life is far more important than my career. Now quick. We don't have much time. Where's Lindsay's purse?"

"I think it's on the floor in front of the desk where we were sitting. The desk in the middle. The one with the cookies on it." Allison started to turn around, but Nic grabbed her shoulder before she could present her face to the room.

"I already said that it was you under that sheet. But having your purse next to the body is crucial. The medical examiner will be the one to make the final ID, and he'll be looking at the driver's license as well as going off his own personal knowledge. How well does Tony know you? Does he know you have a sister?"

"He doesn't know me that well, and he doesn't know my sister at all." Allison's voice was shaking. "I don't think he even knows I have one."

"I'll make the switch." Leif held out his hand, and Allison handed over her purse. "Is your phone in it?"

She nodded, looking dazed.

"While you do that, I'll get her outside," Nic said. "We'll meet at your car." Her sunglasses were still on top of her head. Now she took them off and handed them to Allison, thankful that they were oversized. "Here. Put these on. And button your jacket so no one can see the blood on your throat."

Allison did as she was told.

With his big hands Leif managed to nearly fold the purse in half, and then he clamped it under his muscled arm so that only an edge showed. No one seemed to be paying them any mind. Keeping to the edge of the room, Nic and Allison made for the door. Just before they reached it, Nic looked back and saw Leif crouch down as if he were looking at something on the carpet. When he stood up, he still had a black purse under his arm, but Nic knew it was Lindsay's.

Watching the way he slipped through the crowd, somehow managing not to draw attention to himself, she was filled with gratitude. There was no way she could pull this off by herself. She probably couldn't even pull it off with Leif, but at least she could try.

She flashed her badge at the cop manning the door. Back out in the flat heat of the day, she half pushed, half pulled Allison toward Leif's car. The poor girl was barely able to put one foot in front of the other. Leif came up and took Allison's other elbow. He was talking on his cell phone. From the half of the conversation Nic could overhear, he was telling, not asking, Ophelia that she would need to shelter Allison, at least for a few hours.

Once they reached his car, Leif opened the door and helped Allison inside.

What other loose ends were there? Nic leaned in. "What's the name of the loan officer you were meeting with?" she asked Allison.

"Annie Botinelli. I remember thinking it was such a lovely name." Her head lolled on her neck, and her voice sounded floaty.

"Okay, I'm going to go back in there and talk to her. Get her to keep quiet about Lindsay being here too. Leif will take you to Ophelia's. We'll meet later and figure out what else we need to do to keep you safe."

"What about Marshall?" Allison asked.

Nic hadn't thought of that. She hadn't thought of anything. There had been no time.

"I'll go to him before the police do," she said, thinking out loud. "I'll tell him the truth and tell him to get out of town and tell people he's in seclusion. It will be too hard for him to pretend you're dead if he knows otherwise. And that will keep him safe." She stepped back. "Now you two need to go before anyone spots you."

When Nic reentered the bank, Karl Zehner, another agent, hurried up to her, his face set and pale. "Oh, Nicole, I just heard. I'm so, so sorry. I can't believe Allison is dead. What a stupid waste. The tellers are saying they handed over the money. They didn't need to kill anyone—let alone one of the best federal prosecutors in the country."

"I can't believe it either," Nic said, which wasn't really a lie. She had lit the fire, and it was already sparking to life. When Karl turned away, she hurried over to a man wearing a name tag. "Which one is Annie Botinelli?"

He pointed at a tall woman with curly blond hair. She was talking to Theodore, one of the new agents. Maybe Nic's luck was holding. She was with them in two long strides.

"Excuse me, Theodore, let me take over for you. I want to interview this woman myself."

He looked confused, but nodded and left.

"How far had you gotten in telling him what happened?"

"I was telling him about the robbers. Not that there's much to tell. The minute they fired their guns, I knew we were in trouble. We've been robbed before, but I've never known anyone who was in a robbery where a customer was killed." Her voice shook.

"And that was your customer, right?"

"One of them. It was a woman and her sister. One went to the bathroom and the other one was shot. She seemed so nice, too, and they were both close. You could tell. They even looked like each other."

"Look, Annie, I'm not asking you to lie." Which was a lie. "I'm just asking you to leave something out. Whoever killed Lindsay thought they were killing Allison."

"I don't understand. Wasn't it just a random shooting?"

"We don't know that yet. I'm going to interview you and take down all your information. And when you talk to anyone else, just tell them exactly what happened—how these men came in, what they said, what they did, and how as they left, they shot your client. The only part I'm asking you to leave out is that Lindsay was here. Just for right now, don't tell anyone else but me that the woman killed was here with her sister. We're going to say it was Allison who was killed and then put her into protective custody for the time being—but that's on a need-to-know basis only." She said *we're* as if she meant the FBI. "We can't risk the killer finding out he shot the wrong woman."

Annie hesitated. "What about the other people who were here when it happened? I won't tell anyone, but what about everybody else?"

"All they're going to be focused on is the robbery. On the guns. Once people see guns, they don't pay attention to anything else." This had been Nic's experience, but now, when Allison's life depended on it, would it hold? "Trust me, even their descriptions of the robbers are going to be all over the map. The chances that one of them will mention you had two customers, and not one, a few minutes before these guys walked in and started shooting are nil."

Looking dazed, Annie nodded. But Nic knew she wouldn't keep quiet forever.

CHAPTER 26

Feeling as if she were floating above her own body, Allison had stumbled forward through the bank's parking lot. Past the police cars, past the ambulance, past the gawkers. Her sweaty feet slipped in her shoes, but at the same time she shook with chills. Nicole's hand under her elbow was the only thing that kept her on her feet. Nicole had warned her in a whisper to keep her head down, but Allison didn't have to fake it.

Her sister was dead.

Her baby sister.

Lindsay.

Dead.

She'd kept staggering forward, but her mind was still back in the bank, reliving what had just happened a few minutes earlier.

After she had left the safety of the bathroom, Allison had crouched in the hallway between the two restroom doors and tried to figure out what to do. Slowly, slowly she had raised her head until she could see through the small glass window set into the door.

Where was Lindsay? Why had her sister's voice been abruptly silenced? She could see only a small section of the loan area with a loan officer and two customers, all on their feet with their hands raised. But no Lindsay. All three people were staring openmouthed at something just out of Allison's range of vision.

While she couldn't see the tellers, she was pretty sure it was one of them that kept screaming and screaming. A few of the tellers' customers were in her line of sight. One man in a pinstriped suit was crouched on the floor, while a middle-aged woman had her arm around an old lady with a walker. All of them were staring in the same direction the others had, at the spot Allison couldn't see.

A second gunshot roared and faded. The shock of it stole Allison's breath. Now everyone was shrieking and moaning, all of them staring at whatever it was. She risked raising her head another inch, but it wasn't far enough for her to see anything.

A short, plump man dressed in black suddenly burst from the direction of the teller area and into her line of vision, running for the door. Allison's first incongruous thought was how hot his black ski mask must be. He had a gun in one hand and a second in his waistband, and he was clutching a bulging white pillowcase. And here came a second man, this one from the loan area. He was also wearing a mask and dark clothes. Taller and more fit, he loped after the first man, a gun in his fist.

"Don't anyone try to be a hero," the second man shouted back over his shoulder. "You've seen what happens." And then both men were through the front door and out of her line of vision.

The bank robbery was over, Allison realized. Over almost before it had begun. But the teller didn't stop screaming. And the loan officer's expression didn't ease. Her lips were still pulled back from her teeth in an expression that mingled horror and disbelief. The old woman in front of the teller's window was crossing herself. And everyone was still staring at that same spot.

Staring at someone, she realized. They weren't staring at something but at *someone*.

Allison shouldered open the door. Then she stopped so abruptly she almost fell.

In front of Annie's desk, Lindsay lay on her back. Her eyes were closed. One hand was limp on her chest, the other flung back to rest by her head, her fingers curled like a sleeping child's.

No. Not Lindsay. No. There wasn't much blood, just some bright splashes on the white blouse she had borrowed from Allison that morning. Maybe she had simply fainted.

Then Allison saw two dark holes. Right over her sister's heart.

Lindsay's eyes fluttered open. Her gaze sharpened when she saw Allison's face. "You!" she said urgently. Allison read her lips more than heard the word.

Falling to her knees, she pressed her hand over the wounds as she put her ear next to her sister's lips. Lindsay's hand rose and touched the side of Allison's face. Her fingertips smelled of coppery blood.

Lindsay labored to speak. "He . . . thought . . . I . . . was . . . you."

Allison pulled back and stared at her sister. Scarlet blood was frothing on her lips. Her skin was bone white. "What?"

Each word was followed by a panting gasp. "He said . . . say . . . hello . . . to . . . Cassidy . . . Allison."

Allison stilled. "Did he say anything else, Lindsay?"

She watched her sister's lips, but they didn't move anymore. Her eyes were open, but fixed. A bubble of blood appeared between her lips and then burst. But that bubble meant she was still breathing, didn't it? Didn't it?

"Lindsay? Lindsay?" Allison patted her cheek, gently at first and then harder. She couldn't even form a prayer, just a wordless cry for help. "Stay with me! Stay with me!"

And for a moment the spark of life returned to Lindsay's eyes. Reaching up with one wavering finger, she touched Allison's cross. Then her gaze shifted to something past Allison, something above her, and she smiled, her expression radiant.

Then her eyes went fixed and still. Her face slackened and settled back, empty of all expression.

Allison's frantic fingers searched for the pulse in her sister's neck. Searched and found nothing. Lindsay was dead.

A second later a wave of nausea had hit Allison so forcefully that she had barely made it back to the bathroom. She had vomited again and again, vomited as if the evil was actually inside her instead of loose in the world. Five minutes later the police had burst in. Five minutes too late for Lindsay.

As Leif and Nicole hurried her into the car, Allison tried to make herself believe that what had happened back in the bank was real. Believe that it was really supposed to have been her, lying with her eyes open, a sterile sheet over her face. Not playing dead but really dead. As dead as poor Lindsay was now.

Nicole talked about Marshall, about the loan officer, but Allison was mostly on autopilot, not really in her body.

After Nicole left, Leif touched Allison's arm and said, "Keep your head down like you're looking for something on the floor. I need to get you out of here without anyone noticing you."

Allison did as she was told, her face pressed against one knee. As the car took a quick series of sharp turns, she fought off waves of dizziness. Her memory kept replaying what had happened. The horror on people's faces. The fear that had almost paralyzed her. How her bones had turned to water when she finally saw what they were looking at. The way Lindsay had used her last bit of breath to warn her. The bright blood that had bubbled between her lips.

"Okay, you can sit up now," Leif said after a few minutes. "I looped back to make sure that no one was following us."

Allison straightened up. She hadn't thought of that, that someone might be watching the bank, making sure the killing had gone off without a hitch. If Nicole's plan didn't work, then sooner or later they would come after her again. And she would be the one dying on cheap blue carpeting.

"Somebody put some planning into this," Leif said. "Who knew you were going to be at the bank today?"

Allison barely heard him. An endless loop kept playing in her head. Lindsay touching her cross and then slumping back to the floor. The light going out of her eyes. The feel of the cool, slick skin of her throat, a throat that no longer held a pulse.

"Allison." Leif shook her shoulder, summoning her back to reality. "Help me out. Who knew you were going to be at the bank today?"

She thought of Lindsay's joyful pride. "Lindsay probably told a bunch of people. She was always talking about her coffee cart."

"It doesn't matter how many people she told, because none of them would have shown up looking for you," Leif pointed out. "These guys obviously didn't know your sister was going to be there. So who else knew?"

"Marshall knew, our mom knew . . . and . . ." Allison realized what was missing. "And people in my office. We all keep our calendars online. Dan likes us to. It makes meeting planning a lot easier."

"Did your calendar say you would be at the bank with Lindsay?"

Allison concentrated. "No. Just something like Loan Officer, 2 p.m., Seventh Avenue Oregon Federal."

"And who has access to your calendar? Just the secretaries?"

"No. Everyone in the office."

Leif's eyes widened. "How many people is that?"

Allison tried to focus. "Probably over a hundred."

Leif swore under his breath. "I think that it's possible someone at your job gave out the information."

She straightened up. "Knowing I was going to be killed?"

"Probably not. It's likely that someone just got pretexted. This guy could have called around, pretended to be someone he's not, gone fishing until he caught someone who was a little too chatty. But it's also possible that whoever gave up your schedule knew exactly what they were doing, and now they think you're dead. That's why we can't give anyone a reason to think differently." Leif said what she had been thinking. "Because if they know you're still alive, they'll come back. Only next time, they'll make sure you really are dead."

Allison was at risk, but she realized Leif was putting himself in a different kind of danger by helping her. "This isn't safe for you either. I appreciate everything you've done, but I think you should just drop me off at a bus stop. Give me the address, and I'll figure out where Ophelia's house is on my own."

"What are you talking about, Allison? Of course I'm going to drive you there. You've just had the biggest shock in the world. You could barely walk to the car."

Some of the strength came back into Allison as she focused, not on the dead, but on the living. "Nicole told me she already got a lecture from Bond about nosing around Cassidy's death. You could both end your careers if Bond finds out you helped me switch identities with Lindsay."

"It doesn't matter." A muscle tensed in Leif's jaw. "You're not safe if the truth gets out. And Nic genuinely thought that was you dead on the floor back there, at least at first. So it's not even that much of a lie. More like a misunderstanding."

Allison had a feeling Bond wouldn't see it that way. "Isn't someone going to ask questions about why you left the bank?"

"I'm not on the bank robbery squad, so it's not like I'm expected to be there. With luck, things are still so chaotic that no one even noticed us leaving. But the killing of a bystander at a bank robbery is going to make this everyone's business. And killing a federal prosecutor? They're going to want all hands on deck."

Allison remembered the reading of Ecclesiastes at Cassidy's funeral. There was a time for weeping and a time for war. She pulled her shoulders back and gritted her teeth. No more weeping. Not right now. Right now, it was war. She gritted her teeth.

"This guy just killed my baby sister. He killed her just when she was turning her life around. I'm not going to rest until I get him. And when I do, I'm going to make sure he goes to jail and stays there for the rest of his life."

"That's what we all want," Leif said. "Just before we came to the bank, Nic told me about the prints on the knife, about how someone framed Rick. Did you see the guy who shot your sister? Was it a bald white guy?"

Allison tried to remember what she had seen when she had only been looking for Lindsay. "He was tall and thin, that's all I know. He was dressed all in black and wearing gloves and a ski mask, with no skin showing. He could have been a bald white guy or a black guy with dreads for all I know."

"Dark clothes and a ski mask are going to stand out on a 102-degree day," Leif said. "Let's hope they got rid of some of that near the bank and we can get touch DNA."

"Whoever shot Lindsay thinking it was me has to be the same guy who killed Cassidy. He tried to make it look like a coincidence, but when he bragged to her, he gave away the truth." Allison was sickened, thinking of how he had boasted to one dying woman about killing another. "And the main thing Cassidy and I have in common are our jobs. Crime."

"The Triple Threat," Leif said.

"Right. Cassidy didn't cover every story that we did, but Nicole and I work together on nearly everything. I think that's why this guy went to the trouble to frame Rick, and why he staged a robbery this afternoon. Because he wants to get all of us. And that means he's hoping to be able to get close to Nicole without her knowing she's in danger."

It hit Allison full force, the huge flaw in Leif and Nicole's hastily cobbled-together plan.

"And now that he thinks both Cassidy and I are dead," Allison said, "he'll go after Nicole."

CHAPTER 27

Is Marshall in the office today?" Nic asked the girl with two slender silver rings in her right nostril. With the help of her badge and some fast talking, Nic had persuaded a young patrol office who had just arrived at the scene of the bank robbery to take her to the ad agency where Marshall worked. During the short drive she had thought about what needed to happen next for the fiction she and Leif had created to hold together. The only way Allison could stay alive would be if everyone continued to think she was dead.

The receptionist was sitting behind a curved waist-high stainless steel counter inset with glowing translucent inserts shaped vaguely like fish. To Nic, who spent most of her time at bureaucracies with government-issued furniture made of laminate over particleboard, the advertising agency's reception desk seemed like something out of a dream.

Suddenly she was so tired. All she wanted to do was curl up on the polished cement floor, pillow her head on her arm, and go to sleep. And wake up in a world where Cassidy and Lindsay were still alive, and no one had to worry about being a target.

"Yes, Mr. Pierce is working today." Marshall was the agency's art director. The girl was already reaching for the phone. "Shall I tell him he has a visitor?"

"Tell him Nicole Hedges is here."

"Okay." After a brief conversation the girl put down the phone and pointed to an office in the corner.

Marshall was already opening the door by the time Nic got to it. Behind him, a single pristine cobalt blue and acid green athletic shoe sat in the middle of his black polished desk.

"Nicole?" Marshall's thick, dark eyebrows were raised. "What's wrong? Why are you here? Is Allison all right?" His blue eyes pleaded with her as the color drained from his face.

She gestured at him to step back into his office, then followed him inside and closed the door. Leaning against it, Nic said quickly, "This isn't about Allison. She's okay. It's about Lindsay."

"What?" His forehead wrinkled. "Lindsay?"

"Listen to me carefully, Marshall. Lindsay and Allison were at a bank today when it was robbed. Allison was in the bathroom when the robbers came in. In the course of the robbery, Lindsay was shot." She paused, met his confused eyes. "I'm afraid that the wound was fatal. Lindsay is dead, Marshall."

He moved over to his desk and sat down heavily. "Oh no. No. Poor Lindsay. That's terrible." He rubbed his hand over his mouth. Then his eyes flashed up to hers. "But what about Allison?"

"Here's the thing, Marshall. Before Lindsay died, she told Allison that the man who shot her thought *she* was Allison. Remember how I said Allison was in the bathroom when the robbery started? Well, this guy called Lindsay by Allison's name after he shot her. And he told her to say hello to Cassidy. Then he shot her in the chest."

Marshall touched his own chest. "Wait. What? I'm not sure I'm following you. Someone killed Lindsay but thought it was Allison? Are you sure? Are you sure it's Lindsay that's dead?" His eyes were the color of gas flames. "How do you know it isn't Allison?"

"Because I saw them both myself. I saw Lindsay dead and I saw Allison alive. But when I first saw Lindsay's body, before I saw Allison, I made the same mistake the killer must have." Even remembering the horror of that moment nearly overwhelmed her. "Because for some reason, today Allison and Lindsay looked like twins."

Marshall leaned forward and rested his head in his hands. "They had an appointment with a loan officer about Lindsay's coffee cart. Lindsay wanted to make a good impression, so Allison gave her one of her old court outfits to wear to the meeting. She even fixed Lindsay's hair." Marshall raised his head, his hands balling into fists. "But I still don't understand. Why would anyone want to kill Allison?"

"I don't understand it either, Marshall. All I know is that it means that the murders of Lindsay and Cassidy must be connected. And that neither of them is what it seems to be. Earlier today we found evidence that someone framed Rick for Cassidy's murder. And whoever was in that bank just now wanted to make it look like a robbery gone bad, so he could cover up killing Allison. I think the same man is responsible for both murders."

"But what happens when he finds out he killed the wrong person?" Marshall asked.

"Then he'll come after her again. Which is why we're going to make sure he doesn't find out. We're going to let whoever shot poor Lindsay think that he accomplished exactly what he set out to do. I identified Lindsay's body as Allison's and then sneaked her out of the bank. Right now, Leif is taking her . . ." Nic hesitated. It wasn't inconceivable that if the killer found out Allison wasn't dead, he would hunt down Marshall and force him to say where his wife was. "He's taking her someplace safe."

Marshall scraped a hand through his hair, leaving furrows. "I don't understand why you did any of this. Why did Allison leave the bank? Why did you say Lindsay was Allison? Why didn't you just tell the authorities what really happened?"

"Because someone let these killers know that Allison would be at the bank today." Nic had puzzled it out on the way over. "I think it must have been someone in the federal prosecutor's office. Until we have time to figure out what's going on, the fewer people who know she's alive, the better. Even if we just told a few of the higher-ups, I don't think they could keep a lid on it. And I don't think they would agree to telling the world that Allison is dead." Nic took a deep, shuddering breath. "Look, Marshall. When I realized it wasn't Allison but Lindsay lying on the floor, I knew I had a choice. To tell the truth or to let the lie stand. Maybe I made the wrong choice, but I think it's safer for Allison, at least for right now, if she stays dead."

"Do you really think you can pull this off?"

"I have no idea," she said honestly. "But I'll do anything to keep Allison safe, and I know you will too. Pretty soon, homicide is going to show up here and give you the news. They're going to say that Allison is dead. And you'll need to convince them that you believe that your wife was murdered and that you're falling apart."

There was something like a challenge in Marshall's eyes. "So I'm supposed to act as if I really believe it's true?"

"With the homicide detective, yes. And then you need to get out of town as soon as possible. Tell your office that you need some time alone. They'll understand. Go home, pack a bag, and then go hole up someplace quiet at the beach or the mountains and don't answer your cell phone."

"Are you kidding me?" Marshall made a *puh* sound. "Allison's life is in danger, and you want me to go on vacation?"

"What do you think you'll be able to accomplish if you stay here?

We can't risk Allison coming to you or you going to Allison. If the killer has any doubts about what really happened in the bank, he could be watching you. That's why you need to get out of sight and go someplace where you don't know anyone. Because if you stay here, people are going to be coming to you, crying because their hearts are breaking, and I guarantee you that they'll realize that something's off about your reaction."

Marshall looked as though he wanted to argue, then he closed his eyes and nodded. "Okay, fine. I'll get out of town—but on one condition." He stood up and grabbed his suit jacket from a coatrack in the corner. "I'm taking Allison with me."

Nic was painfully aware of the seconds ticking by. "We can't risk that either, Marshall. It will get around that the victim's husband is off with another woman. Or if the killer has someone take a closer look at you, they'll report that you're not alone. Either way, this guy could put two and two together."

Marshall said stubbornly, "I am not going to turn tail and run and leave Allison here all by herself to face a murderer."

Nic's adrenaline was running so high that patience was difficult. "I'm not asking you to leave her on her own. Leif and I will be with her. But our best shot at keeping her alive is if everyone thinks she's dead. And that means you need to stay away from her."

"So you really expect me to take part in this charade?"

"I'm putting my career on the line for what you're calling a charade. So is Leif. We're doing it because we believe it's the only way to keep Allison safe." Nic's voice softened. "Look, I'm only saying get out of town for a day or two, until we can figure out who leaked Allison's schedule. Until we can figure out who would want both Cassidy and Allison dead."

"So why aren't you going out of town?" Marshall challenged her.

"Why do you think you can lie to people about your best friend and I can't?"

"Because I don't have any choice. Even if I left, it wouldn't make any difference. Because if this guy killed Cassidy and Lindsay, then I'm next. Everything that Allison and Cassidy had in common, I did too. We all three worked or covered the same cases."

Marshall's eyes widened. "The Triple Threat."

"Right. In fact, I think he already tried once to kill me. On the same day Cassidy was murdered, a car almost ran me over. At the time I thought it was an accident. I'm not going to sit and wait for him to come after me again. Allison and Leif and I are going to figure out who he is and then hunt him down."

"I don't know," Marshall said.

Nic could tell he was wavering, but not enough.

"I have to talk to her. I have to talk to Allison."

She wanted to shake him, but instead she just said, "Does Lindsay have a phone?" When he nodded she said, "If it was in Lindsay's purse, then Allison has it, because we traded their purses before she left the bank. Call her on it now, and maybe she'll pick up when she sees who it is. But if she does answer, make it quick. We don't need someone from homicide showing up and finding you on the phone with your supposedly dead wife."

Nic was walking out of the agency when she heard the voice of the man she most didn't want to see right now. Detective Jensen.

"What are you doing here, Hedges?"

She wiped all expression from her face. "I didn't want Marshall to hear the news from a stranger."

He looked at her with a jaundiced eye. "You keep turning up in the wrong place, do you know that?"

CHAPTER 28

Gina Hodson used her car key to slit open the clear packing tape on the brown cardboard box the mailman had left on her porch. The box was plain on the outside, but when she turned back the flaps they read *Fruit by the Foot*. The sender had separated the box at the seams and taped it back together, inside out, before packing her messenger bag inside.

People who sold a lot of stuff on eBay figured out how to do it for the cheapest way possible. They recycled boxes, stuck new address labels on old envelopes, and used wadded-up newspapers instead of packing peanuts.

Gina's entire wardrobe came from eBay. Even her underwear, just as long as it was listed as "new without tags." When you were putting yourself through Arizona State, you had to save money any way you could. So she ate Ramen, hunted out used textbooks, and shopped eBay.

When Gina was a kid, she was dressed from head to toe with finds from garage sales and thrift stores. Her mom had had money once, before her family cut her off for marrying Gina's dad. They'd said he was bad news, and they were right. He left before Gina learned to walk.

But her mom taught her that if you knew what you were looking for, the signs of quality, you could still dress nicely, if you didn't mind that what you were wearing had once belonged to someone else. Rich people got tired of perfectly good things all the time. Sometimes things they hadn't even gotten around to wearing.

Her mom was a dedicated Goodwill shopper, but Gina didn't like the sour smell of mothballs and mildew that hung in the air. Browsing and buying on eBay involved no smells at all; it was like Goodwill to the nth power. And a lot of items were brand-new, bought by compulsive shoppers or by people who lived near outlet malls and marked their finds back up a little, making their money on volume. Over the last two years, Gina had learned the best way to bid on eBay. She made an offer in the last two minutes, for an odd amount, and as high as she was willing to pay. And she nearly always won.

Now from the balled-up newspapers stuffed in the old fruit leather box, she pulled out a black canvas messenger bag. It looked brand-new. And she had paid only $5.13 with free shipping. The eBay seller, who went by the name LiveFree, had ended up practically giving it away. That's what he got for listing it at nearly midnight, West Coast time, when many potential buyers were already in bed.

Before bidding, Gina had checked online. Messenger bags from the same company normally sold for forty bucks.

This one had lots of handy little pockets. She slipped pens in one, lip gloss in another, and paper clips in the third. One zippered pocket was located deep inside the main compartment. Gina's mom had drilled into her the importance of always carrying an emergency twenty-dollar bill, and this seemed a good place for it, hidden but accessible.

Gina unzipped the compartment and started to slip the folded bill inside. Her fingers touched something loose and rubbery. Before she could think better of it, she hooked the item with her index finger and pulled it out.

Dangling in front of her horrified eyes was a white vinyl glove, so thin it was nearly translucent. It was inside out, the fingers still half pushed back into themselves. Whatever the glove had been used to handle had left behind a sticky, dark red residue.

Something that looked very much like blood.

Gina let out a little scream. Dropping the glove, the twenty-dollar bill, and the messenger bag, she jumped back as if the glove were a living thing and could bite her.

Then she tried to reason with herself. Maybe LiveFree was a doctor. Or a hobbyist who had cut himself.

Steeling herself, she picked up the bag and probed the compartment again. Inside was a second glove. There was blood inside this one too. Several longish blond hairs had been trapped in the blood and now dangled from the cuff of the inside-out glove. Gina set the bag and the glove on the floor next to the other glove.

LiveFree must have done something bad.

Very bad.

With shaking hands, Gina smoothed out one of the sheets of crumpled newspaper that had cushioned the messenger bag. It was from the *Oregonian*. She checked the return address on the box. It was a PO box in Portland.

Then she called 9-1-1.

CHAPTER 29

Okay," Leif told Allison as he pulled up in the driveway of a 1950s ranch-style house in Southeast Portland. "This must be Ophelia's place."

It was the newest and plainest of houses in a neighborhood full of century-old homes with ornamental woodwork, cedar siding, and gardens with crayon-bright flowers. Many of the homes probably had views of the Willamette from their second floors, but it must not have occurred to whoever built Ophelia's one-story house that such a thing was possible.

Long and low, the structure had about as much personality as the shoe box Allison and Lindsay used to pretend that Barbie and Ken lived in. It was painted a dull white, down to the trim. The lawn was neatly mowed, but there wasn't a single flowering plant, not even Portland's ubiquitous rhododendron.

As Leif put the car in park, Ophelia half opened the door and beckoned to Allison. She turned to Leif. "If the FBI figures out the truth, you guys should tell them whatever you need to, to keep out of trouble. Tell them it was all my idea, or that you made a mistake. I don't want you to flush your careers."

Leif nodded, but didn't say anything. Allison knew he would do what he thought was right, not what he thought was easy. Finally he said, "We'll be back in touch tonight once we know more."

"And you'll keep Nicole safe?" Allison asked. "Just in case that guy does have his eye on her?"

"Of course," he said gruffly. "Now, you'd better get inside before Ophelia has a meltdown."

Ophelia had stepped closer to the doorway and was gesturing more urgently. Allison took a deep breath and stepped out of the still-running car and into the heat of the day. It was like stepping into an oven. She hurried up the walkway.

As soon as she was inside, Ophelia closed the door behind her. The house was blessedly cool.

"Most of my neighbors work during the day," Ophelia said, "but I don't want anyone wondering who you are or remembering what you look like."

"If you don't feel safe having me here," Allison said, "I could go." She had only met this girl yesterday, and now she was asking to be sheltered from a killer. Then again, their lack of a preexisting relationship make it unlikely anyone would look for her here.

"No," Ophelia said after a long pause. "It's okay."

White spots were dancing in front of Allison's eyes. "Do you mind if I sit down?" she asked. "I'm feeling kind of shaky."

Allison waited for Ophelia to ask a question or demand an explanation. All she said was, "Sure." She seemed devoid of curiosity. It was oddly soothing, allowing Allison to try to float in the in-between, to push away the thoughts of what had just happened.

For places to sit, she had her choice of a well-used green leather recliner or a navy blue futon couch. She chose the couch. The center-piece of the room's decor was not the small flat-screen TV but a carpeted cat-climbing structure with multilevel platforms and even a few ramps. A ginger tabby rested on top, and a small black cat with bright green eyes sprawled on another level. Something was missing from the room.

It took Allison a few seconds to figure out what it was. There wasn't a single picture on the wall.

A black-and-white cat slinked out from under the couch. It wound its way around Ophelia's ankles, letting out plaintive meows.

"Maizy wants to go outside, but I don't let her," Ophelia said, bending down to pet her. "It's destructive to native bird species, plus she would run the risk of being struck by a car."

Allison felt as though she had stepped onto another planet. Only a few minutes ago her sister had died in her arms. Now she was having a conversation about the ethics of keeping an indoor pet.

Tinny music began to play. Allison jumped. It was coming from Lindsay's purse, which she was holding on her lap.

"It's my sister's phone."

"Don't answer it."

"Let me just see who it is." Allison opened the purse and tried to locate the phone with just her eyes. It scared her to touch it, as if it would somehow broadcast the fact that she was alive. But then she saw the display. "It's my husband." She flipped it open and turned away, giving herself the illusion of privacy.

"Hello." She kept it short and neutral, just in case.

"Oh, darling, you're alive." Marshall's voice broke with relief. "Oh, Allison, when Nicole walked into my office just now, I thought you were dead."

"I'm alive, Marshall. But Lindsay really *is* dead." Hot tears filled her eyes. "This guy pretending to be a bank robber shot her. I talked to her before she died. One minute she was there and the next minute she was just . . . gone."

"Nicole told me."

"The terrible thing is that he shot her because he thought she was me."

"Nicole told me that too."

"She died in my stead, Marshall." The tears spilled down Allison's cheeks. "It's my fault that my sister's dead."

"You can't tell yourself that, Allison. You have to look at reality. When we took her in, Lindsay was headed for death. You saved her."

"Saved her for what?" Allison said bitterly. "Saved her so she could be murdered in my place? It's such a waste! All those years I spent worrying. I thought she would die of an overdose, or be murdered by one of her customers, or that Chris would finally kill her. But for this to happen now? Just as she was getting her life back together?" Allison wept at the injustice of it, at how her sister's plans and dreams and endless practice espressos all added up to nothing. "It's not fair. Lindsay finally turned her life around, and now it's all ended before it even began."

"But it did begin, Allison," Marshall's low voice insisted. "She had a year sober. A year where she had dreams and worked to make them come true. It's terrible that she won't get to see them fulfilled, but how much worse would it have been if she had never had a dream at all?"

"But she's only thirty-one, Marshall. She's just a baby, and now she's dead. She's never going to fall in love with the right man or have kids or grow old." Just as Cassidy would never get that Emmy she had always longed for. "Why is everyone dying?" Her voice broke.

"Allison, listen to me. We're all dying. All of us. We don't know the day or the hour. It could be tomorrow or it could be in fifty years. But we are all appointed to die. And Lindsay must have come close to death a dozen times. A hundred. Would you rather she had died in some nameless alley with a bullet in her chest or a needle in her arm?" He took a deep breath. "Instead, your sister died right with God and happy about her life. She died with you there to comfort her.

She died knowing she was loved. And she died fast. A lot of people can only wish for those things."

Was Marshall right? It was true that Lindsay had died when her life had meaning and purpose. Not when she was hating herself, as she had for years and years. Allison took a hitching breath and swiped at her eyes. "It's just so hard."

"Of course it is, babe. I wish I could be there with you." He paused. "But I think I'd better go for now. Nicole said a detective could be here any minute to give me the news. I'm going to have to pretend that she already told me that you're dead, and make him believe that I believe it. And then she said I should get out of town so I won't have to worry about letting the truth slip. We argued about it. I still don't know if it's the right thing to leave you all alone."

"But I'm not alone. And I'm safe now. I'm safe as long as the killer thinks I'm dead." And Marshall himself would be safer out of town. Allison couldn't bear to lose both her sister and her husband.

Suddenly she realized another flaw with the little plan they had made. "Marshall, what about my mom? She needs to know the truth. If we let her think that I'm dead and then she learns it's really Lindsay, that's even crueler than the truth. Can you tell her what really happened?"

"But once I do that, the cat's out of the bag. If Nicole thinks I can't keep quiet, then your mom certainly won't be able to."

It was true. Her mother had never been a good liar. "I think you probably need to take her with you."

"Your mom?"

In Marshall's tone, Allison could hear his resistance. Then he heaved a sigh.

"You're probably right. This whole thing feels so rushed, but I guess we don't have any other choice," Marshall said. "Oh. Someone just pulled into the parking lot—I think it's a cop. I'd better go."

"I love you." She meant those three words more than she ever had before.

"I love you too. Remember the psalm we memorized last year? Hang on to those words."

Allison snapped the phone closed. Then she put her hands over her wet face. What were they doing? What was going to happen to them?

She knew the verses Marshall was referring to. When their Bible study group chose Psalm 27 to memorize, she was sure none of them had dreamed of taking the meaning quite so literally. *The Lord is my light and my salvation—whom shall I fear? . . . When the wicked advance against me to devour me, it is my enemies and my foes who will stumble and fall.*

She started when Ophelia pressed a paper towel into her hands. Allison wiped her eyes and blew her nose on the thick paper.

The other woman looked at her and then away. "I'm sorry about your sister," she muttered. "I don't have a sister, but Felicity, one of my cats, died a few months ago and I was very sad."

Allison digested this in silence and finally settled on saying, "Thank you for your sympathy."

She just wanted to lie down and close her eyes, but Ophelia had other ideas.

"Okay." She cocked her head and made a humming noise, regarding Allison. "The first thing we're going to need to do is change your appearance. Everyone always wants to go blond, but I think you would look more convincing as a redhead." She cleared her throat. "Maybe while I'm at the drugstore getting the hair dye, you should take a shower. You still have some, um, blood, here." Ophelia touched the hollow of her throat. "By your cross."

Allison thought of how Lindsay's eyes had lit up just before she died. What had her sister seen? "Okay."

"Let me show you the guest room and the bathroom." Ophelia turned to go down the hall, and Allison followed.

"Your house is so quiet."

"When I moved in I had extra insulation blown in the walls. The blinds are also noise-reducing."

The same white honeycomb shades Allison had seen in the living and dining rooms were in the guest room as well.

"You don't like sounds?" Allison asked.

"Street noise is very distracting. And now because it's so hot, I have to have the central air on. That *whoosh*ing sound is a constant annoyance."

Allison nodded, even though she had been unaware of it.

On the counter of the small bathroom, Ophelia had laid out a neatly folded but much washed T-shirt and soft cotton drawstring shorts. They sat between a brand-new white towel and a lidded glass bowl filled with cotton balls. "I figured you'll probably want to change. The waist on the shorts is elastic, so they should fit you. And the towel is for you. It's the guest towel. So please don't touch my towel." She pointed at a faded lavender bath towel hanging on the towel rack.

"Okay. I won't touch your towel."

Ophelia nodded, looking satisfied, apparently oblivious to the note in Allison's voice.

"When you're at the drugstore, could you get me something too?"

Allison told Ophelia what she wanted, then threw the dead bolt after Ophelia left. She was turning to go back to the guest room when her eye caught on Lindsay's purse. Taking a deep breath, she sat down on the couch and shook out its contents. Doodled sketches of signs for

Lindsay's Lattes and More. Plastic chips from Narcotics Anonymous that looked like poker chips but marking varying milestones of sobriety: one month, two months, six months. ChapStick. Lipstick. A pair of earrings made from peacock feathers.

And a plastic accordion of snapshots. Some were of people she didn't recognize. One was of Lindsay's old boyfriend, Chris, and Allison found herself hoping it was truly old, as if she still needed to save Lindsay from him.

Another photo was of the two sisters in front of a Christmas tree. Allison was about ten, Lindsay seven, both in their pajamas, half dazed with sleep.

Here were she and Lindsay sitting on the hood of the station wagon, two sets of long tanned legs in cutoff shorts. They were making bunny ears behind each other's heads, grinning as widely as they could. Allison didn't remember the picture, but she knew who had taken it. Their dad.

Out of the two dozen or so photos, there was only one that showed him. He was leaning against an old red Mustang he had sold the year she was born. His hair was longer than she ever remembered it being, his face open and without care. He had been younger than she was now.

Allison flipped through the rest of the photos, looking for more of their dad, but didn't find any. Yet he was in every photo Lindsay had kept of their family, because it was his eyes that had framed the shot, his voice that had directed them, his hand that had pressed the button.

And suddenly Allison was crying again, crying for the loss of Lindsay, the loss of her father, the loss of her family. Only she and her mom were left.

When Ophelia returned thirty minutes later, Allison was dressed in the clothes the other woman had left her, her hair still wrapped in the towel. She was beginning to feel as if she had entered some strange limbo, a place between heaven and hell, between the pain of Lindsay's death and the knowledge that it had been meant for her, between grief and revenge.

"I purchased what you asked for." Ophelia held out the plastic bag from Rite Aid.

Without a word, Allison went into the bathroom. Three minutes later she was staring at a pink plus sign on a white plastic wand.

Allison was pregnant.

Her sister was dead, and she was carrying a new life.

CHAPTER 30

When she saw the plus sign on the pregnancy test, Allison's first reaction was a fear so strong it nearly overwhelmed her. A voice inside her screamed that she had to get out of this house, get out of this city, get out of this state. She had to run away and hide. Not just to save herself, but to save the new life inside her.

But where would she go? Where could she guarantee that the killer couldn't find her? Where could she live freely and without fear? In her bones Allison knew that if the man who had killed her sister discovered she was still alive, he would hunt her down and correct his mistake.

But she couldn't die. Not when she was carrying a new life. Allison rested both hands on her still-flat abdomen. She had prayed for this pregnancy, begged for it, longed for it.

But for her prayer to be answered now? Now, when her friend was dead, her sister was dead, and her own life was on the line? When everything could be over before it even began?

Why now? Allison asked God silently.

The answer came to her like a lamp being lit in the darkness. *For I know the plans I have for you . . . plans to prosper you and not to harm you, plans to give you hope and a future.*

Allison made herself take a deep breath. God did have a plan for her, she reminded herself, and this baby must be part of it. This pregnancy was a reminder that she still had hope and had a future.

And she wanted to live! To live without fear. And to do that, she could not hide. She would not. Instead, she would find this guy and make sure he was locked up for good. In the mirror, Allison met her own shadowed eyes, then lifted her chin.

When she came out of the bathroom, she found Ophelia sitting at the dining room table, which was empty except for a pen and a notebook. The black-and-white cat was in her lap. Even standing ten feet away, Allison could hear it purring.

"I took that test you got for me. I'm pregnant."

Ophelia looked down at the cat and rubbed behind its ears. "Is that such a good idea?"

If Allison had been expecting congratulations, she hadn't been factoring Ophelia into the equation.

"Well, it's not exactly like I planned to be the target of a killer at this point in my life. But my husband and I have been wanting a baby."

Not exactly trying, though. They had been too scared to try on purpose, too scared to even talk about it. If they didn't voice their hopes, it wouldn't hurt so much when they were dashed.

Setting the cat on the floor, Ophelia said, "Do you feel okay?"

"I feel fine." Allison remembered the parking lot at the VQ, the bathroom at the bank. "Although I have thrown up twice in the last few days. I figured it was just from the heat and the stress."

Ophelia shot a glance at her belly. "You don't look pregnant."

"Of course I don't. I'm only a few weeks along. About as early as you can be and still have it show up on the test. You don't really start to show until the second trimester."

Eighteen months ago Allison and Marshall had greeted that first pregnancy with such joy. He had gone with her to every doctor's visit, pored over *What to Expect When You're Expecting*, held her in bed at night while they giddily batted back and forth ridiculous baby names. ("Opal Moon!" "Twelve!" "Oak!" "Rotator Cuff!")

Allison had just been entering her second trimester when things went horribly wrong. She remembered Dr. Dubruski's intent face as she moved the ultrasound wand over Allison's belly. Slowly the doctor's expression had changed from concentration to consternation. Even though she had been flat on her back, Allison had felt as if she were falling. Marshall had gripped her hand, and it had felt like the only thing tethering her to the earth.

A few days later she had joined the invisible club of mothers who had miscarried. Her dreams for their baby had ended in blood and pain, in sadness and even shame that she must have done something wrong, no matter what Dr. Dubruski said.

Now the only person who knew about the new life within her was this strange woman Allison had met just yesterday.

"I should call my husband." She walked over and picked up Lindsay's phone from the mantelpiece where she had put it earlier.

"Wait a second," Ophelia said. "Didn't you want your husband to leave town? Because if he learns that you're pregnant, he might feel that he needs to stay to protect you."

And just when Allison had been thinking this odd woman didn't understand human beings at all . . .

"You're right. Having the killer think I'm dead is the only advantage we have." She set down the phone. "And we have to get this guy. We have to. For Lindsay and for Cassidy." The thought of her sister and her friend gave Allison new strength. She remembered the almost jaunty way the man had loped out of the bank. "I'm not going to be whimpering in some corner, waiting for him to come back for me. The only real way I can protect this baby is not to hide, but to go after this guy and get him before he gets me."

"The hunted becomes the hunter," Ophelia said, offering Allison a small smile.

"Exactly. Only to do that, I need you to help me track him down."

"Today we have a different problem from the one you presented me with yesterday." Ophelia steepled her fingers. "It's both more complicated and perhaps more easily solved. We need to figure out why someone would want to kill both Cassidy *and* you."

"It has to be somehow connected with what we do." Allison took a seat across from her. "Our personal lives do overlap, but that's all grown out of our professional ones."

"The Triple Threat," Ophelia said.

"That's right. And I think all three of us have actually been targets. On the day Cassidy was murdered, Nicole told me that someone had tried to run her down while she was out jogging. At the time she thought it was just a careless driver, but now I don't think it was any coincidence. I think it was somebody trying to cover his tracks. Then Cassidy was murdered and Rick was framed for it. And I'm supposed to be dead in a bank robbery gone wrong. For some reason, someone wants to kill the three of us. But I can't think of anything we've done that merits three murders."

Ophelia said, "I have come to understand that people act the way they do to correct what they perceive as an imbalance in the world."

"What do you mean?"

"For example, a shoplifter might feel deprived—of love, of money, of attention—so she steals things to make up for it."

"But surely the store she steals from didn't deprive her of those things." Allison wondered where Ophelia was going with this. "And stealing won't really give her the underlying thing she needs."

Unperturbed, Ophelia continued to stroke the cat. "However, it does give her something, and perhaps she figures something is better than nothing. I'm not saying it makes sense to us. But it makes sense to the people who do these things. And whoever is trying to kill the three of you feels that doing so will correct some sort of imbalance, an injustice."

"But in all the years I have been a federal prosecutor, I have never asked for the death penalty. Never." Allison slapped her hand on the table for emphasis. "Yet something we've done is worth all of our lives?"

Ophelia shrugged. "It may not be logical to anyone but the man who's after you. But I'm not sure the *why* is even important. What we really need to figure out is the *who*. There are two ways to approach this, and I think we need to utilize both. One is to look at all the people you three helped put away. There's a database I can access to find all your prosecutions, and another database I can cross-reference to find out if Nicole was involved. What I won't be able to look up as easily is whether Cassidy covered them. I need you to make a list of those so I can start narrowing it down." She slid the notebook and pen toward Allison.

"That's not going to narrow it down much. I prosecute some-where between fifty and seventy-five cases a year. Nicole and I work as a team more often than not, and Cassidy covered most of our cases. That's got to add up to hundreds of defendants." The idea was overwhelming but then Allison thought of a way to whittle it down. "Except it has to be a recent case, right? Because why would someone suddenly want revenge for an old case?"

"It could be a recent case," Ophelia said. "But not necessarily. It could be someone who has served his term and been released and now wants to punish you. Or someone whose sentence was overturned.

Or a relative who has now decided to take revenge because an appeal was recently turned down or it's the anniversary of a sentencing. Try to think about some of the bigger cases you handled, ones where Cassidy might have done a whole series of stories instead of just one. It wouldn't be logical to kill her just for covering a story once."

"Nothing about this is logical," Allison said. The world felt like it had gone topsy-turvy.

"But what's happening is logical to the killer," Ophelia said. "And if we knew who he was, it would go a long way toward stopping him." She tapped her lips with her index finger. "You know, these guys carried off a bank robbery pretty well. Maybe we should first consider any bank robbers you prosecuted."

"Maybe. But prison is like college for criminals. They go in knowing about one kind of crime and come out with an education in all the others. And one of the things cons talk about most is the best way to rob a bank." Allison looked at the pen and notepad, but didn't pick them up. "You said there were two ways. What's the other?"

"We can also try to work backward by figuring out more about the man you saw in the bank. Two of our witnesses have talked about a bald man, perhaps with a droop on one side of his face. Do you remember prosecuting any bald guys? Any bald guys who'd had a head injury or suffered a stroke?"

"The only bald guy I can think of was a biker in the Mongols who went by the name Little Man." Allison saw him in her mind's eye, glowering at her from the defense table. "But he had to be close to four hundred pounds. He's in prison for racketeering and drug dealing."

"Well, if the person who killed your sister is the same person Roland and Angel saw, then we know he's thin, bald, tall, and has intense eyes. And possibly a droop on the left side of his face. Does that sound like anyone you know?"

It didn't, did it? Something nagged at her, but when Allison tried to focus on it, it slipped away.

Ophelia tried again. "You're the only one who's seen this guy, who has probably met him before. Was there anything about him that was at all familiar?"

Allison thought of the man she had seen loping away from her. "I only saw him and the other guy, the one with the bag of money, for a few seconds. And mostly from behind. I barely paid attention to either of them. All I was focused on was finding my sister." Allison felt a jolt of electricity. "Wait a minute!" She straightened up. "The bank will have surveillance footage! We can get Nicole to get us a copy. There should have been at least three or four cameras that taped the robbery. I'll be able to see him from all different angles."

"You'll also probably be able to see him shoot your sister." Ophelia cleared her throat. "Do you think you can handle that?"

CHAPTER 31

While they waited to see if Nicole could get the tapes for them, Ophelia had Allison dye her hair and then took a pair of scissors to it.

Allison had never thought of her hair as heavy, but having ten inches gone left her head feeling unexpectedly light. Or maybe the feeling was a side effect of the whole crazy day. She had learned about Rick's probable innocence, held her dying sister in her arms, and discovered she was pregnant. It should have all been too much, but instead of feeling overwhelmed, she felt blank and empty. As if her head were a balloon and she might just float away into the sky. The feeling reminded her of when they had found Cassidy's body. Maybe her body and mind were conspiring to protect her.

Leif and Nicole called to say they were coming by around eight. When Ophelia let them in, they both stopped short and stared. Between the new short cap of dark red curls and the loose-fitting shorts and T-shirt, Allison's look had changed dramatically from the woman who had walked into the bank six hours earlier.

"Wow!" Nicole blinked. "If I didn't know that was you, Allison, I would never guess."

Leif turned to Ophelia. "You did a great job."

"It's a little uneven, but I did the best I could."

Leif set a plastic bag on the table and began to pull out white takeout boxes. "We thought you guys might be hungry, so we picked up Chinese."

At the sight of pot stickers and the smell of broccoli beef, Allison's stomach rumbled and her mouth watered. How could she be hungry when her sister was dead? But the answer was as near as her belly.

Allison had asked Ophelia not to share the news of her pregnancy. She wanted the focus to stay on finding the man who had killed her sister and Cassidy. And if she managed to get out of this situation alive, then the person who should hear the news first was Marshall.

Nicole held out a thumb drive. "Here's the footage from the surveillance. I figure I must know this guy too, so I've watched it and watched it. But when I look at the guy who shot Lindsay, he doesn't ring any bells." She laid a cool hand on Allison's arm. "I don't know if you should eat before or after you see this. Because I'll warn you, some of it will make you sick. It did me."

"Lindsay can't be any more dead than she is. And I'll do anything to find her killer." Maybe it was better her emotions were already walled off, Allison thought. She would watch the video dispassionately. Like a computer. Like Ophelia.

They dished up plates of food and then Ophelia led them into her office. It was yet another plain room, this one with a blond wood desk and a silver Macintosh desktop with the largest screen Allison had ever seen.

Ophelia inserted the thumb drive and clicked to open it. There were a half-dozen files.

Leif said, "We have footage from six cameras altogether. Four from the teller area—that's one behind each teller. One camera showed the lobby. And one was outside the bank's entrance. Once the alarm was triggered, the cameras were programmed to automatically save the footage from fifteen minutes before the alarm and continue for fifteen minutes after. Oregon Federal has gone to all digital film." A lot of banks just shot a frame or two per second, which was why most footage of a robbery looked herky-jerky.

"Let's start with the exterior camera," Nicole said, pointing over Ophelia's shoulder. "That should be the easiest to watch."

Ophelia opened the file, which began with an overhead view of two ATMs and a stretch of sidewalk, but no people.

Leif said, "Go up to fourteen minutes fifteen seconds on the tape. The car appears a few seconds after that."

Ophelia dragged the playhead to the right. A small dark-colored car pulled up just past the ATMs.

"It appears to be a navy blue or dark green 2002 or 2003 Toyota Tercel," Leif said. "We already have an APB on it. The camera wasn't at the right angle to see the plates, but they were probably stolen anyway."

Simultaneously, the rear passenger doors swung open and two men got out. Allison stiffened. Their masks were already on, their dark outfits identical, their hands gloved. The shorter, fatter one was closest to the camera. It was the other one, the taller, thinner one, who stopped the breath in her throat. Here he was. This was the man who had killed her sister.

But as he ran ahead of the other man and then flung open the door and disappeared inside, nothing about him seemed familiar at all.

The two robbers were now out of sight of the exterior camera. The driver stayed in the getaway car, waiting, just a blurry figure also wearing a mask. It was hard even to tell if it was a man or a woman.

"You can fast-forward to the seventeen-minute mark," Leif told Ophelia. "That's when they appear on the tape again."

Allison took a ragged breath. So it had taken less than three minutes to end her sister's life. Less than three minutes to forever scar every person who had been in that bank.

Ophelia dragged the playhead farther to the right. A few seconds later the men ran out the door. Two or three loose bills fluttered from the pillowcase in the shorter man's hands. He started to turn back, but the taller man yanked him roughly forward, his mouth moving. And then they were jumping in the car and the car was peeling away.

Ophelia half turned. "Anything about the tall one seem familiar at all? His gait, the way he moved his hands, how he held himself when he was angry?"

"I don't think so," Allison said, not wanting to admit she had seen nothing that sparked a memory.

"Let's run through the tellers' cameras," Leif said, "although there's not a lot you can see." He turned to Allison. "For better or worse, only the camera in the lobby shows what happened to Lindsay."

Ophelia clicked on the first of the four files. The camera was placed too high, a common problem with banks. Allison had heard that banks had initially wanted unobtrusive cameras that wouldn't detract from the beauty of their grand lobbies. The practice had continued even as cameras became smaller and most banks had all the charm of a fast food outlet. These robbers had face masks, but any bank robber who visited this branch wearing a baseball cap would have had his face hidden by the bill.

Each of the four clips showed a slightly different soundless slice of the same scene. Lindsay entered the bank and then five minutes later, Allison, at which point they both walked into the loan officers' area and out of sight of the camera. A few minutes later the two men ran in. The tall one pulled one pistol from his belt, the short one produced two. Then simultaneously they pointed the guns at the ceiling and fired. The tellers flinched at the sound of three gunshots.

"Wait," Allison said the first time she saw this maneuver, and Ophelia obediently clicked on the pause button.

"Is that like any bank robbery we dealt with?" she asked Nicole. "With the robbers firing at the ceiling?"

"No. But before we came here, I sent a memo out to all the FBI field offices, asking them to check for similars," Nicole said. "Shots in the ceiling. One guy watching the customers, one going over the counter. Maybe we'll get lucky and get a match."

And maybe not, Allison knew. Professional bank robbers, as opposed to the mopes who were just looking to score enough to buy a few days' worth of their drug of choice, were always looking for ways to refine their technique. To increase their haul and decrease their chances of being caught.

"Okay," she said to Ophelia, and the other woman clicked the play button.

After the guns were fired, the tall man walked rapidly toward the loan officers' area, his mouth moving. Allison knew he was shouting the commands about alarms and dye packs that she had heard in the bathroom.

On each of the four files from the cameras located behind the counter, they saw the customers' faces stretch into masks of fear before they obeyed the command to get down and then disappeared below the level of the counter. Three of the tellers raised their hands, but one with hair dyed a platinum blond just put her hands over her mouth. The shorter man put one gun in the back of his waistband, pulled a pillowcase from under his shirt, and moved from window to window, making the tellers fill the case with money.

And on each bit of film, there were two times when the customers and tellers started in terror. Even the other robber seemed surprised, jerking his head around. And the blond teller lost it, hands on either side of her head, mouth stretched wide in a scream.

Even though it was out of sight, Allison knew this was when her sister was shot, but she managed to watch it four times through without breaking down.

She also didn't see anything she recognized about the shooter.

Nicole took Allison's hand. "There's only one more clip to watch, but it's the one where Lindsay gets shot. It has the best images of the guy who killed her, though."

Allison's whole body tightened. "I'm ready."

Ophelia clicked Play and moved the playhead to the point where Lindsay first appeared, pacing nervously and looking out the bank's window. This camera must have been somewhere above the swinging door, but it showed much more than Allison had seen looking through the small window. She watched herself walk into the bank and then the two of them move to sit with Annie.

Allison's eyes filled with tears as she watched her sister hand over her business plan. Seen from this distance, Lindsay looked poised, confident.

"You do look like twins," Nicole said. "Even I had trouble telling you apart when I first looked at this."

Allison watched the woman she had been a lifetime ago. She watched Annie point her in the direction of the restroom. She watched her old self walk toward the camera and then disappear, and Lindsay offer Annie a box of cookies.

And she watched the bank robbers run in and the same sequence begin for the fifth time. Her breathing speeded up. Her palms got wet.

This camera showed what the others had not—Lindsay cowering, the man yelling at her, Lindsay raising her hands as the man stalked over to her. He raised the gun even as she pleaded. And then he fired. She fell back on her elbows and tried to lift herself up. He watched her futile efforts, a sneer twisting his lips. And finally he took two steps toward her and leaned down, his lips moving, and shot her again.

And then the two men were out the door.

Allison saw herself suddenly reenter the frame and fall on her knees by her sister. "That's enough," she said hoarsely as the other Allison, the Allison who still had a sister, took Lindsay in her arms. "That's enough."

Ophelia closed the file.

Allison realized that Nicole was still holding her hand.

"Did you see anything?"

"I don't know." Something nagged at her. "I feel like I did, but I don't know what it is. Or if it's just wishful thinking."

They went through the files again and again, until Leif and then Nicole stretched and moved away, talking quietly. Allison continued to look over Ophelia's shoulder as she slowed the files down. They watched each video second by second, beginning with the footage from the exterior camera and ending with the one that showed Lindsay dying.

Allison concentrated. What was it that bothered her? Was it the way the tall man moved? She watched for a limp, a gesture, an odd tilt of the head, but saw nothing. Was it something out of place? Something so small she hadn't completely registered it? Something that should have been there, but wasn't? The more she focused on the feeling that she was missing something, the more it receded.

She groaned and rubbed the back of her neck. "I know there's something that bothers me, but no matter how many times we watch these videos, there's nothing about the tall guy that's familiar."

"Wait a second." Ophelia clicked on one of the teller tapes again and then leaned forward. "That's it. It's not him."

"What do you mean?"

"It's the other guy. The guy who didn't shoot your sister."

Nicole looked up.

"What do you mean?" Leif asked.

"Watch," Ophelia said, and pressed Play. "Just watch the second guy."

It was the same scene they had already watched a dozen times. "I don't see anything," Allison said. "He shoots two guns into the ceiling, he takes the money, he runs out."

Ophelia pressed the mouse, ran the video back a few seconds, then froze the image. "Look at that." She tapped on the screen. "Look how he's pulling the trigger on the gun in his left hand."

She clicked, and the screen came to life again. With his right hand, the gunman pulled the trigger back with his index finger. But with his left hand, it was the middle finger that was inside the trigger guard. In front of it, his gloved index finger looked floppy. Ophelia froze the image again.

Allison and Nicole looked at each other, wide-eyed.

"Why would someone pull a trigger with his middle finger?" Allison squinted at the screen. "It certainly wouldn't come naturally."

Leif held out his hand and moved his index and then his middle finger experimentally. "It looks like there's something wrong with his index finger."

"That might be enough for us to find the second man," Nicole said. "And if we can find him, then we can find the man who murdered Cassidy and Lindsay."

CHAPTER 32

At three in the morning Ophelia got up to use the bathroom. Padding down the hall, she heard hitching breaths coming from behind the guest room door. Allison. Quietly sobbing.

Should she ignore it? But that seemed cruel. However, she wasn't certain how to respond. Finally she went to the bathroom and then came back to Allison's door with a pill bottle in her hand. She knocked softly.

The sounds stopped. Ophelia wondered if Allison would simply sit in silence until she eventually went away. It was how she herself might act, but she wasn't a neurotypical.

Finally, just as Ophelia was turning to go back to her room, Allison called softly, "Come in."

She was sitting on the end of the bed, the sheets twisted and tangled behind her. Only now did Ophelia realize she should have offered her some different clothing to sleep in. As her pupils adjusted to light, she could see that Allison's eyes were swollen from weeping.

"Would you like a sleeping pill?" She held out the bottle. She used them herself on the nights she woke from nightmares about her stepfather.

"No." Allison shook her head. "I'll be okay." Her voice was not at all convincing.

"I have a pill cutter," Ophelia offered. "You could try just taking half."

Allison put one hand across her belly. "I don't think I should."

Ophelia had forgotten about the baby. The thought of being pregnant had always unnerved her. Something with a life of its own growing inside you? It reminded her too much of the sci-fi movie *Alien*, the look of horror on that one character's face as the monster burst from his abdominal cavity.

What would a neurotypical do in this situation? She steeled herself. "Would a hug help?"

Allison was silent for a long moment. Ophelia was just beginning to relax when she answered. "Yes, I think it would."

Ophelia sat down, turned toward her, and slowly reached out, tentatively putting her hands on the other woman's shoulder blades. Suddenly she was locked in a tight embrace, with Allison's warm, wet face on her neck. Ophelia stiffened, although she tried not to show it.

"I just can't believe she's gone," Allison mumbled. "My little sister. And she died because of me."

Ophelia pulled back until she could see the other woman's face, contorted with grief.

"Not because of you." It wasn't logical to blame oneself for someone else's deeds. "It's because an evil man decided to target you."

"So? I'm the one who chose to be a prosecutor. I'm the one who put myself in daily contact with criminals. I'm the one who *made* myself a target."

"From what I understand, your sister used to have a much more risky lifestyle than you have ever had," Ophelia said reasonably. "And if it weren't for people like you, even more criminals would be out on the street. You do good things, Allison. It's not your fault that other people choose to do evil."

"I know you're right." Allison took a shaky breath. "I know that. I can't let my emotions get the better of me. Not when we're so close to catching this guy."

"You can't change the past." Ophelia spoke from personal experience. "No matter how much you might wish that things had been different, you can't go back. All you can do is go forward. And maybe try to make things better for the future."

"Thank you." Allison squeezed her hand, then, to Ophelia's relief, released it. The two women sat side by side in silence for several more minutes, until Ophelia judged it would be okay to return to her room.

In the morning the house was silent, the door to the guest room closed. Ophelia could almost pretend it was a normal day, one she would spend quietly in her office, with the occasional cat jumping on her lap or desk.

She began writing a computer program that she could send slipping through back doors to examine and compare online databases. While it would leave no trace and alter nothing, it might give her the information they needed to catch the man who had killed Cassidy Shaw and Lindsay Mitchell.

First she generated a list of the 356 people whose crimes had been investigated by Nicole and prosecuted by Allison. Since every witness had reported the suspect as male, the next step was eliminating the 59 convicted female felons from the list. She identified 6 men who had died since they had been sentenced.

Next she looked for inmates who had already served their time, and who would thus be free to cause mischief. That was still a substantial number: 78. And of course she couldn't be sure that the killer wasn't someone acting on another criminal's behalf.

But if he *was* one of the 78, it would help to have the name of the man with the damaged finger. Then she would be able to create a list of men who had been investigated by Nicole, prosecuted by Allison,

and incarcerated with the man with the damaged finger. Her working hypothesis was that the killer and the second bank robber had
met in prison. Once she had the name of the second man, she could
start work on proving—or disproving—the hypothesis.

Ophelia worked until lunch, when she ate what she always did—a
peanut butter and grape jelly sandwich on whole wheat bread, accompanied by a banana. It was healthy and filling, and she saw no need to
vary it. After some thought, she made a second sandwich and covered
it with plastic wrap.

Despite the near constant *whoosh* of the central air-conditioning,
the air inside the house felt heavy and muggy. In Oregon, so much
humidity meant only one thing: a storm was coming. The three
cats—Maizy, Amber, and Cinders—sprawled on different platforms
of their cat tree, lazy in the heat.

Ophelia was just finishing the last bite of her sandwich when
Allison walked into the dining room.

"Good morn—" Ophelia looked at her watch. "Good afternoon.
I figured you needed your sleep."

"Thanks." Allison's eyes were so shadowed they looked bruised.
"Thanks for letting me sleep. And thanks for talking to me last night.
I was just feeling so overwhelmed."

Ophelia's cell phone rang, saving her from another awkward
discussion of Allison's feelings. It was Nicole, calling with a possible
match for the bank robber with a damaged finger: a recently released
con named Denny Elliot.

And the news got even better. Not only had Elliot just gotten out
of prison for bank robbery, but they had his cell phone number and
should be able to figure out where he was through either cell phone
tower triangulation or, if it was a more modern phone, GPS. And
with luck, where Elliot was, there would the killer be also.

But of course they couldn't count on that. Ophelia wrote a new program that compared where Elliot had been imprisoned with the incarceration records of the 78 former prisoners she had previously identified. That cut the number down somewhat, but 33 people were still too many to consider them all viable suspects.

She needed a new angle. She went back into the dining room, where Allison sat with her sandwich. She had taken only a single bite. Ophelia hoped she wasn't allergic to peanut butter. She should have asked.

"Would you like something different to eat?" she said.

"What?" Allison gave her head a little shake, as if she had been someplace far away. "Oh no, I'm fine. I'm just not very hungry."

"Oh. Okay. So, I've got it down to 33 possibilities from 356. All of them are men sentenced in cases that involved you and Nicole and who are currently out of prison."

"Wow—that's pretty impressive."

Ophelia felt a warm glow of pride. "It still is higher than I would like. I was wondering if you remembered anyone who particularly threatened you and Nicole during their case."

"We get a lot of dirty looks," Allison said, "but threats are pretty rare. People usually manage to hold it together. There are only two people I can think of: Doug Halvorsen and this guy named MT Young. Both of them had to be removed by the U.S. marshals because they wouldn't stop screaming at us. The Young guy even made a run at us, but he got tackled."

"Young and Halvorsen," Ophelia said. "I'll check them out." But two minutes later she had learned that neither of them had been released and nothing had recently changed about their status.

The day dragged itself forward as they waited for further word from Nicole. Ophelia made a print-out of the remaining 33 names and then ran them past Allison.

"Jayson Forrester."

Allison looked up, remembering. "Worker safety issues. His company was going down the tubes, so he started cutting corners—and as a result two people were injured and one was killed. But he was over sixty and frail when he was sentenced five years ago—he's certainly not the guy who shot Lindsay."

Ophelia ran a line through Forrester's name. "How about Freddie Riding?"

"Freddie Riding. Freddie Riding," Allison repeated. "Oh yeah, mail fraud. He cried when he was found guilty. Sobbed, actually. Prison might have toughened him up, but not to the point where he became a stone-cold killer."

Ophelia crossed his name off. And so it went.

Jed Bitton.

A definite no.

Noe Crossley.

So scared he had begged the judge at his sentencing.

Two or three times Ophelia mentioned a name Allison thought was slightly more likely to have turned killer than others, but none of them made her straighten up and say, "That's him!"

Ophelia was starting to think they had come to a dead end. Where had she gone wrong?

"Who's next?" Allison asked, drumming her fingers on the arm of the couch.

"That's it. There aren't any more."

"Then what are we going to do? We have to find that guy before he kills Nicole. We have to."

It was worse than that, Ophelia thought. If she failed, not only would Nicole die, but it seemed likely that Allison would too.

CHAPTER 33

Dressed as a housekeeper, Nic stood in front of Room 16 at the Castaways Motel. From behind the door came muffled conversation and the low thump of music. A woman laughed. One of the men's voices, Nic realized, must belong to the guy who had killed Cassidy and Lindsay.

He was partying with his buddies and whoever else they had picked up along the way. Celebrating the taking of $8,720 and a woman's life.

The hair rose on the back of her neck.

After leaving Ophelia's the night before, Nic and Leif had gone back to the field office to track down the lead about the finger. The best photos of the two masked men captured from the surveillance video had been sent to law enforcement agencies across the country, along with information about the crime, the probability that the shorter suspect had a damaged or missing index finger, and a request for ID.

Late this afternoon their efforts had paid off. The FBI had gotten a call from a corrections officer at Lompoc. He thought the short plump bank robber was quite possibly Denny Elliot, a con originally from the Portland area who had been released from federal prison a month ago. While Elliot was in Lompoc, another inmate had bit off the top third of his index finger in the exercise yard. The gloves he had worn at the bank had helped camouflage the missing finger.

Had Elliot taken part in Cassidy's killing? But Nicole hadn't investigated his crimes, and when she asked Ophelia to check the database, it showed that Allison hadn't ever prosecuted him. It seemed likely that the killer was acting on his own, and had enlisted Elliot to help him cover his tracks as he picked off the three women one by one.

Elliot's parole officer said he was staying with his sister. The sister said she hadn't seen him for a couple of days, but she did have his cell phone number. An hour ago the cell phone had been tracked to this motel. The GPS records showed that it had been in the same location since midnight. A plan was quickly pulled together.

Now Nic rapped again on the peeling white paint of the door, hard enough that her knuckles stung. The sun pressed between her shoulder blades like a brand. Even though it was nearly six o'clock, the heat showed no signs of abating. The air felt thick, and dark clouds were massing on the horizon. A storm was coming. It couldn't come fast enough for Nic.

"Housekeeping!" she repeated. Loud enough that they should be able to hear her. But the noise didn't falter. They must be too drunk or too high to care.

When someone finally did look out the peephole, all they would see was a housekeeper standing in front of a laundry cart. Nic looked the part, what with her dark skin and her borrowed uniform of a pink short-sleeved polyester shirt and maroon elastic-waist pants. What wouldn't be seen through the peephole was the Kevlar vest she wore underneath the shirt, or the Glock tucked in the back of the waistband of her pants. The person on the other side of the door also wouldn't see Leif pressed against the wall on one side of Nic and Karl Zehner on the other. Or the dozen other agents scattered throughout the complex, all ready to rush in.

In private Leif had argued with the plan. "You should not be the one going to the door," he had told her after pulling her into the copy room. "What if he makes you? You might as well be wearing a sign around your neck that says 'I'm Nicole Hedges, go ahead and shoot me.' "

"Who else are we going to send to get these guys to open the door, Leif? It's going to be hard enough not to spook them, having someone show up at this hour. A housekeeper is the best option we have."

"We can get Manny to put on a uniform shirt and pose as a maintenance worker."

"Yeah, and how many times do you think a maintenance guy knocks on the door at that place? No one has done any maintenance there since the 1950s. Let's face it, I'm the only female agent of color we have right now in the field office, and a dark-skinned housekeeper is going to be the only person they might open the door to at six p.m. And don't worry, I won't look anything like Nicole Hedges."

Nic had watched the film of Lindsay being shot over and over. She knew the killer wouldn't hesitate to do the same to her—*if* he recognized her. Which was why she was wearing a bandana over her hair and clear glasses over her eyes. To disguise the shape of her face, she had stuffed a wad of cotton in each cheek. With makeup she had added shadows under her eyes and hollowed out her face. Now she looked two decades older, a woman who had a close relationship with hard work and hard times.

And hard times were what the motels along this stretch of North Interstate Avenue were all about. They catered to people who weren't too choosy—hookers, parolees, people one step up from homeless. The Castaways was a perfect place for three bank robbers to go to ground, count their money, and maybe invite a girl or two over to celebrate with them.

The manager had sketched the layout of the room for them. Once Nic was inside, she would find an open alcove with a sink to her immediate right. Past that lay a small bathroom with another sink, a toilet, and a shower. Straight back from the door and again to the right, half hidden by the wall behind the alcove and the bathroom, she would see two beds.

The room on one side hadn't been rented. The room on the other was occupied by a couple, but the manager had called them three times and gotten no answer. If they came back while the arrests were still going down, the perimeter team would snag them before they could get too close. The remaining guests—there weren't many—had been contacted by phone and warned to stay in their rooms.

"Housekeeping!" Nic called again. She rapped so hard her knuckles felt bruised. The conversation didn't pause. The music kept thumping. The woman laughed again, setting Nic's teeth on edge. At least they were probably too wasted to pose a threat.

At a nod from Leif, Nic slipped the card key in the slot, her sweaty fingers sliding on the plastic. The light under the handle turned green, followed by a faint beep. She threw the door open at the same time as she grabbed her gun and entered the darkened room. Immediately, she stepped to the side so she wasn't silhouetted against the bright light of the day. The FBI had a name for entryways—vertical coffins.

"FBI—freeze!" Gun in hand, Nic blinked in the sudden darkness. Leif and Karl darted in behind her, their guns also at the ready. Nic narrowed her eyes to slits, trying to force them to adjust to the dimness. She saw no one, just the bottom halves of the two unmade beds and a dozen empty beer bottles scattered across the threadbare carpet.

But she could still hear music, still hear people talking in voices too quiet to understand. The woman laughed again. Some part of Nic had already known the woman was going to laugh.

Her eyes found the source of the party sounds. She could just see the corner of an open laptop sitting on the cheap dresser between the two beds. The computer was broadcasting in an endless loop. The party sounds weren't real at all.

Nic still saw no one.

But the air was heavy and hot with the scent of blood.

All this took only a second or two to process. More agents were crowding in. Leif kicked open the bathroom door. Karl crouched low and then burst around the corner and into the main section of the room.

And a second later they all knew where the stink of carnage was coming from.

The plump man Nic recognized from his mug shots as Denny Elliot lay sprawled in the bathtub with a slug in his heart. In the sleeping area, between one of the beds and a wall, lay a redheaded man she didn't recognize.

The reason Nic didn't recognize him might have had something to do with the fact that he had been shot in the face. Still, even if he had been bald, he was too heavily muscled to be the man who had killed Lindsay.

The room was no longer a criminals' hideout. It was a crime scene. As the team leader for the FBI's Evidence Recovery Team, Leif arranged for two agents to guard the room and dismissed everyone else who wasn't part of the team. Then Leif, Nic, and the other ERT members went back to their cars in the parking lot to put on shoe coverings, hairnets, and white Tyvek suits. The lookie-loos were already gathering at the yellow perimeter tape—informally known as flypaper for its ability to snag gawkers. Nic paid them no mind as she pulled the wads of cotton from her mouth, then covered her hair and pulled on rubber gloves. She tried not to think about how hot it was.

Or the fact that their one lead was dead.

Within the ERT Leif had a dual role: team leader and photographer. He put Nic in charge of the photo log, and together they went back in alone to document the scene before the others processed it.

"How long do you think they've been dead?" Leif asked as he snapped a photo of Denny Elliot. Elliot's eyes were wide and surprised, a neat hole in his chest.

She leaned closer, trying not to be grossed out by the silverfish skittering on the bottom of the tub in a vain effort to hide from the light. "Judging by the color of the blood and how tacky it looks, I'd say several hours. Maybe even longer."

Nic imagined the bald man standing a few steps from the door and shooting Elliot as he opened the door to the john, then pivoting and shooting the man next to the bed. While it was possible he had relied on the street noise outside to cover the crack of the shots, she thought it likely that he had used a silencer.

They moved into the main room where Leif began taking photos that showed the two beds and the redheaded man. Someone had turned down the sound on the computer. Soon it would be wrapped in a pink antistatic bag and delivered to the FBI's computer forensics lab.

Nic realized that something else was missing. The pillowcase with the cash was nowhere in evidence. She pointed it out to Leif. "Do you think he killed them because he didn't want to split the money?"

"I think first he hired them. And then he fired them," Leif said, keeping his voice low because the other ERT agents were waiting just on the other side of the door. "With a gun. He wanted everyone to think it was a bank robbery, just like he wanted everyone to think that Cassidy died at Rick's hands."

"And now we're back at square one," Nic said. "Because I doubt very much that he left any fingerprints behind. This whole scene didn't bother him one whit. He kills these two guys and then he has the presence of mind to download a loop of party sounds."

"It feels like he's methodically ticking things off a list," Leif said. "And since I think you're one of them, you're staying at my place again tonight."

Nic tilted her head. "You say that like I don't have a choice."

"You don't, Nic. Not when this guy is still out there, and he's looking for you. I don't want to give him an opening." Leif snapped a photo of the laptop and the beer bottles on the dresser.

"Wait." Nic pointed. "What's that? It looks like a cell phone."

He leaned closer to get a picture. Then they both blinked in surprise. For a second, the cell phone had flickered to life and then gone dark.

Leif's eyes narrowed and then he cursed under his breath.

A light went on for Nic. "He's been listening to us this whole time, right?"

Leif looked disgusted. "Who needs to go to Radio Shack to get a bug? All he needed were two phones. Before he left here, he called one with the other, answered, and then put this one down where he could hear what went on in this room."

Nic tried to think how they could use his trick to their own advantage. "We can get the number that called this phone and trace it."

"It won't matter. He'll already have dumped the other one. I'm betting both of them originally belonged to our two dead guys."

"But, Leif—" Nic cut to the heart of the matter. "What exactly did we say? How much do you think he overheard?"

In the motel's parking lot, a bald man wearing a baseball cap slipped the battery from the phone he had been using to eavesdrop on Nicole Hedges and Leif Larsen. So she was staying with Larsen? He would have to figure out how to separate them. And when he did, Nicole Hedges was a dead woman.

Before he left, the bald man dropped to one knee beside Nicole's Crown Victoria as if he were tying his shoelace. Instead he stuck a black GPS tracker the size of a domino to the underside of the bumper.

CHAPTER 34

Nicole had called to say that the FBI had found Denny Elliot at a cheap motel in North Portland. That was the good news.

The bad news was that they hadn't been able to talk to Elliot because he was dead. Shot in the heart.

But as far as Ophelia was concerned, there was more good news that helped ameliorate the bad. Because a second man had been found dead along with Elliot. He had been identified by his fingerprints as Reggie Bates, another ex-con. Nicole and Leif thought it likely that he had been the getaway driver at Oregon Federal.

With both of the other participants dead, it seemed clear that whoever had masterminded the bank robbery had decided to get rid of any loose ends. It fit their theory that the robbery was merely a cover designed to disguise the fact that someone was going after Cassidy, Allison, and Nicole. Elliot and Bates had played their parts and were no longer needed.

For dinner, Ophelia heated up two Healthy Choice frozen meals and opened a bagged salad. Because Allison was there, she got out her place mats, but she ended up eating in her office. Now that she had a second name, she sliced and diced the data again, seeing if any of the thirty-three people they had identified earlier had been incarcerated with both Denny Elliot and Reggie Bates.

She cut the list down to eleven names. Eleven. They were so close now. She knew it.

She walked back into the dining room with the list she had printed out. Allison was pushing the contents of her frozen dinner back and forth in its box. It looked like she hadn't eaten any of it. Wasn't she supposed to be eating for two?

Ophelia read the list of names out a second time, pausing after each one. It should be easier to pick the real culprit now that it was shorter. And Allison had had a bit of time to think more about the possibilities.

As she went down the list, Ophelia was undaunted by Allison's flat reaction to each name. She was probably still recovering from the brutal murder of her sister.

Undaunted, that is, until Allison had rejected all eleven names.

"None of them?" Ophelia asked. "Are you sure?"

"I can't see any of them doing it. They're all too old, too weak, or too stupid."

"But it has to be someone on the list," Ophelia insisted. "If you had to pick one of them, who would it be?"

"I told you." Allison set her jaw. "None."

But that wasn't possible, was it? Ophelia went back to her office and started again from the beginning. She checked her logic, examined her computer code, and occasionally came out to question Allison again. Had she gone wrong in one of her assumptions? Or was Allison displaying a lack of imagination, unable to recognize who was capable of exacting such terrible revenge?

And suddenly it came to Ophelia, the realization so abrupt she almost felt like she was falling. There was one parameter she hadn't even thought to check. How could she have been so stupid?

It was true that a prisoner who was released would be free to hunt Allison down.

   But so would a prisoner who had escaped. Ophelia's fingers flew over her computer keyboard.

   A few minutes later she was staring at the answer.

   Lucas Maul. A convicted bank robber. And until twelve days ago, an inmate of United States Penitentiary Lee in Pennington Gap, Virginia. Then he had been transported to the hospital for some sort of medical problem, where he had escaped. Authorities in Virginia were still hunting him.

   But he wasn't in Virginia, Ophelia realized. He was in Portland.

   Getting his revenge.

CHAPTER 35

Eli Winkler, the Phoenix patrolman who had responded to Gina Hodson's call, put on gloves of his own and then tested one of the gloves from the messenger bag. He used a plastic wand that looked like a pregnancy test. In less than three minutes, Eli was looking at two blue lines that meant the dark red sticky substance was not just blood, but human blood.

Eli bagged and tagged the bloody gloves, the messenger bag, the box, and the crumpled balls of newspaper. Then he delivered them to the Arizona State Police.

The Arizona State Police called the Portland Police Bureau, who in turn got in touch with eBay to find out the real name of the person who had sold Gina her messenger bag.

LiveFree, eBay staff informed the Portland police, was really one Jerome Harford, a frequent eBay seller. Jerome didn't seem to specialize in any one type of item, and he had a 99.8 percent approval rating on eBay.

Jerome was brought in for questioning, and once he figured out that he wasn't in trouble for his habit of Dumpster diving, he stopped stammering and wouldn't stop talking. According to him,

businesses and individuals threw out lots of perfectly good stuff—
shoes, clothes, ballpoint pens, lamps with the plug-ins cut off. You
never knew what you would find, which was why Jerome checked
every Dumpster he passed. He kept whatever took his fancy and sold
a lot of the rest on eBay.

Including the messenger bag.

Then Jerome led the police to the Dumpster where he had found
the messenger bag on the evening of Cassidy's death.

It was just two blocks from her condominium.

At about the same time as Detective Jensen was being notified
about the messenger bag and the bloody gloves, Shannon Coffelt, an
Arizona State Police crime scene technologist, was taking a sample of
blood from the glove for a DNA test.

Next, Shannon worked to see if she could get prints from the
inside of the gloves. Since the gloves had been discarded already
inside out, she left them as they were. She began by inserting a narrow piece of PVC tubing into one of the thumbs, shoving it up until
the tip was pushed completely inside out. Since there was no way
to tell whether the glove had been worn on the left or right hand,
she carefully rolled the entire thumb of the glove, over and over,
along a length of black gelatin lifter. Slowly, the ridges and whorls
of a thumbprint began to emerge. Shannon smiled and grabbed her
Nikon.

"And you thought you were so smart wearing gloves, didn't you?"
she said out loud. It was moments like this that Shannon lived for.

In a few hours IAFIS had suggested a match to the two complete fingerprints Shannon was able to obtain. The latent fingerprint
examiner confirmed it.

Neither belonged to Jerome Harford. Instead, the fingerprints belonged to a federal prisoner named Lucas Maul.

Six years earlier Lucas Maul had had a head of thick black hair. He was also a career bank robber who worked as a team with a guy named Axel Schmidt. Unlike most bank robbers who had no plans beyond writing a note, Maul and Schmidt carefully planned their robberies, staking out targets for weeks beforehand. They also picked times—like right after a department store deposited the weekend take—that would yield the greatest amount of cash.

Their luck ran out the day a plainclothes cop happened to be depositing his paycheck in the same bank that they were trying to rob. The resulting gun battle left the cop wounded and Axel dead.

Maul managed two more weeks of precious freedom.

Even though he had never fired his gun, FBI Special Agent Nicole Hedges dubbed Maul the Dueling Bandit.

He hated that name. It was catchy, and he supposed that was all that mattered to her. Not the truth.

Then Cassidy Shaw on Channel Four showed his picture again and again on the news. Crying crocodile tears about the wounded cop—who wouldn't have been hurt if he hadn't pulled his gun—she urged the station's viewers to be on the lookout for Lucas Maul and to call 9-1-1 if they spotted him. Which a bartender eventually did.

Nicole Hedges also gathered the evidence that helped federal prosecutor Allison Pierce put Maul away. Cassidy continued to cover the story, especially when it came out that much of the money taken in the robberies could not be accounted for.

And Maul certainly wasn't talking, not even when he was sentenced to twenty-four years in federal prison.

After his sentencing he ended up on the other side of the country in a federal prison in Virginia. Six years ticked by, years when he thought about the three women who had worked together to put him in prison and the judge who had sentenced him.

Then the left side of Maul's face started to droop. The prison's doctor suspected a stroke, but he lacked the sophisticated equipment needed to scan his brain. So Maul was taken under armed guard to a hospital.

That night, after a series of tests, the neurologist came to talk to Maul in his hospital room. Maul's wrists and ankles were shackled to the bed, but the corrections officer still stood in the corner with his hands clasped in front of him, openly eavesdropping.

Maul was told he hadn't suffered a stroke. Instead he had an incurable brain tumor. It was twined around his brain stem and couldn't be treated. Not with surgery, not with radiation, not with chemotherapy. The doctor told him that he could expect to live about a year, maybe eighteen months. It was likely that he would feel perfectly fine until close to the end, when he would spend the last few weeks bedridden and blind. At that point, the neurologist said, doctors would take "comfort measures."

Even the guard blinked at that.

Accepting the sheaf of brochures and printouts the doctor handed him, Maul took the news with a stoic expression. But his thoughts were in turmoil. He was going to die in prison. Blind and incontinent in a prison infirmary.

Maul was six years into a twenty-four-year sentence, but as a model inmate he could reasonably expect to be released after twenty. He had resigned himself to patiently serving out the remaining fourteen years, knowing that when he got out he'd have almost a million dollars waiting for him. It made the waiting almost bearable. He would be forty-eight, not impossibly old. He could still have a good life.

Now he would never get that life. Never get that freedom. Never get a chance to spend the money he had hidden. It was unaccept-able. If he had only a year to live, he had to be free. Free to go where he wanted, eat what he chose, sleep with whatever woman caught his fancy. And first, and most important, free to extract his revenge.

After the neurologist left, an aide brought Maul's dinner. The guard took off the wrist shackles so that he could eat, leaving his ankles still secured to the hospital bed. He said nothing before he resumed his post in the hallway, but his look said volumes. It said, *It sucks to be you.* It said, *Being in this hospital room is as close to free as you are going to get, buddy.*

As soon the door closed behind him, Maul went to work. Shackles and handcuffs were not particularly sophisticated. Most opened with a universal key. A key he didn't have, but that didn't mean he couldn't open them.

The brochures the doctor had given him were held together with a small binder clip. Maul pinched the metal wire until one silver arm slipped free of the black clip. The arm was already bent at a ninety-degree angle. He slid it into the lock of the shackle and wiggled it. In less than a minute he had both legs free.

That still left the guard just outside the door. The guard and his gun. So that way was out. The window in his hospital room didn't open. And Maul was dressed, if you could call it that, in only a hos-pital gown.

Fifteen minutes later, when the guard checked on Maul, he found the bed empty and the bathroom door locked. The guard wasn't par-ticularly worried, except by the possibility that Maul was in there trying to kill himself. A maintenance man was summoned to help circumvent the lock.

Meanwhile, Maul had already climbed up on the sink, pushed aside an acoustical tile, and crawled up into the ceiling. If any of the patients along the hall had happened to look up from their bed at just the right moment, they might have seen one of Maul's brown eyes peeping at them. Six rooms down the hall from where he began, he saw what he wanted—a sleeping male patient who looked about his size. He dropped through the ceiling tiles into the man's bathroom. Later the patient would wake up to find his shirt, jeans, baseball cap, and Nikes missing from the hospital room's closet, as well as a vase of flowers from his bedside.

And by the time the guard figured out what had happened, Lucas Maul was long gone and on his way back to Portland.

Portland, where his money was.

Portland, where the people who were to blame for his incarceration were.

Cassidy Shaw, the reporter who had harped on how he had to be found.

Nicole Hedges, the FBI agent who had given him his ill-fitting moniker and then arrested him.

Allison Pierce, the prosecutor who had persecuted him.

And Nate Grenfels, the judge who had sentenced him.

The last one, the judge, had already died. But not the rest.

Not yet.

But as Maul had made his way to Portland, he vowed to change that.

CHAPTER 36

It's Lucas Maul," Ophelia said. She had found Allison in the dining room, stroking Cinders. "Lucas Maul."

Allison's eyes opened wide. "He was a bank robber, right?"

"Right. I apologize for not realizing it earlier." Ophelia felt her cheeks redden. "I didn't think of checking for escaped offenders until just now. And Maul escaped from prison in Virginia a little less than two weeks ago."

"Lucas Maul," Allison repeated.

"I have his booking photo up on my computer screen if you want to see it."

Allison followed her back into her office. Maul stared out at them with his chin lifted and his teeth clenched. His dark eyes offered them a silent challenge. Ophelia could see why Angel had called them intense.

Maul also had a thick head of black hair.

"He must have shaved it," Allison said.

"Or he may have had it shaved for him," Ophelia said. "I found a story about him online. He had been diagnosed with a brain tumor, and it sounds like he doesn't have that long to live. When he started showing symptoms—which must account for that droop on the left side of his face—the prison didn't have the equipment they needed to diagnose him, so they sent him to a large hospital. He escaped from there. I looked for other stories about it, but I didn't find that many." Ophelia figured authorities had been embarrassed.

"So Maul finds out he doesn't have long to live and then he decides that his priority is to kill everyone who held him to account for the things he did? And that's why he killed Cassidy and Lindsay?" Allison exhaled sharply through her nose. "What a waste. What a stupid thing to die for."

While Allison was speaking, Ophelia heard the sound of cars turning into her driveway. She went to the window and twitched aside the blind. Nicole and Leif pulled up in separate cars.

Ophelia braced herself. She was proud of her computer programming skills. While she would be able to tell them she had solved the puzzle of the killer's identity, it would be difficult to do so without also revealing that the reason it had taken so long was that she had overlooked one obvious parameter.

But as soon as she let them in the house, Nicole started chattering away about bloody gloves and eBay and fingerprints. And about Lucas Maul. Just before they had left the motel, Detective Jensen had called Nicole with the news that a lead from Arizona had been traced back to a Dumpster two blocks from Cassidy's apartment—and to Maul's fingerprints being identified on a pair of bloody gloves.

Now they knew who had killed Cassidy and Lindsay. But knowing who he was, the four of them realized as they talked, was not the same as finding him. Maul had no family and no known associates aside from the two men they had found dead in the motel. All authorities could do was keep casting the net, trying to figure out a way to track him down. They planned to release his photo to the media, although it turned out they didn't have any that showed him bald.

"Nic is staying with me for the time being," Leif told them, putting his arm around her shoulders. "It's not safe for her to be at home, not when Maul might be looking for her. Not when he thinks she might be the last one of the Triple Threat standing. And we'll have an agent watching my house in case he shows up there."

Nicole ducked her head. Ophelia wasn't certain what emotion Nicole was feeling. She couldn't tell if the other woman was embarrassed or happy about this turn of events.

Ophelia was also distracted by Nicole's clothes. She was wearing a pink and maroon outfit made of some shiny polyester material. It looked like a uniform.

"Is something wrong?" Nicole asked, and Ophelia realized she had been staring. Neurotypicals were not comfortable with open scrutiny. It was fine to stare—it just wasn't fine to get caught.

"Your clothes are a different style from what you normally wear." Ophelia liked people to be predictable, which meant Nicole should have been wearing a dark pantsuit.

"I borrowed a housekeeper's uniform from the motel tonight to help me talk my way into the room." Nicole grimaced. "That was before we knew the only people in there were dead. The day manager locked up my clothes for safekeeping, but he left while we were still processing the scene, and it turns out the night guy doesn't have a key to that closet." She tugged at the white round collar, and Ophelia caught a flash of a black layer she wore underneath. "I can't wait to go home and change."

"It's been a long day," Leif said.

Nicole yawned, making an almost musical vocalization, and Allison followed suit. Ophelia was normally immune to neurotypicals' contagious emotions, but other people's yawns were sometimes infectious. She yawned as well.

"I think we should call it a night," Leif said, stifling his own yawn. "We can regroup tomorrow and decide what we should do next. There must be some way we can figure out how to find Maul."

"Sure." Allison blinked slowly, as if she were already half asleep.

A few minutes later Nicole and Leif left, after hugging Allison good-bye. To forestall either of them touching her, Ophelia crossed her arms.

"I'm exhausted," Allison said as soon as the door closed. "I'm going to bed. It's been a long day."

She'd only been up for about ten hours, but Ophelia understood that time could be subjective.

Maizy and Cinders were unsettled, pacing back and forth, crying occasionally. Amber was hiding someplace, probably behind the refrigerator or under the couch. Like Ophelia, the cats were unused to having strangers in the house, bringing with them their smells and sounds and odd, unpredictable behaviors. She was stroking Maizy when she heard a faint tinkling sound. Glass breaking. It had come from down the hall.

"Allison?" She stood up and started down the dark hallway. She hoped the other woman hadn't been looking through her bathroom cabinets. Maybe she had knocked over the glass jar that held the cotton balls.

Suddenly a big hand reached out of the darkness and grabbed Ophelia's shoulder. She gasped.

"Don't scream or I'll kill you," a man whispered. In his hand she saw the silhouette of a gun with a long barrel. His shaven head gleamed in the faint light. The left side of his mouth drooped, although it didn't seem to affect his speech.

Had he heard her say Allison's name? And what about Allison? Was she still awake? Did she know that Lucas Maul was right here, only a few feet away?

"I won't scream," Ophelia said. She modulated her voice so that it was louder than normal, hoping that Allison would hear. Hear and understand. Understand and react.

But what could Allison do? The guest room held no weapons, not even something that could be an improvised weapon. She hoped that Allison had Lindsay's cell phone with her. That she was even now calling for help.

Ophelia's eyes had adjusted to the dim light. Past Maul she could see into her own bedroom through the now open door. The window above her bed had been broken, the blinds twisted to one side, the glass pushed out of the frame so that it now lay on her bed in glinting knife-life shards. She didn't like to think about the tiny slivers of glass that must have slipped among the downy feathers of her comforter, or of how he must have trampled it with his shoes.

"What do you want?" she asked.

For an answer, Maul marched her back into the living room, holding her so close to himself that they bumped into each other at every step. He smelled sharply of sweat and beer. The scent took her back to a bad place.

When they stepped out into the light, she saw the silencer screwed onto the barrel of his gun. Maizy came toward them, meowing.

His foot shot out. It was so quick that Ophelia was still opening her mouth to shout a protest when he kicked the cat, almost casually, about three feet into the air. Maizy twisted in midair and managed to land on her feet, then darted under the couch, her ears flat against her head.

Ophelia was shocked. "Why did you do that?"

"Because I can," Maul said, smiling lazily. "I can do anything I want." There was no dissonance in his face or his body. He believed what he was telling her. "You're very pretty, you know." He reached his free hand toward her, and she flinched.

Maul laughed and stroked her cheek with his knuckles. She could feel the promise in them. He could caress her or kill her. His choice, and either was easy. Dark memories stirred in her gut.

"And because I can do what I want, you should do what I ask or I'll do more bad things. And what I want is for you to get Nicole Hedges to come back here. By herself."

"Why?" Ophelia asked. "What are you going to do to her?"

"I don't think that's any concern of yours, do you?" Maul offered her a smile that even she could tell was fake. He tightened his grip on her upper arm. In the morning there would be bruises shaped like fingerprints. She wondered if she would be alive to see them.

"How am I supposed to accomplish that?" Did she hear some soft movement from the back of the house, where Allison was? She reminded herself not to look in that direction, not to change expression.

"I can tell you're a smart girl. Make something up. Just make sure she comes back without that Leif."

"How do you know his name?"

"It's my business to know things." Maul's eyes narrowed. "Not yours. So stop asking questions and do what you're told."

Amber walked down the hall and into the room, tail switching. It was clear she sensed something was wrong. Ophelia wished she knew where the cat had come from. Had it been with Allison and slipped out when she opened the door to listen?

Maul's lip curled as he looked at Amber. "What are you, the crazy cat lady? How many cats do you have?"

Ophelia couldn't work out whether it was better to lie, or if so, what that lie should be, so she simply said, "Three."

"If you don't get Nicole Hedges here really fast, you're only going to have two." He turned and sighted casually at Amber, then Cinders. "Or maybe one. I need a little target practice." He swung the gun back to Ophelia.

Over Maul's shoulder, Ophelia saw a cell phone lying on the mantel. Her heart fell. Not her phone, but Lindsay's. Which meant Allison had no way to alert anyone. Even if she was hearing every word of Maul's, what could she do?

There. Another sound in the back. She knew every creak and groan of this house, and this wasn't one of them. With difficulty, she kept her face blank and did not look toward the hall.

Then she remembered the broken window in her room, the blinds twisted to one side. It could be that the sounds she was attributing to Allison were actually common night sounds she normally didn't hear through the closed window and the noise-reducing blinds. It was possible that Allison was sound asleep, unaware that the man who thought he had killed her was only a few feet away.

"Where's your phone?" Maul looked around the room.

"I don't have a landline. Just a cell phone."

"Aren't you modern?" Maul smirked. "Call Nicole. But put it on speaker phone. I want to hear everything both of you say. And to make sure you play nice, I'm going to be holding your cat Daisy here, and if I don't like what I hear, I'm going to hurt her."

Still keeping his gun pointed at Ophelia, he leaned down and scooped up Maizy with his free hand and held her against one hip. He obviously had no idea how to hold a cat, how she didn't like her feet dangling in space. The cat writhed, but was no match for his strong hand.

"Maizy," Ophelia said, knowing it was stupid to correct him, but unable to stop herself. "Her name is Maizy."

"Whatever. Just make sure Nicole comes alone, or I'll be forced to kill the cat—or you."

It seemed probable that he would kill her either way. But what could she do? Ophelia took her phone out of her pocket, set it down on the dining room table, pressed the button for the speaker phone, and called Nicole.

"What's up, Ophelia?"

Maul was making her lie, but she tried to insert a kind of truth. "I think I might have made a mistake. A big one. Can you come back here for a minute? There's something I need to talk to you about, but not in front of Leif."

"What is it?"

She hesitated. Maul squeezed Maizy until she let out a pained yowl.

"I don't want to say over the phone." Improvisation had never been one of Ophelia's skills. "It's, um, something I have to show you."

"Is it something to do with Allison?"

She couldn't let Nicole say anything more about Allison, couldn't let her give away that she was still alive. "In a way. Just come back for a second. Please, Nicole? I need you."

And then she pressed the key to end the conversation.

CHAPTER 37

Allison fell asleep as soon as she put her head on the pillow. She bobbed a little closer to consciousness, heard voices, decided Ophelia was watching TV, and dived back into the deep. Sleep was an ocean, and she wanted to drown.

A cat yowled, pulling her back onto shore. Ophelia and her cats. She seemed more comfortable with them than she did with people. She must have stepped on one's tail. Allison had already seen how they could get underfoot, especially if they sensed the possibility of food.

Half in, half out of sleep, Allison listened to the rhythm of voices the way she would listen to the rush of the surf. A lulling background noise.

But one of the voices belonged to Ophelia. Not TV, then. The waves receded further. Who could she be talking to? And this late at night?

How much did she know about Ophelia, anyway?

Allison's eyes sprang open.

She slipped from bed and padded to the door, holding her breath so nothing would interfere with her ability to hear. Sickeningly, she was reminded of how she had waited and listened at the bank, hesitated while her sister died in her place.

Slowly, slowly, she turned the knob. The hair on her arms rose. She knew it was irrational, but it felt like someone was waiting for her on the other side, just a few inches away, and as soon as she opened the door, she would be face-to-face with whoever it was.

With agonizing slowness, she inched the door open. And nearly cried out when the ginger tabby tried to butt its head through the crack. She pushed it back with her foot, but it persisted. Finally it made a little noise of protest, then turned and went down the hall.

She could hear the voices much more clearly now. One definitely belonged to Ophelia. The other voice was a man's. It was not a voice that Allison knew well, but it was familiar nonetheless. The man ordered Ophelia to call Nicole and persuade her to return. When she hesitated, he threatened to kill Ophelia's cat. And then he threatened to kill Ophelia.

Lucas Maul. It was Lucas Maul. The floor felt like it was falling away from beneath her feet. Allison tightened her grip on the doorknob, willing herself to stand upright. Lucas Maul, the man who had killed her friend. Who had killed her sister. Who had tried to kill Nicole. Who thought he had killed her.

And who now was no more than twenty feet away.

Allison had nothing to defend herself with. No gun, no mace, not even a baseball bat. Not even—her gaze darted to the blank top of the dresser—Lindsay's phone, which she remembered leaving in the living room.

Allison listened as Ophelia followed Maul's demands. She called Nicole and asked her to come back, ending the conversation shortly after Nicole used Allison's name.

Had Maul picked up on that? Did he already know she was alive? Did he know she was here? Was he just tormenting her, knowing she had nowhere to run?

"Very good, Ophelia. You've bought yourself some time," she heard him say. "Something I don't have very much of these days. I have a terminal illness, Ophelia. When I learned that, I decided that if I'm going to die young, so will the people who ruined my life. They don't deserve to be enjoying themselves when I'm not walking around on the earth anymore. They don't deserve to eat, drink, feel the sunshine. I decided they all should be dead and buried long before I am."

Allison had to get out of this room. Escape Maul, warn Nic, help Ophelia. She went to her window, but the only way out was through the top section. It was hard to imagine how she would be able to clamber out without making a lot of noise. And then Maul would catch her midway. He would shoot her on the spot, while she still had one leg over.

She crept back to the door. Maul was still ranting.

"I watched Cassidy's eyes change as she realized she was going to die. I saw the terror on her face. I heard her beg and then I made her be quiet. I felt her pulse go still under my fingers."

Allison swallowed her nausea. She had to think. She couldn't be ruled by her disgust and fear.

"Why frame Rick McEwan for it though?" Ophelia asked.

"I didn't want to warn the other two. It was just a bonus that I figured out how to blame it on a cop. Then when I killed Allison, I told her to say hello to Cassidy. I wanted her to know that her death wasn't random after all."

But Lindsay's had been. Lindsay had died in her place. Allison had to stop him. Maybe she could rush down the hall and surprise him? Somehow snatch the gun from his hands? If he was standing with his back to the hall, it could possibly work.

But it probably wouldn't.

Suddenly a flash of lightning lit up the hall, making Allison gasp. A gust of warm, damp wind blew against her right cheek.

She froze. Had Maul heard her?

No. He was still lecturing Ophelia, apparently enjoying an audience. Meanwhile, time was ticking away. She had to find a way to escape and warn Nicole.

Wait. Why could she feel a breeze? Then she realized that Ophelia's door was open. Allison opened her own door another inch, two, until she could see into Ophelia's room. The glass had been broken out from the window, the blinds twisted to one side.

It was a way out. Once she was outside she could warn Nicole. And Nicole could summon help for Ophelia.

But depending on where Maul was, Allison might die trying.

Last time she had waited. Last time she had been cautious.

And last time Lindsay had died.

Before she could think about it too much, she ducked low, scurried into Ophelia's room, and leapt up on the bed. She was holding her breath. Maul's rant didn't pause. A shard of glass sliced her foot, just a slippery sensation at first, followed by a sharp pain. She bit her lip. She should have slipped on some shoes, but there was no time to think about that now.

She jumped out of the broken window, landing painfully on her hands and knees. It was raining hard, and one palm slipped on the wet grass, wrenching her shoulder. With a muffled grunt, Allison pushed herself to her feet. Scrambling around the corner, out of sight of the front door, she pressed her back against the side of the house. She looked up and down the block. There was no one in sight. The street was wide and empty, lit up by streetlights. It looked like a stage set, like it was just waiting for Gene Kelly to dance down it, singing about the rain.

It did not look like a place to hide.

It was raining so hard the drops hit the street and then bounced up again. Allison swiped the water from her eyes. Most of the houses had porch lights on, but past each of those she could see only darkness. If people were up, they were watching TV in the dark. No house looked clearly occupied by someone who would immediately answer the door if she pounded on it.

And even if she did get someone to respond to her frantic knocking, how long would it take to explain to them why they should contact the authorities? Or to persuade them to let her use a phone to warn Nicole? Three minutes? Five? Far too long.

Another flash of lightning, followed almost immediately by the crack of thunder. Didn't that mean the lightning was less than a mile away?

When Allison peeked around the corner again, Nicole's car was already in the driveway, and Nicole was raising her fist to knock on the door.

"No, Nicole, no, don't!" As she screamed a warning, the thunder cracked again.

Nicole turned to look over her shoulder. Her hand was moving toward her gun.

The door opened.

A man stood silhouetted against the light. Both arms were held straight out in front of him, and in his hands was a gun with what looked like a silencer on the end. "Welcome to hell, Nicole Hedges," he shouted over the rain. "Save a place for Lucas Maul."

Then he fired, and Nic fell backward off the steps.

"No!" Allison screamed. She was too overwhelmed with horror to think, to realize that she was giving herself away. "Nic!"

Maul jerked his head to the left. His eyes met Allison's. They widened as he recognized her. The gun snapped up again. Pointed right at her.

Allison turned and ran.

CHAPTER 38

Allison's legs moved up and down like pistons in an engine being pushed to its limit. Her fists punched the air with each step. Desperately she zigged and zagged, her bare feet beating against the wet pavement.

Pi-choo! A bullet whined past her ear. Trying to present as small a target as possible, she squeezed her arms tight to her sides and bent forward as she ran even faster. The rain lashed her skin. She only hoped it was also obscuring the outlines of her body.

She paid no attention to the stinging rain, or the cut on her foot, or the burning in her lungs. The only thing that mattered was staying alive.

She had to. Even though Nicole was lying dead somewhere behind her. Even though so many people she loved were dead now. Not only Nicole, but Cassidy and Lindsay. She had to live because of the new life growing inside her.

And because if she died, then Lucas Maul would win. His twisted version of justice would triumph.

Risking a glance over her shoulder, Allison saw that Maul was about a block behind her, running flat-out. He held the gun down at his side. At least he was no longer aiming it at her. Not right this second, anyway.

Where could she go? This street was too open. Just a long straight stretch of empty road, lit up by streetlights and the occasional flickering bolt of lightning. If Allison tried to hide behind a garage or cut into a side yard, Maul could follow her all too easily. Probably with the helpful addition of motion-activated security lights.

Even if a car appeared and she ran to it, how would they be able to save her? She would just end up getting any possible Good Samaritan killed, gunned down alongside her.

Ophelia must have called the cops by now. Unless Maul had shot her too. Allison couldn't think about that right now. Even if Ophelia had managed to alert the authorities, Maul would get to Allison long before any of them responded. She had to get off this empty, brightly lit street and to someplace he couldn't see or follow her as easily.

Where? Where? Where? The question pounded in her brain.

The road curved to the left, and she crossed over to the other side, the side with no houses. Instead there was just a grassy strip of bluff about twenty feet wide. Below it the land dipped steeply down toward the Willamette River about a mile away. She could see the headlights of cars crossing the Sellwood Bridge, the lights of a boat sailing down the river in the darkness. And in between her and the river lay—what?

Closest to the river was Oaks Amusement Park, where Allison had attended many birthday parties and summer outings when she was a kid. The Ferris wheel was still lit up, and a few spotlights had been left on, but most of the park was dark, the rides shut down, closed up for the night.

And in between Allison and that Ferris wheel was a deep, velvety darkness, shadow upon shadow. Precious darkness, where she might be able to hide.

But what was in the darkness, exactly? Then she remembered. It was some kind of wildlife refuge for birds. Oaks Bottom, that's what it was called. It had a shallow lake, trees, shrubs, wildflowers, trails for city dwellers who wanted a taste of the wild without leaving the city. And dozens and dozens of birds: hawks, hummingbirds, ducks, woodpeckers, and eagles.

She and Marshall had been there once, years ago, before they were even married. Her memory conjured up a short paved path and a longer, narrower, muddier trail, which was the one they had taken. While they were walking, a great blue heron had lifted off nearly in front of them, uttering a deep, hoarse croak. Its huge wing span had been awe-inspiring, as if they had traveled back to the time of flying dinosaurs. And later they had seen an osprey dive steeply into the river and come up with a still flopping silver fish in its claws.

Thinking of all this took only a second, and meanwhile Allison's feet kept right on slapping the pavement. The wetlands offered more cover than the illuminated city street. She chose them without a second thought. Darting across the bluff, she bolted into the darkness that lay below. It was so steep her first step off the bluff felt like it covered yards and yards, like she was an astronaut bounding endlessly in zero gravity.

Then she landed so hard that the pain jolted all the way from her heel to her jaw. Her teeth caught her tongue, and blood flooded her mouth. Still she didn't stop. She hurtled blindly down the hill, hands in front of her, willing her eyes to adjust to the darkness.

With her next step, Allison's toe caught a root. She went tumbling head over heels, jolting over what felt like hundreds of small stones. Each time she landed on her shoulder or her hip or the back of her neck, she worried that she had broken something, but the slope was so abrupt that she could do nothing to slow herself down. She was like one of those daredevils who had gone over Niagara Falls in a barrel. At a certain point, you gave yourself up to whatever came next.

As she rolled and tumbled down the hill, she again heard *pi-choo, pi-choo,* this time above her. Maul must be standing on the edge of the bluff, shooting down at her. Shooting blindly, she hoped.

Finally she slowed down enough that she managed to regain her feet. She stumbled forward and kept moving, not stopping for anything, trying not to think about the various parts of her body that were now screaming in pain.

To run was to live. To stop was to die.

And then she was in the trees, lurching between them, branches slapping her face, ripping out hanks of her hair. Another lightning bolt zigzagged down to her left, lighting up the sky so that for a split second it was as bright as day. It had hit only yards from her, close enough that the back of her neck prickled. The thunder came right on its heels.

Allison kept running.

She could hear Maul some distance behind her, stumbling and cursing. The sounds gave wings to her feet. Pushing her way through the wet tangled underbrush, she was heedless of the brambles and sticks that clawed at her bare skin.

The night itself was far from quiet. Frogs peeped, the occasional mosquito whined in her ears, and the rain still drummed on the thirsty ground, although it seemed to be letting up a little. The earth was so dry and cracked that it was turning to mud, making it even harder to move quickly.

Allison ran and fell and picked herself up and ran again, feet sliding out from under her at every step. She never looked back. Her right ankle throbbed. She thought it might be sprained, but her fear was bigger than the pain. Her eyes had adjusted by now so she could avoid the trunks of big trees, but roots and rocks still tripped her up, brambles and smaller branches still tore and slashed at her. She splashed through a small stream and worried that she was making so much noise that Maul could easily follow her. But it seemed more important to put distance between them than to be silent and slow.

The lake was off to her right, wasn't it? She hoped it was, because if she blundered into it, he would surely hear her.

When she tore half her left big toenail off on a sharp rock, Allison gritted her teeth to keep from screaming. At least she hoped it was half her toenail and not half her toe. The pain was such that either seemed possible, and she couldn't afford the time to reach down to check.

Her skin was slick with rain, her hair plastered to her head. To stop the sodden cloth of her borrowed shorts from simply sliding off her body, she had to keep yanking on the waistband.

And then she burst from a stand of trees into a clearing. Ahead of her was a railroad track, and then a chain-link fence and a short stretch of weeds that dropped down to a narrow paved road. On the other side of the road was a wrought-iron fence and the imposing circle of the Ferris wheel.

She had run out of wetland.

Ahead of her were two fences and the amusement park.

Behind her Lucas Maul.

The choice seemed easy.

CHAPTER 39

Allison darted across the railroad tracks and managed to climb over the chain-link fence, using her bruised bare toes like a monkey's. She scuttled across the road, the skin between her shoulder blades itching. If Maul spotted her, she'd be an easy target. The resulting spurt of adrenaline gave her the extra push she needed to clamber over the metal fence that ran around the amusement park. The tops of the black bars ended in dull points, and one dug painfully into her thigh.

She landed on her poor feet, which were by now so bruised and cut that she barely bothered to wince. There were now two fences between her and Maul. With luck, he was still hunting for her in the wildlife refuge. She could find a security guard or maybe a pay phone—some way to connect with the outside world and let the cops, who were hopefully looking for her by now, know exactly where she was.

Keeping to the shadows, she ran through the parking lot and between the two huge toy soldiers on either side of the entrance. Corrugated metal shutters covered the windows and doors of the gift shop and booths that sold lemonade and snacks. The ticket booths all had white Closed signs in their windows. To her left, the roller coaster looked much tamer than she remembered. Across the way was the big pink slide that had been a fixture at the park since she was a child. Did children still slide down it on burlap sacks? Did burlap sacks even exist anymore?

Allison remembered the first time she had climbed to the top of the slide, how her father had held her hand up the seemingly endless series of steps. Once they reached the platform, the only thing separating them from the long fall to the ground was a chain-link fence. Five-year-old Allison had frozen in fear. She didn't want to stay on the open platform. She didn't want to slide down the slide. She didn't even want to turn around and go back down the stairs to where her mother waited with Lindsay. All three choices seemed impossibly dangerous.

Allison remembered the fear so well. What she didn't remember was what had happened next. Had she slid down the slide, discovered it was fun, and begged to go again? Or had she been carried, sobbing, back down in her father's arms?

Then the danger had all been in her mind. Now it was real. So real it could kill her.

She turned to look at the slide again and walked full-tilt into a metal garbage can. The round lid crashed to the pavement. The noisy clang was as loud as the clash of cymbals. It was unmuffled by the rain, which had died down to a light patter. The lid rolled over and over, making more noise with each revolution before finally coming to a halt.

Allison froze. Holding her breath, she listened as hard she could.

Nothing but the faint sound of the rain.

She was just exhaling when she heard footsteps swiftly crossing the road. Heading straight toward the amusement park.

No. No, no, no.

Where could she hide? While there were plenty of shadows, they didn't offer enough concealment. Everything here was out in the

open and squared off—no recesses, no unevenness, no projections to
hide behind. The wide and open walkways had been designed with
children in mind, so they couldn't slip out of sight of their parents.

But now that openness meant there was no place for Allison to
hide from the man who was determined to kill her.

She heard him grunt as he scaled the fence and dropped down on
the other side. His footsteps began again. And now they were getting
closer.

Where could she hide? The nearest ride was the carousel. She
hurried over to it and stepped up on the outer edge of the platform.
The rain pinged off the roof. Until now, Allison had been wishing
for shoes. Suddenly she was thankful for her bare feet, which moved
soundlessly. She threaded her way around the carousel, past a pranc-
ing black horse, a brown kangaroo, a gray emu, a white unicorn with
a golden horn. Finally she crouched down behind a large elephant
designed to hold at least two riders. She peeped past the elephant's
short curly tail.

Go away, she told Maul silently. *Go away, go away, go away.*

Instead, he stepped into view in front of the Tilt-A-Whirl. Allison
would not have recognized this thin man with the shaved head as the
same man she had helped bring to justice six years ago.

Maul pulled a small black rectangle from his back pocket. A
phone. He tapped on it with one thumb. His other hand still held the
gun. It seemed a strange time to send a text. Then the whole screen
glowed a bright white, and Allison realized he had been opening a
flashlight app.

After a spurt of fear, she relaxed a little. The phone as flashlight
was nowhere nearly as bright as a real one. It illuminated an area only
about five feet in front of him.

Then Maul leaned over the wide paved path. What was he looking at? He held his phone a few inches above the ground. And Allison saw what had caught his attention. Half a bloody footprint. Bent double, he shuffled forward, waving the light back and forth until he found the next. And the next.

They were leading in a line straight to the carousel.

He stepped up on the carousel, and it shifted a little under his weight. Allison risked another glance. Holding the phone in one hand and the gun in the other, Maul slowly began to circle the ride.

If she moved, he would shoot her. If she stayed still, he would find her and still shoot her.

Was there anything she could wrench off one of the wooden animals and throw at him? Or better yet throw into the distance so he would hear the sound and think she was someplace else? Her eyes darted back and forth, but of course there was nothing loose on the ride, nothing that some determined child could pry off and turn into a safety hazard.

And then she saw Maul's shoes. They stopped about five feet from her.

"Get up," he said. His voice was more weary than angry. "Get up or I'll shoot you right now."

She stood. He skirted the elephant's wooden trunk until only a few feet separated them. In silence they stared at each other. Water still ran in rivulets from his bald head. Very little about him looked like the Lucas Maul from his booking photos. Except for the eyes. They were the same. Challenging. Threatening.

"You." Maul shook his head. "How can you be alive? I killed you. I shot you twice in the heart."

"You shot my little sister. Lindsay Mitchell. Not me."

"No. I've seen your sister. Some skanky tramp with pink streaks in her hair. I've seen her sneaking cigarettes outside your house."

"That *skanky tramp* was going to be a businesswoman," Allison spat. "You didn't know her. You didn't know her at all. She never did anything to you, and you took her out of this world."

Maul let out an angry snort. "Did you know *me*? Did I ever do anything to *you*? No. But you still sent me off to do twenty-four years in prison."

Over the rain softly drumming on the metal roof of the carousel, Allison heard a faint ululation. Sirens. More than one. Ophelia had done what she could, had called the police. But they were too far away to do Allison any good. Maul's head lifted a fraction and she could tell he heard them too.

"But you robbed banks," she said slowly, wondering how she could buy just a little more time. "Lindsay did nothing but dress in my clothes one day. She just wanted to impress the loan officer. But instead you killed her. Not me. Her."

"Don't worry," Maul said, and he lifted the gun so it again was pointed right at her heart. "I won't make the same mistake twice."

"Freeze!" a voice shouted. Allison and Maul both started, their heads whipping around.

It was Nicole.

Nicole.

And while the maid's uniform was soaking wet, it was with water, not blood.

Nicole stood next to the carousel, her arms straight out in front of her, her Glock pointed right at Lucas Maul.

Maul's mouth fell open. "Why does this keep happening to me?" he said wonderingly. "Why aren't you dead?"

Allison lunged for his gun.

And suddenly they were both grappling for it. She yanked it to one side and up, hoping to pull his finger out of the trigger guard.

Nicole was shouting, and Allison also heard Ophelia's voice. But she could only pay attention to Maul and what she knew would be a fight to the death.

He elbowed her in the face, hard enough that fresh blood flooded her mouth as he smashed her lips. She did not slacken her grip on the gun. Instead she kicked him in the shins, wishing again for shoes. He twisted the gun until her wrist threatened to snap. She took a half step to one side, then drove her shoulder into his solar plexus.

He grunted, the air going out in a *whoosh*. And suddenly Allison was the only one holding the gun. She turned and pressed it against his chest, right at his heart. Over his shoulder, she saw Nicole circling them, trying to find an angle that would let her shoot Maul without injuring her. But now Allison had the gun. Her face and Maul's were just inches apart. His sharp breath was hot on her face. She had never been this close to another person without kissing them, but now all she wanted to do was kill.

Exultation sang in her veins. All she had to do was pull the trigger and Maul would be dead. She wanted it more than she'd ever wanted anything in her life. Her vision narrowed so that only his face filled it. His fierce gaze locked with hers.

He deserved to die.

The trigger was under her finger. The weight of the gun felt good in her hand. She would end this thing—right here, right now, with a single pull. Maul's heart would cease beating, his mind would stop its twisted fiendish plotting, his tongue would no longer be a restless evil.

But when Allison looked into his burning eyes, it was like looking into her own. The same rage consumed them both. They were different sides of the same coin.

But justice wasn't in her hands any more than it was in his. She wasn't God.

Something like a smile stretched across Maul's face. "Go ahead," he said. "Do it. Do it for Cassidy. Do it for Lindsay. I killed them. And I enjoyed every second of it."

The anger surged back. She saw Cassidy shoved under the kitchen sink like garbage, heard Lindsay's last breaths.

"Do it!" he shouted. His fingers closed on her throat, trying to force her to pull the trigger. With her free hand, Allison clawed at her neck, trying to pry his fingers loose. A line burned across her neck and then her necklace snapped. The silver cross went flying into the darkness behind him.

Her father had put that necklace around her neck. Now Maul had taken it away. In pursuit of what he thought was justice, Lucas Maul had killed Cassidy and Lindsay and shot Nicole. Justice meted out by him. Outside of any court of law.

But Allison had taken an oath to faithfully discharge the duties of her office. And those duties were to be a prosecutor. Not judge. Not jury. Not executioner. No matter how much she wanted it. No matter how much Maul wanted it too.

"Sorry," Allison said, and stepped back as Nicole pushed the nose of her gun between Maul's shoulder blades, ordering him to put his hands on top of his head. "Whether you live or die is not for me to decide."

Ophelia ran up, breathing heavily.

"Cuff him for me," Nicole said to Ophelia, taking the handcuffs from her belt. Maul put his hands behind his back without protest. All the fight seemed to have gone out of him.

"Oh, Nic." Allison's voice caught. "I thought you were dead too."

"Thank God for whoever invented Kevlar." Nicole smiled. "I'm pretty sure I've got a few cracked ribs, and I definitely had the wind knocked out of me." She had to raise her voice because a dozen vehicles—police cars, unmarked vehicles, and an ambulance—were now pulling up outside of the amusement park, sirens wailing. "But cracked ribs sure beat the alternative."

Cracked ribs or no cracked ribs, Allison knew that as soon as Maul was safely in custody she was giving Nicole a huge hug.

Maybe Ophelia too, if she would allow it.

CHAPTER 40

When the hostess at the Laurelhurst Market led the three women to their table, Ophelia chose to sit with her back to the crowd. Allison made a mental note that next time they should look for a quieter venue.

"Did you ever go to this restaurant with Cassidy?" Ophelia asked as she opened her menu.

"No," Allison said, feeling a momentary pang.

"What would Cassidy have ordered if she were here?"

There was no sense in asking why Ophelia wanted to know, Allison was beginning to realize. Ophelia was Ophelia, and her reasons made sense to her.

Allison looked over the menu. "Probably the flat iron steak and the roasted potatoes with black garlic butter and hazelnuts." Cassidy had always been tempted by rich food, happily ignoring calorie counts and cholesterol. "She used to say, 'Sin now, Spin class later.'"

"Then I'll have the beet salad with chevre." Ophelia closed the menu with a snap.

Nicole raised an eyebrow. "Are you a vegetarian?"

Laurelhurst Market was known for its steaks and chops.

"No. I just don't want you to think I'm trying to take Cassidy's place."

"You can't," Nicole said, and Allison winced. But then Nicole leaned forward and said, "And that's okay. You may not be like any-one else I know, but like my mama says, 'God don't make no junk.'"

Ophelia busied herself lining up her silverware. "I know it will sound wrong, but if Cassidy hadn't died, I wouldn't have met you guys. And you have changed my life."

"What do you mean?" Allison asked.

"When I started school, I was good at reading and math. In fact, I was better than anyone else. But after a while I realized that everyone else had friends and I didn't." Ophelia raised her head and shot each of them a darting glance. A rare smile transformed her face, making her suddenly beautiful. "Now I do."

"Thank you," Nicole murmured.

Allison touched the spot above her heart. "Well, I've learned a lot from you too, Ophelia."

She nodded. "Yeah, I think you probably did."

Allison tried hard not to laugh, but then she met Nicole's eyes, and it was all over for both of them.

She expected Ophelia to shrink back, but instead she said, "Sorry. I think I was inappropriately blunt just now. I'm not good with praise." She looked down at her hands. "I know that I'm different from other people. But you two don't seem to mind."

"Everyone's a little bit different once you get to know them," Allison said. "Your differences are just more visible than most people's."

"Maybe, but you two are different too."

"What do you mean?" Nicole asked.

"The way you work together. Other people have to talk things through, but you two can accomplish something together saying hardly a word. All it takes are a few glances and some body language, and all of a sudden you have a common purpose. I admire that, but

I'll probably never be able to do it. I know you take it for granted, but it's really amazing."

Allison had never considered it, but it was true that she and Nicole could say volumes without speaking.

The waiter took their order. When Nicole handed back the menu, Allison spotted something glinting on the finger of her left hand.

"What is that?" Allison held out her own hand, palm up.

Nicole ducked her head so that Allison couldn't see her expression. Without speaking, she slowly put her left hand in Allison's.

What Allison had glimpsed was a small but sparkling diamond set on a plain gold ring.

"It appears to be an engagement ring," Ophelia said.

"It's beautiful." Allison gave Nicole's cool fingers a squeeze and then released them. "Congratulations. You couldn't do any better than Leif."

Nicole blinked rapidly and then turned her eyes up to the ceiling. Biting her lip, she held herself still, keeping her unblinking eyes wide open.

Ophelia glanced up, looking puzzled.

"Why are you crying?" Allison asked.

"I'm not crying." Nicole dropped her gaze and looked at Allison. "At least I'm trying not to. It's just that I know Cassidy would have noticed first thing, even if I hid my hand behind my back. She would have grabbed my hand the minute I walked in the door."

"I noticed the ring," Ophelia objected. "I just didn't know if it was polite to mention it."

"Cassidy would have been so happy for you," Allison said. And maybe a little bit jealous, but she chose not to say that. Still, she was trying to hold on to all of her memories of Cassidy, to remember the real woman and not some plaster saint, perfect and unmoving.

"And Cassidy would have noticed that you're wearing your necklace again," Nicole said.

Allison touched the cross gently with her fingertips. "Thanks to you, Ophelia. If you hadn't found where the cross went when Maul broke the chain, it probably would have been lost forever. And you have no idea how much it means to me."

"Sometimes it's helpful to have an eye for detail," Ophelia said.

The jeweler had suggested replacing the chain, saying it would be impossible to make it perfectly smooth again. There would always be a mended place in the links, he explained, that Allison would feel against her skin even if she couldn't see it.

She had refused. The chain was the one her father had given her. And somehow, the mended spot felt right, as if it belonged.

The waiter approached with their food, and Allison waited until he left before she said, "In a way, I'm lucky Maul broke the chain. He wanted me to kill him. And he has no idea how close I came." Maul would go to meet his Maker, but in God's time, not hers.

"He didn't want to go back to prison," Ophelia said. "He wanted to die a free man." She lifted her fork and took a tentative nibble of her salad.

"I don't know," Allison said slowly, thinking of the expression in Maul's eyes. "I think it was more than that. I think he wanted to turn me into himself. He wanted to show me that there wasn't any line between us. And he nearly succeeded."

"But he didn't," Nicole said.

"It was close," Allison said. "Too close."

The waiter returned and leaned in. "And how's your food, ladies?"

Ophelia said, "I realized I don't like goat cheese that much."

"Oh." He paused. "Um, would you like to order something else?"

"How about some of those black butter roasted potatoes?"

"Sure."

Later, when they were handed the dessert menus, Ophelia looked at hers and said, "Do you want to split the chocolate mousse cake with roasted pistachio ice cream?"

"I thought you said that sharing was a good way to spread germs," Nicole said.

"I've been rethinking that." Ophelia set her menu down. "There's something called the hygiene hypothesis. It says that when people have an overly sanitary lifestyle, their immune system doesn't get enough practice fighting off bacteria and viruses. As a result, it tends to overreact by having allergic reactions to harmless substances like pollen. Scientists think it might explain why there are more allergies now."

"So?" Nicole asked.

"So what it means is that by allowing your immune system to be challenged occasionally you might actually strengthen it."

"So you're saying we should make it one dessert and three forks?" Allison asked.

Ophelia nodded. "Exactly."

And when the cake came, Allison raised her water glass. "To old friends—and new."

"Here, here!" Nicole said, raising her wine glass.

And with a grin, Ophelia followed suit.

1. Have you ever lost a good friend? How did it affect you?

2. What would you change if you knew that one of your good friends or a family member would die in the next 12 months? Would you save more emails? Be kinder? Say yes to spending more time together? Not multi-task when you talk together on the phone? Take more photos?

3. Have you ever known anyone like Ophelia? While no one in the book uses the term "Asperger's Syndrome," do you think Ophelia has it? When you were a child, did that diagnosis exist? Do you think people have changed or that medicine has?

4. Do you think our society appreciates that differences are strengths as well as weaknesses?

5. Have you ever been tempted to get revenge on your own, even for something small? Did you follow through? What were the results?

6. Do you trust the legal system to always do what is right?

7. A government study estimates that one in six women has been stalked. Have you ever been stalked or known someone who has? What happened? Were the police involved or was it more benign?

8. While on vacation in Florida, Channel Four's previous coanchor, Alissa Fontaine, performed an impromptu striptease. After it ended up on the Internet, she was offered a job on a reality show. Do you think some reality shows have gone too far, or that there are too many of them? Have reality TV shows changed your viewing habits?

9. Nic and Allison see the degrading terms people couple with Cassidy's name (i.e. "breasts," "nose job") when searching for her

on the Web. Do you think the Internet has coarsened our cul-
ture? Or is it merely a tool, like the printing press?

10. Would you ever risk your career for a friend?

11. One of the characters dies just when her life is turning around.
Some of the other characters think this is a cruel irony—just
when her life held such promise! Others think it's better that she
died when she had hopes and dreams than when she was down
and out. What do you think?

ACKNOWLEDGMENTS

Dear Reader, you've come to the acknowledgments, so you know what happened to Cassidy. So, thank you, Cassidy, for your amazing spirit, zest for life, and quest for a good story. Speaking of quest for good stories, the wonderful folks at Thomas Nelson also carry that torch: Allen Arnold, Senior Vice President and Publisher of Fiction (a true visionary and friend); Ami McConnell, Senior Acquisitions Editor (I'm proud to call you my friend as well as editor); Editor L.B. Norton (a/k/a eagle eye); thank you Natalie Hanemann, Senior Editor; Jodi Hughes; Belinda Bass; Kristen Vasgaard; Daisy Hutton, and Becky Monds . . . it is an honor to work with you. And the Thomas Nelson sales team's enthusiasm is inspiring . . . thank you Doug Miller; Rick Spruill; Heather McCulloch; and Kathy Carabajal, just to name a few. Last, but certainly not least, in the Thomas Nelson team are the marketing whizzes who have imagination and stamina to be envied: Katie Bond; Eric Mullett; Ashley Schneider; and Ruthie Dean. Thank you.

Thank you, O'Reilly, from Wiehl. And Roger Ailes (who took a chance on hiring a certain Legal Analyst). And Don and Deirdre Imus. And special thanks to Dolores Brandi.

Research is key to any good story, so thank you Joe Collins (paramedic and firefighter); Robin Burcell (author and former cop and forensic artist); and all our friends in law enforcement who consulted and advised without attribution.

Our book agents, Todd Shuster and Lane Zachary of the Zachary,

Shuster, and Harmsworth Literary Agency, and Wendy Schmalz of the Wendy Schmalz Agency—you made the Triple Threat happen.

To my Mom and Dad, who always told me to follow my moral compass. You were right all along.

And thank you to Ed Lemos, who had the inspiration for the title.

All of the mistakes are ours. All the credit is theirs. Thank you!

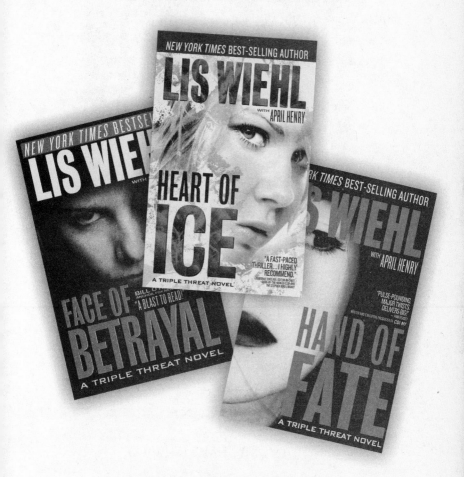

The Supernatural Series from

Lis Wiehl
with Pete Nelson

BOOK ONE
in the
EAST SALEM TRILOGY

ALSO AVAILABLE IN AUDIO AND E-BOOK

TO FIND OUT MORE, VISIT

LISWIEHLBOOKS.COM

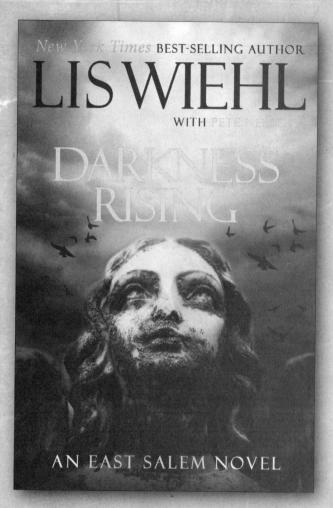

New York Times BEST-SELLING AUTHOR
LIS WIEHL
WITH PETE NELSON

DARKNESS RISING

AN EAST SALEM NOVEL

The evil that's in East Salem is no
longer content to hide in the shadows.
The stakes—and the darkness—are rising.

ARRIVING 10.2.12

TO FIND OUT MORE, VISIT
LISWIEHLBOOKS.COM

Tommy Gunderson woke in the middle of the night to the howling of the wind and the siren of his home's security system. *Probably an animal*, he thought, still half dreaming. But the system deployed a pattern recognition program calibrated to avoid false alarms from deer or raccoons. The alarm meant an intruder of the two-legged kind, intent unknown.

The swoop of the alarm seemed to deepen as Tommy threw the covers off and rolled out of bed. He pulled on a hooded black sweatshirt to match the black sweatpants he slept in and stepped sockless into a pair of running shoes. Fully awake now, he strode down the hallway to the kitchen, where he tapped on the space bar of his computer's keyboard and, when the machine lit up, clicked on the video feed to see what was going on. Thermal imaging revealed the orange heat signature of a human, crouched low by the edge of his fishpond.

Tommy moved quickly down the hallway again and threw open the door to his father's bedroom. Still sleeping, present and accounted for. He'd given the older man's caregiver the night off. Whoever was crouching by the pond was definitely uninvited.

Tommy didn't like uninvited guests.

He walked swiftly to the back door, grabbed the heavy black flashlight that hung from a hook by its strap, and hid it in the pouch of his sweatshirt. The moon was full, casting light on the yard, across the pond, and out toward the woods beyond.

He felt his heart rate quicken and was bracing himself for the cold when his cell phone rang from the kitchen counter where he'd left it to charge.

"Mr. Gunderson?" a woman's voice said.

"You got him."

"Sorry to wake you—this is the East Salem police. We have an auto-mated alert from your system. Is everything all right?"

"You guys are fast," he said, keeping his voice low. In a community of wealthy estates like his, the police took special care to assist the residents whose taxes paid their salaries and funded their children's schools.

"Do you need assistance?" the dispatcher asked. "We already have a car in the area."

He quickly considered. "If it's no bother. I'll meet him at the gate."

Armed with his flashlight, Tommy went to the front door, tapped the security code on the keypad to disarm the system, then stepped out into the darkness. He walked briskly, keeping to the shadows, rounded the side of the house, and trotted up the driveway. Gold and rust-colored leaves had started to drop from the trees. He avoided stepping on them, lest he alert the intruder.

Tommy recognized the cop in the squad car waiting at the gate. Frank DeGidio, like most of the local cops, worked out at Tommy's gym. Frank was a burly bear of a man with a swarthy complexion, thick black eyebrows, a permanent five o'clock shadow, and bloodshot eyes.

"What's he doing by the pond?" DeGidio asked, staring in the direction of the intruder. Tommy's house sat on ten landscaped acres, with another twelve acres of woods beyond the cleared lot. The half-acre pond was at the edge of the woods, about a hundred yards from the house.

"I stocked it with rainbow," Tommy replied. "Maybe he's fishing?"

"Without a license," DeGidio rasped, "at three in the morning? That's gotta be illegal."

"Probably a kid," Tommy guessed. "Just give him a warning and a ride home."

DeGidio opened the trunk of the squad car and handed Tommy a Kevlar vest. Tommy hesitated.

"Probably a kid, but you never know," the cop said.

"Does this make me look fat?" Tommy asked.

"Donuts make you look fat," DeGidio said. "I speak from experience."

The vest fit tightly over Tommy's muscular physique. The cop adjusted his jacket to make sure he could reach both the Glock 9 on his right hip and the Taser on his left.

They moved quietly, Tommy leading the way. As they neared the water's edge, Tommy saw that whoever was there was dressed in white.

Ten feet away, their presence still undetected, he saw that the intruder was a woman. Stepping closer, he heard a low animal-like sound.

"Can I help you?" he asked, exchanging glances with DeGidio.

She turned. She was elderly, probably well into her nineties, her pale face a desiccated mask of leathery wrinkles. Coarse black whiskers protruded from her chin. Her thin, cracked lips curled inward, her hair a wild snarl of unruly white wisps, so thin that in spots the moonlight shone off her age-spotted scalp. Her eyes were dark and watery, darting about. She was barefoot. Her nightgown was muddy. A strand of spittle hung from the corner of her mouth.

Tommy knelt down beside her and spoke softly. "It must be past your bedtime," he said. "I think we need to find out where you live."

She paid no attention to him but shook her head violently back and forth, speaking to herself in a low mutter. "No, no, no . . ."

He leaned in closer.

"Luck's fairy tale can go the real diamond."

"Ma'am?" Tommy said, louder now.

No response.

DeGidio made a circular motion around his ear. "Alzheimer's," he said. "That or rabies."

Tommy tried again. "Can we give you a ride home?"

This time she looked at him. "*Lux ferre,*" she said, her eyes widening. "*Le ali congoleare di mondo.*"

"Somebody's off her meds," the cop said. "What's she saying?"

"Something about luck's fairy," Tommy said. "Hang on."

He found his cell phone, tapped the camcorder icon, and held the phone a few inches from the woman's face. It was too dark to get a video image, but at least he could record her words.

"Good idea," DeGidio said. "I'm guessing she left her ID in her other nightgown."

The old woman turned to Tommy. "Do you know what I've got?" she asked, suddenly sounding quite lucid.

"What, dear?" he said. "Do you have something you want to show me?"

She extended her bony fingers toward him, cupped together the way a child might hold her hands in prayer. She opened them.

"A dead frog?" Tommy said.

"Take it."

"Thank you." He let her place the frog in his hands. It was cold and slimy and reeked.

"Do you believe in extispicium?" she asked.

"I'm sorry?"

The frog's entrails spilled from its belly. It had been ripped open, probably by an owl or a hawk. Unless she'd ripped it open herself.

"Extispicium," she repeated. "Do you see?"

"Do I see what?" he asked her. "What is it you want me to see?"

"This," she said. *"Ecce haruspices."*

DeGidio shone his flashlight on the disemboweled frog in Tommy's hands. The old woman poked through the frog's innards with her index finger, as if looking for a lost penny. She was shaking her head even more ferociously now, and muttering intently. She looked up.

"These are only the first to go," she whispered. "You'll be the last." She looked at Tommy again and seemed to recognize him. "You play football," she said.

"Not anymore."

"Ecce extispicium!" she said, now growling and looking Tommy in the eye. *"Ecce haruspices!"*

"That sounds like Latin," DeGidio said.

Tommy shifted the dead frog to his left hand, wiped his right hand on the back of his sweatpants, and touched the old woman lightly on the arm.

"Let's go back to the house and get you some warm clothes," he said.

"Lux ferre!" she screamed, rising suddenly from where she crouched by the water, springing toward Tommy and locking her thin web of fingers around his throat.

She bowled him over, driving him into the weeds.

Her nails pressed in against his windpipe as he grabbed her thin wrists. Tommy bench-pressed 350 pounds easily, but somehow he found it impossible to break the old woman's grip. He pulled as hard as he could, trying to throw her off of him.

He needed oxygen. Blood to the brain. His head was about to explode. *Where is her strength coming from? I'm losing consciousness. I'm dying . . .*

Suddenly Tommy felt a sharp electric buzzing. His vision sizzled, and he felt pain in his fingertips, his toes, and his hair. Something screeched in his ears. He smelled burnt rubber. Then the old woman went limp and fell on top of him, still holding him by the throat.

He pulled her hands from around his neck and rolled onto his stomach.

Tommy gasped for air and coughed violently, turning on his side now to see Frank DeGidio removing the Taser darts from where he'd fired them into the old woman's back.

"You all right?" he asked.

Tommy nodded, still unable to speak.

"Sorry about that," the cop said. "I couldn't get her without getting you too, as long as her hands completed the circuit."

"That's all right," Tommy said, rubbing his throat where her nails had scratched him and coughing again. He glanced over his shoulder to see an ambulance flashing its lights at the gate. "What was that?

How . . . ?" He got to his feet while the cop bound the old woman's hands behind her back with orange plastic flex cuffs.

"Adrenaline," DeGidio said.

Two EMTs took charge of his intruder. As they got her sedated and resting comfortably in the back of the ambulance, a third person examined Tommy's throat and advised him to wash his scratches with a disinfectant.

"You're lucky her fingernails weren't longer, dude," the man said with a gravel voice and an accent that sounded like he was from Texas or Oklahoma.

He looked more like a biker than a doctor, in black boots and jeans and a tattered jean jacket with the sleeves cut off. His arms and chest were tattooed and he wore silver chains around his neck. But after all the other strange happenings tonight, why not a biker-doctor too?

"You hold fast," he said, and headed back toward the ambulance.

DeGidio reappeared then and told Tommy they were already making calls to all the nearby nursing homes.

"We'll figure out where she belongs," he said. "My cousin works in a nursing home—she says this stuff happens all the time. A lot of old people get mellow, but some just turn violent. They don't know what they're doing anymore. It's like all the anger they've suppressed their whole lives comes out at the end."

"That's one explanation," Tommy said.

"We'll take care of her," DeGidio said. "Just for the record, you pressing charges? Trespassing? Assault?"

"Nope," Tommy said, watching as the ambulance pulled away. "Just let me know who she is when you figure it out."

"Will do."

Tommy walked him to his car.

"You'd be shocked at how much ground folks with Alzheimer's can cover when they get the notion," the cop said. "You ever see her before tonight?"

"Not to my knowledge," Tommy said. "She seemed to know who I was."

"Everybody knows who you are." DeGidio opened the door to his car. "I'm guessing you probably don't want the boys at the gym knowing a hundred-pound old lady beat you like a redheaded stepchild . . ."

Tommy offered a friendly smile, but something about the woman deeply disturbed him . . . a feeling that she hadn't arrived in his backyard by chance. He could have been killed tonight, yet somehow he knew she hadn't come to kill him.

"Fuggedaboutit," DeGidio said. "What happens in Tommy Gunderson's backyard *stays* in Tommy Gunderson's backyard."

"Thanks for stopping by," Tommy said, feeling his throat again.

"Anytime."

The officer drove away, and Tommy walked back to the edge of the pond. He saw the frog the old woman had given him, floating belly up, torn open, guts exposed.

He crouched low to examine it again. Why had she wanted him to see it? Her words, if they were Latin as DeGidio suspected, might have been the genus or species. What was she looking for?

It made no sense to him, but he supposed it might make sense to somebody else. She'd been clear about one thing—the message she wanted him to understand had something to do with the disemboweled frog.

He reached down to pick it up, thinking he could throw it in the freezer and send it to a biologist or laboratory. But when his fingers touched the amphibian, they passed right through it, and the animal that minutes earlier had been solid in his hand simply dissolved like bath salts, a murky gray cloud that dissipated in the dark water. He pulled his hand back reflexively. He found a stick and stirred the water, then threw the stick into the pond when there was nothing more to see.

These were the first to go, she'd said. *"You'll be the last."*

He was nearly back in bed when his cell phone rang.

"Tommy, it's Frank—you're still up, right? I didn't wake you?"

"Still up," Tommy told the cop.

"You said to call when we found out who she is. We got a missing persons from High Ridge Manor. Her name's Abigail Gardener. You know her?"

"Not personally," Tommy said. "She used to be the town historian."

"You okay?"

"A little shaken, to tell the truth," Tommy said. "The doctor said I was lucky her fingernails weren't longer."

"You already saw a doctor?" DeGidio asked.

"The one on the ambulance," Tommy said. "Blue jean vest and tattoos? Looked sort of like a biker?"

"What are you talking about?" the cop said. "There wasn't any doctor there—just the two EMTs, Jose and Martin. And nobody who looked like a biker."

Tommy thanked Frank and said good night. Then he went to his computer, hoping his surveillance system might solve the mystery. His property was covered by both high-definition video and infrared cameras capable of registering the heat signatures of warm-bodied visitors. The video feed showed only darkness at first, and then, once the ambulance arrived with its headlights pointed directly at the camera and its lights flashing brightly in the night, he saw only silhouettes crossing back and forth, making it impossible to count the number of people present, even in slow motion.

The infrared imaging was slightly more useful but still inconclusive. It clearly showed his own silhouette, and Frank's, and the old woman's, but once the ambulance arrived, the bright red heat signatures from the engine and the headlights again made it hard to sort out what he was seeing. Sometimes it looked like there were five images, sometimes six. He even saw some sort of digital shadow or negative ghost image in blue, flickering in and out of view.

He was tired and he'd given it too much thought already.

He knew what he knew—he'd spoken to a man who looked like a biker. Frank just must have missed him.

AUTHOR BIOGRAPHIES

Lis Wiehl is a *New York Times* best-selling author, Harvard Law School graduate, and former federal prosecutor. A popular legal analyst and commentator for the Fox News Channel, Wiehl appears on *The O'Reilly Factor* and was co-host with Bill O'Reilly on the radio for seven years.

April Henry is the *New York Times* best-selling author of mysteries and thrillers. Her books have been short-listed for the Agatha Award, the Anthony Award, and the Oregon Book Award. April lives in Portland, Oregon, with her husband and daughter.